Back from Bora Bora

Sondra Luger

GOTHAM BOOKS

Gotham Books
30 N Gould St.
Ste. 20820, Sheridan, WY 82801
https://gothambooksinc.com/

Phone: 1 (307) 464-7800

Published by Gotham Books (February 9, 2023)

ISBN: 979-8-88775-228-0 (h)
ISBN: 978-1-956349-42-9 (sc)
ISBN: 978-1-956349-43-6 (e)

This is a work of fiction. The characters, incidents, and dialogues are products of the author's imagination and are not to be construed as real. Any resemblance to actual events, entities, or persons, living or dead, is entirely coincidental.

Also by Sondra Luger

Rich, Never Married, Rich

To the Romantics
of the World

Chapter One

Eve heard the birds outside her window, but kept her eyes shut. Morning sleep was the best because one was rested enough to enjoy it.

"Why won't you marry me?"

She turned on her side to ponder that.

"You're too rich." No, that was stupid. "You're not rich enough." No, greed would not wash. "You're ugly." But that was untrue.

"Then why won't you marry me?"

"Because," she addressed the empty room, "I've got to get dressed and go to work."

And she jumped out of bed ten minutes before the alarm rang to do just that. It was easier than answering the question that other women knew better than to pose, even in their dreams. She would not marry him because he would never ask her.

The tweed suit affected her thinking, as had the nightgown half an hour before, and sipping the coffee slowly was not a device for prolonging morning rest, but for reviewing, date book in hand, the planned business of the day and annotating listed activities with possible procedures—persuasive, practical, and new. Eve Nelson would be second to none in sales. Boredom had taught her to excel.

The ravine enclosed the masses en route to their hectic glamour and drudgery-ridden niches in the enclave called Wall Street. Eve cast an upward glance at that perpendicular inspiration that was Williams, Wetcliff, and Snell. At their office on 55th Street, she had spoken and waved hellos. Here she merely nodded, in greeting, recognition, or affirmation of a colleague's existence. It didn't matter which. Mr. Snell, however, was awarded her voice. She had overtaken him in the hall near the parting of office ways.

"Good morning, George."

"Good morning, Eve. Have you got a few minutes to discuss Igor's file?"

"A midnight call?"

"Supper."

"I'll be there in a few minutes."

The Gregory Igor type was rarely worth even a few minutes of discussion. Discussion! "Discussion" and "few minutes" were not handmaidens. Fortunately, Igors were rare, but were as disagreeable to Eve as the like in steak, and as costly. He was one of W.W.&S.'s best accounts, even better since Eve had acquired it. She hung up her coat, opened the blinds, and retrieved the file. Hardly "minutes." She strode from the office.

"Good morning, Miss Kay," she perversely informed her secretary, who was settling into her chair.

"Cancel my luncheon appointment."

"But what will your mother say!"

"Get married, probably."

When she closed Snell's door behind her, she allowed her boss to begin.

"Igor thinks you're churning his account."

She placed the file on his desk. "I am, and he'll be grateful within a year."

"A year of evening phone calls," Snell grumbled. "Igor is magnanimous in accepting income, but not in sharing it with us." He glanced down the sheets. "All these commission-generating short-term investments. Not so lovely for us if we lose him. These short-term municipals especially, with interest at half the long-term rate." He shook his head.

"Interest rates are about to skyrocket. If I keep him long, we'll lose him for sure."

"The firm is recommending intermediate terms," Snell suggested.

"That won't be good enough for our Mr. Igor. He'll count every fraction of a cent he's missed."

"He's started counting already, and he's not a patient man. I'm relieving you of his account."

She was stunned, speechless.

"Eve, I'm not ungrateful. I know what you've done for us, but if you're right on this, Fergueson won't satisfy, and Igor will be begging to come back to you. Meanwhile, we've kept a major client and reduced our chances of acquiring an ulcer apiece. Doesn't this make sense?"

Her mother's favorite question required an answer in its business context. "It's not at all sensible for the client, but whatever Igor wants, Igor gets – and deserves. I hope that by the end of the year, he hasn't done himself an injury – like tearing the hair out of his toupee."

Snell laughed appreciatively. He was proud of his own thick, white hair.

Miss Kay had just cradled the receiver as her boss approached.

"Your mother just called to remind you about lunch, and I gave her the bad news. Then she gave me the bad news. She's coming anyway. And so you won't consider it a waste, she'll buy a share of something. Find her something suitable for a senior citizen not yet eligible for Social Security who rarely sees her daughter."

"We have lunch once a week," protested Eve.

"Apparently, one out of seven is not her idea of respectable odds. The poor woman's a widow."

Miss Kay's mother lived in Fort Lauderdale. Eve had a fleeting desire to book her secretary for lunch with Mrs. Nelson once a week. Only then would she understand.

She opened her office door. The brass plate expounded truth and irony: Eve Nelson, Senior Sales. The special accounts, the problem accounts, the challenging accounts requiring the ultimate in management belonged to the "Senior," who would one day graduate to V.P., if she lived long enough – none of the V.P.'s had reached age fifty.

Of course they could be enticed away by more lucrative or prestigious offers – Board chairman, CEO – but so could she, so could she. It had been an exciting prospect when she started at W.W.&S. ten years earlier. It was exciting no more. Mother would have an explanation for that, but all her explanations, her circumlocutions on topics from headaches to careers, led to the same conclusion. And that was where the senior in sales was a freshman, struggling from grade to grade with no expectation of graduation. She had never been able to sell herself. It was a circumstance one had to accept, and only one of them had. She pressed a button on her desk.

"Pete, account of Robert Madison: Sell 500 Asarco, buy 500 Harris Graphics."

"Think they'll merge with AM International?"

"Know so. News before the hour's out."

"Right-O."

Eve stared at the mahogany wood waist-high on the wall. Her desk seemed small in the room's expanse, overpowered by the 12-foot ceiling and absorbed into the woodwork. She pictured the congenial confusion of the floor below. Broker on top of broker, desk on top of desk, and papers everywhere, spilling from tabletops, overflowing the wastebaskets. And the noise – phones, voices, buzzers. And the clientele – ordinary people mostly, with ordinary desires and needs: to survive, to be secure, to enjoy little pleasures. There wasn't much money in helping these people, so you worked like blazes, first to avoid being fired and then to move into a less debilitating climate which was more lucrative – she gazed around the room – and strangely less profitable. Well, there was work to be done, a job to be accomplished. As she checked the opening market quotations, she reflected sadly that after ten years, this job was what her career had become.

Margaret Nelson eyed her watch. If she added up the minutes her daughter had kept her waiting in the past ten years, she was sure they would amount to enough time for an ocean voyage to the South Pole and a one-month stay on the

Polar Cap. Mrs. Nelson was a punctual woman, a fairly exact and exacting woman when it suited her, and with a recalcitrant offspring, it suited her. Mrs. Nelson would have been an astute financial advisor had such a path been open to women forty years earlier, but her excellence lay in her power of persuasion. She had entered the fields of public relations and advertising all the while disguised as a housewife, and she had promoted her husband in his own eyes and those of others to success in retail. The withdrawn, contemplative man had come to own the largest men's clothing store in Bayside, Queens, and when he died – some said from a heart attack, others said in retaliation against his wife – she had entrusted the store management to a young Harvard Business School graduate. With a knowledgeable man at the helm of the business on a profit-sharing plan, and with her brief but sharp-eyed weekly perusal of the books, she was able to devote the bulk of her time to the career of mother. Dan and Phyllis had turned out splendidly, that is, according to her wishes. The boy was a doctor, the girl a mother – supported in the style to which Mrs. Nelson had insisted she become accustomed. Only Eve had balked at her mother's command. With the retiring character of her father and the courage of her mother, she had balked. True, Eve was not beautiful, but beauty was of minor importance to men. Some of the ugliest women married the handsomest men. Even high-class whores like Cleopatra, who looked revolting, got their men because they had more to offer than looks, and Mrs. Nelson didn't mean a stock portfolio. Eve had that something more, and she was by no means ugly. Plainness was a blessing, like the classic black dress, wonderful for all occasions, dressed up or down with pearls or scarf. Oh, there was so much one could do with basic black! But basic Eve defied persuasion. It was a blow to Margaret Nelson. And where, pray tell, was her daughter? Framed in the doorway of the eatery was the culprit. Mrs. Nelson could not disguise her admiration for the long-limbed executive striding toward her. Eve pecked her cheek.

"How are you, Mother?" It was the wrong question.

"Not too well. I have this pain near my heart. The doctor has prescribed a dose of at least five grandchildren, and since Dan and Phyllis have provided me with a total of only four—"

"What you need is a plate of cream cheese blintzes with heaps of sour cream and strawberries."

"But my heart!"

"You haven't got one, you lovable ogre, or you'd stop torturing me with innuendos and commands that break my heart. I love you, Mother. I'm doing the best I can in all departments of life. I can't force men I like to fall in love with me, nor I with them. At least I've got a career you can be proud of."

Mrs. Nelson touched her daughter's hand. "I'm very proud of you, darling, very proud." She sighed. "But I won't have the blintzes."

As Mrs. Nelson's talk of new broadloom and faulty window shades gave way to old Mrs. Morgan's bad back and the neighborhood mugging, the restaurant filled. It was a popular place with secretaries, typists, and clerks; lunch with the market crowd or lawyers who might know her and be seated within earshot of her mother's voice was anathema to Eve. Those people were welcome to knowledge of her business life and no more. Eve frowned into her salad at the voice behind the partition at her back. It was the voice, she knew, of a ruffles-and-lace, voluptuously-shaped young woman who laughed a lot and whose face was decidedly beautiful. She always ate with a man, sometimes young, sometimes old, and she never paid the check.

"You're not looking at me, Eve."

"I'm sorry, Mother."

"Hmm. You're not preoccupied with some particular man?"

"No."

"Well, that is the only acceptable excuse for not listening to your mother." She paused. "I think we should have our lunches elsewhere. The men here are too puny, poorly clothed, and young."

"Mother, that's not why we get together every week."

"Well, maybe it should be."

The woman behind Eve was laughing now. Eve wondered what she was wearing today. If it was the scallop-edged suit, she was with someone of consequence. If it was a flare skirt and frilly blouse, it was a peer. Just when Eve had thought she understood the dress rationale of the woman, she had arrived one day on the arm of a distinguished-looking, craggy-faced man, but she had worn a Western shirtwaist. Then Eve had not seen her for a long time. She had undoubtedly moved up the luncheon circuit into classier surroundings. But here she was again.

"It's sinful, just sinful," said Mrs. Nelson.

"Fifteen dollars for a pound of cookies! I buy them in the supermarket now. At one-third the price, they taste delicious." She put her coffee cup down with finality, "Now I'm ready for Houston Street. Maybe my luck will be better this time. Well, darling, I'll see you next week." She kissed her daughter on the cheek. "Do find us a more rewarding place to lunch. Somewhere a brisk walk from your office; you look a bit pale. And don't forget, Eve, your mother has a telephone."

As they started for the exit, Eve took a quick look behind her. Skirt and blouse.

Chapter Two

When she got back to her office, she opened her purse and looked into her mirror. The half-block walk had endowed her cheeks with a slight flush. A longer walk would bring a deeper flush, which would be even more becoming. Why, even now, she looked almost pretty. She put the mirror away. But it would fade. The vivacious color would fade, and she would remain. The thought was troubling to her, not because she valued beauty, but because it did not value her. Because even her daytime thoughts were frequently dreams of the handsome Bill Wetcliff Jr. instead of W's business. Her successes could only be in business, and reducing her effectiveness at work endangered her position. Even the best could lose their jobs, and in her unselfish heart, she felt no pleasure in the fact that they could lose their beauty, too.

The board meeting went as usual, with criticisms and proposals ranging from the stately to the staid. Eve barely glanced at Bill Jr. down the table from his father, instead giving undue concentration to the parade of voices. Only when the man himself spoke did she look at him. His Grecian nose and curly, black hair were more Olympus than Wall Street. He spoke slowly and deliberately, an endearing quality at W.W.&S., where good looks and charm were suspect, even in a boss's son. Only full lips and bright devouring eyes hinted at the Wetcliff reputation and non-financial interests. Why Eve dreamed of him so often lately she could not understand. His business acumen, evident even now in his attack on a proposed margin policy, his academic credentials, his art (his nudes were quite good, if the one hastily removed from the reception room last spring was any indication of his talent) all combined in a man who demeaned them. This aberration seemed to be the man, as a business suit and plain sense seemed to be Eve Nelson. But what seemed to be true was not necessarily the truth.

"These requirements will work hardship on some of our best accounts," she heard herself saying, "And while I agree with George that for both their sakes and ours, we should limit risk, we can distinguish between those clients whose businesses are suffering a seasonal or otherwise temporary decline and those whose continued solvency or reasonable prosperity is questionable. If we stiffen our margin requirements beyond those imposed by the Exchange, we should have a defensible, sensible reason to do so."

"I agree with Eve," said Wetcliff Jr. "Those who get 'thumbs down' from us will feel we've seconded their economic slip. They'll take their accounts elsewhere, and when their businesses recover, and who is to say they won't, they will not return to us. This personal guesswork would be discriminatory, time consuming, and probably inaccurate. Why should we spend valuable time checking a mountain of personal financial statements? And why should we think we can predict client solvency, when for the past year we've embarrassed ourselves with predicting the movement of this economy?"

Wetcliff gazed intensely at Eve as he spoke, sharing his fervor with systematic eye contact up and down the table. Eve did not remove her eyes from his face. Only on occasions such as this did she feel she had this unquestioned privilege.

"Then perhaps we should modify our margin requirements," she responded, "so that they are more stringent than the Exchange's but less stringent than originally proposed here. All our accounts will receive equal treatment, but we can eliminate the margin accounts of financially shaky clients who can't comfortably meet higher margin requirements. We'll still have more than the Exchange-ordained protection."

Wetcliff smiled at her and nodded his head. "I can go along with that."

So could everyone else, and for the remainder of the meeting, they attempted to determine the rate at which to fix margin purchases.

Bill Wetcliff patted her shoulder as they left the room. "I originate, you decimate. I retaliate, you conciliate." He laughed. "Picture us on Broadway."

She couldn't, and she resented the pat.

He leaned toward her. "I've got a sensational idea for next month's meeting." Then softly, "Shall we try a little orchestration beforehand?"

The chauvinist thought he was irresistible.

"We've done so well to date without it," she responded, and turned away.

"Solid thinking," said Snell in passing, but Eve only half heard him.

"Whenever will I adapt!" she silently reprimanded herself, thinking of the arm clasp and shoulder pat routines among men. And why had she rejected Bill's offer of a meeting? Did she expect him to see her for any but business reasons? Was she so inept that she could not make the occasion serve a dual purpose? Stupid! Stupid!

She shook hands with the man waiting in her outer office. "It's a pleasure to see you again, Mr. Tillson. I think you'll appreciate the plan I've constructed to accommodate your new financial status."

The thin-lipped, balding man agreed. "Probably. I'd rather lose my latest oil well than your services."

"We have done rather well together," she said as she opened the office door for him.

Eve stared at her bedroom ceiling. She should have said yes. She had tortured herself with that thought for the last hour. They worked at the same business with the same purpose, and she should have said yes. But she hadn't, and she could think of no way to gracefully reverse herself. She had only business associates, no friends to cry to, confide in, or seek advice from. She turned on her side toward the telephone on the night table and dialed.

"Mother? How did the shopping go today?"

There was a momentary silence. "I'm sorry, young lady, but you have the wrong number," came the husky-voiced male response, but in the background, Eve heard her mother's, "Who is it, Harry?"

"I—I'm sorry." Eve replaced the receiver. She lay very still, listening to occasional screeching tires, sonic boom, and the incessant ticking of the clock.

Eve paid elaborate attention to buy and sell orders the next day. She worked through her lunch of a tuna sandwich and a muffin. This was not unusual, but it was done with unnecessary intensity. She left the office late and decided to walk home. Walking relieved tension and unhappiness, and she was feeling both. The extent of her anguish could be gauged by the fact that she lived four miles away. She admired store window displays of elegant clothes she would not buy and passed singles bars with scorn. She stopped along the way for a few minutes each in several houses of worship, but each debilitated her more. The realm of the spirit did not supply the needs of the flesh.

When she got home at seven o'clock, she hurled herself onto her bed. She was exhausted in mind, body, and spirit, and only the oblivion of sleep offered respite. When the phone rang, she did not at first choose to answer it. Her mind was not fit for business now, and she was too depressed to deal with her mother. She allowed it to ring itself out. Then she turned on the radio to blot out her thoughts and the sound of her heartbeat. The soft music brought her to the verge of tears, and when the phone rang again, she answered it. But she could not clear the catch in her voice or regain her composure sufficiently to avoid an exclamation of surprise from the other party.

"Eve! I'm sorry. I never would have called now if I'd thought—What I mean is—Can you talk?"

"Yes, Bill, I can talk."

Her calm and the imagined circumstance struck the caller like a quietly leveled bullet. He hesitated.

"I'd like to know what you've called about," she encouraged badly.

"It can wait."

"No, it can't wait," she insisted. "I'm sure it can't. Please tell me now."

"Well, it's next month's board meeting. I have a rather daring suggestion for our Annual Report, and I wanted to try it out on you first. Get your criticism and suggestions. There's no need for us always to disagree."

"Do we? I think we've always come down on the same side eventually."

"I'd rather it were sooner."

Had she displayed belligerence? Was he hurting? She'd had no idea!

"Whenever you say."

"Well," he laughed, "hardly now. Your friend would probably cut me to pieces, but as soon as you can."

"Tomorrow, then?"

He heaved a sigh. "Well, all right."

"If it's not convenient—"

"It's convenient, it's convenient. Business takes precedence."

She didn't have to ask him over what.

"Why don't we meet at the Union Club library? The place is practically empty on Saturday. Would that be all right? If we're there at ten, we could be finished before noon."

"I'll be there."

"At ten, then, and I apologize again for interrupting."

"I'll have no trouble getting back to what I was doing."

"I'm glad."

The hand that replaced the receiver was shaking. Eve Nelson was furious. The male voice emanating from the radio had just completed his seductive sales pitch for a foreign car. The pitch had obviously eluded Bill Wetcliff, but the male voice had not. But his interest could not have been sufficiently piqued or he would not have selected the romantically sterile setting of the Union Club library. She was sure she did not want Bill Wetcliff. How could any sensible woman want such a man? But he was a convenient challenge. She leaped out of bed and headed for the shower.

"The hell with you, Bill Wetcliff! You're not the only one who can play games."

Wetcliff was already at the library when she arrived promptly at ten. He looked at her with approval and surprise. He had not expected a flowered blue skirt and a powder blue, soft cashmere pull-over. And she smelled good.

He had said he wanted business, he would get business.

"You said we would be finished by noon."

"Definitely." He handed her six stapled pages with each line numbered. "So I can follow your comments on my copy."

They wouldn't even be sharing the same copy.

While Wetcliff strolled the room, Eve read the entire proposal, then discussed it with him point by point, line by line, and page by page. They argued, retreated, offered alternatives, and came to general agreement. It was 11 o'clock.

"Have you time for coffee?"

"Some," she responded evasively.

They sat in an outdoor café and drank espresso.

"If I could have succeeded as an artist, I would have loved it."

"You're a success in our business."

He laughed. "Do you think so? I'd hardly have guessed that from the relish you've taken in trouncing me at meetings and anticipating and promoting my ideas before they've cleared my brain."

"You know that's untrue! I haven't trounced, and our thoughts sometimes just happen to take the same track."

"Do they now? Then guess what's in my mind this minute."

"Won't it stay any longer?"

He laughed again. "Check! But do guess."

She fondled her coffee cup. "The curvaceous blonde with cascading hair you canceled your date with in order to be with me this morning."

He roared. "Close enough! Do you see what I mean?"

They both laughed, he not quite with her, she definitely not with him.

"Your art career could zoom to a lucrative start at the drop of an ad: 'Wall Street artist, skillful depictions of all manner of naked stock certificates. Printing may be added by buyer.'"

"Unfair, unfair." He wagged his finger at her.

"Quite right."

He stared into his coffee cup. "I can't understand why this firm begrudges me little pleasures. A man needs an outlet from all the paperwork and numbers. Our work is tedious, boring, and inhuman. We fuel the dull side of progress, and I think we're entitled to some sunshine on the side. Why should I be lectured and reproved? You'd think Dad and George were ninety, like old Williams out in Bora Bora. And I can imagine what he's doing out there! The world is different today. We all have the right, maybe even the obligation, to be different, too."

That's what people have always said, Eve thought, from the whorehouses and wars of ancient Rome to the wars and "new morality" of today.

"Then you'd surely better stick to those inhuman numbers. They're what provide you the wherewithal to indulge your individuality. Actually, though, your behavior would not be considered 'different' in most other fields."

"May I quote you to Dad?"

"Don't you dare! By the way, when is he returning from Bora Bora?"

"As soon as old Williams lets him go. He was quite a character, Dad says. Stubborn and loud. Everyone sang hosannas when he retired, oh, it must have been twenty years ago. Can't imagine why he wanted to see Dad. They fought like hell for forty years."

A blinding April sun was overhead. Bill Wetcliff moved closer to Eve to avoid the rays that escaped the umbrella on their table, but his eyes were on the people passing by.

"Don't feel too sorry for yourself," she pursued. "You're respected at W.W.&S., and you deserve to be. Your staffing procedures and new ad campaign are superb."

He turned his eyes on her again. "Thank you, Eve."

"And you're always listened to with respect at meetings."

"The boss's son speaks."

"That's not true, Bill. What you say matters. Everyone knows you're fabulously well-prepared for every topic on the agenda. Your attendance is outstanding, regardless of snowstorms or fever, and you're always available to any staff member who needs help."

"I do my best," he said modestly, failing to add the fact that she was his match in preparation and attendance and more than his match in ideas. No one was his match in availability to staff, an availability which was often unsolicited but always appreciated by the women who were its major recipients.

His eyes returned to scanning the sidewalks.

She lunged again. "It must have taken you months to mount our new ad program."

His eyes again met hers, and he leaned closer to her. "I'll tell you a secret. Some of our girls were kind enough to offer their assistance in researching it. I just put the pieces together. I worked like the devil that day."

"That was a very practical approach," she said flatly, realizing she had been "kind enough" to do just that for him now. Was she one of "the girls," too? Were there no "women" on staff?

"You're a very practical person yourself," he said warmly, patting her hands as his eyes took in the street again. "Now, there's a woman who's immune to the practical. It may well cost her a week in bed."

Eve looked at the woman in question as she approached a table at the edge of the café. "Oh!" she exclaimed.

"Have you ever seen such negligence? If her bodice were cut any lower, it would meet her hem. When it's 60 degrees in the sun, that's not what you wear."

But Eve's exclamation had not been over the dress, nor a presentiment of Bill's immediate demand for the check and his hurried goodbye and thanks. It had been over the identity of the woman herself. She watched as Wetcliff humbly requested to join her and her hesitant acquiescence. "Elaine," barely audible, floated towards Eve. The vision now had a name. Eve lifted the coffee cup to her lips and looked away. She was heartily tired of herself.

Chapter Three

From above the datebook she was examining, Eve saw her enter. THE woman. Beige shirtwaist. Amazingly, she was alone. She kept the datebook poised before her face, but the observed one walked disconcertingly in her direction. She felt the Shirtwaist standing beside her and was compelled to look up.

"Please don't think me rude, but may I join you for lunch?"

Eve was about to demur.

"I have more than an apology. I have an explanation."

Eve motioned toward the seat, but the young woman ignored it.

"Your friend said you were a business associate and that you'd had a business brunch, or I would never have allowed him to sit down."

Eve could not disguise a smile. "And if he'd said he was my chauffeur or a friendly burglar, that would not have sufficed?"

Her face went crimson. "I'm usually very discriminating, but I was depressed."

"Low body temperature from undue exposure." Eve sliced another piece of steak.

"That's a cruel thing to say!" The young woman was close to tears. "I didn't know for sure he was your boyfriend. I didn't mean to behave badly."

"Sit down." Elaine up front was less mature than Elaine at a distance.

The younger woman stood stubbornly, her lower lip trembling.

"You may sit down. He's not my boyfriend. He's a business associate, as he said."

Elaine sat down, stunned. "I can't remember when I've met an honest man!"

"Well, don't be hasty and think you've met one now."

They looked at each other, blushed, then looked away.

"I'm sorry anyway, but there was no danger."

"Danger?"

"That he would stay with me. They don't you know. Six months is my limit. They just—go!" She motioned with her hands in the air.

"You haven't found a man you want to stay with you, that's all," suggested Eve.

"Oh, but I have. Dozens. I used to worry about it all the time, but when I decided I just wasn't interesting enough to hold onto them, I stopped getting upset mostly. I'm not well educated— no college, and I'm not into books, so I don't know very much. Women have to be interesting these days, so I watch as many of those educational television programs as I can, but—" She shrugged. "It doesn't help. I think a woman has to be born interesting. Like you."

Eve unsuccessfully stifled a laugh. "How do you know I'm interesting?"

"It's in your face, it's character."

"Character. Is that what I've got? Perhaps you've got more character than you think and it's frightening men away," she mused almost to herself.

"Oh, no. I haven't any character at all. I suppose there is such a thing as too much of it, though. Maybe that's your problem."

Eve stiffened. She had not spoken of herself. How dare this woman, this total stranger, take the liberty of doing so. She had come to apologize, and she had done that. Now she should leave. But there she sat, brazenly giving the waiter her salad order. The apology took character; the intrusion took chutzpah. Eve moved uneasily in her seat. Here was a woman she had long ago singled out, marked for observation.

A woman who had what she lacked—youth, beauty, men. She was sure that with the first two, she could obtain the third. This woman was devious, complimenting her on her character. Bill Wetcliff had abandoned character for beauty. Hollow compliments did not appeal to her. She could not envy a woman so insincere or so stupid. She would not speak. She would eat quickly and leave, and tomorrow she would take a later lunch or eat in the office. There was so much work to do.

"I'm Elaine Dawson. I'm a secretary at Merrill Lynch."

Eve took a forkful of beans and said nothing. Such unmitigated prying!

Elaine Dawson's salad arrived. "You're a somebody, I suppose. Most of them wouldn't be caught dead here, but you come. They say truly big people are that way."

She insisted on turning a snub into a compliment and still wouldn't leave! "Perhaps I come to flaunt being a somebody."

"That's not in your face."

"For such a discerning person, Miss Dawson, you should be more successful with men than you allege you are."

"That's very unkind of you!"

"People of character cannot be unkind." came the even response. "You said you're discriminating in your choice of men. I'm merely repeating what you said."

"I don't want it repeated!" She stuffed salad into her mouth in agitation.

"It's not character you lack, my dear," thought Eve. "I'm sorry," she said aloud.

"Thank you."

No, not character. Eve silently watched Elaine Dawson devour the salad. The ravenous hunger for substance in the insubstantial was obvious and sad. She recalled the words Shakespeare had put into Cleopatra's mouth: "My salad days, when I was young and green." Eve was green too, and she knew it. She and Elaine Dawson amounted to the same thing.

Miss Dawson waved away a second cup of coffee.

"I can't afford to be late again," she explained. "Lengthy lunches," she intoned in a low octave, mimicking her boss.

She laughed, her eyes crinkling with mischief and cheer. "Thank you for allowing me to eat with you and explain things."

Eve smiled. "You're quite welcome. You don't like to eat alone, anyway."

The younger woman flushed slightly. "That, too." She held out her hand. "Thank you again, Miss—"

"Eve Nelson," said Eve, extending hers.

"How do you do, Miss Nelson."

"Fine, thank you, Miss Dawson. I hope your luck with men improves. Goodbye."

Elaine Dawson turned away smiling. Eve watched wistfully as she gracefully maneuvered past waiters and tables. She wondered how she looked negotiating those turns. Well, an appealing face and walk did not pay the rent on a luxury apartment, though of course, they could. For Elaine Dawson, she was sure they did not. So Bill Wetcliff had struck out. "What a fall was there, my countrymen." But Elaine Dawson hadn't said that, had she? Eve had gotten no intimation of their conversation or its consequences. The apology, she brushed aside. Miss Dawson may have been fending off a feared attack from an "associate" who was really a woman scorned. In social situations, anyone who looked as lovely and moved as well as Elaine Dawson could not be trusted. Still, Eve could not conclusively state whether she was ingenious or merely ingenuous. They were not likely to dine together again, because Miss Dawson would doubtless not repeat the aberration of a maleless lunch and because Eve had resolutely determined to patronize another eating establishment. If the Wetcliff-Dawson liaison amounted to anything, she was sure to read it in Bill Wetcliff's face or hear it in his boasts. Her disconcerting brush with the young woman was fortunately over. She had not noticed that Elaine Dawson had not said goodbye.

Chapter Four

The remainder of the week proved gratifying. Eve had seen Bill Wetcliff the usual knots of moments during the business day, and the change of mealtime and restaurant had ensured her inner peace and pleased her mother. Dreams kept to their place, and the mechanics and mental stimulation required during the hours of 9 to 5 banished thoughts of another reality. It was the following Monday, fresh from an early spring weekend in the countryside, that Eve encountered unavoidable change. The morning nod did not work its introductory magic.

"Hi, Eve. Rotten morning isn't it?" asked Fergueson. The elevator door opened.

"I hadn't noticed." The elevator door closed. "Igor?" she questioned.

"Heck, no. It's those two-bit accounts Bill keeps throwing my way. Who has time to work on million-dollar accounts when he's buried under one-hundred-dollar accounts?"

Eve said nothing. With a dozen sales executives ear to ear, such talk was a mistake. She exited with Fergueson.

"Don't those accounts eventually drop away?"

"Not fast enough. I'm the only link these girls have to dear Bill, who naturally is in conference whenever they come to discuss their investments. And do they come! I ask you, Eve, is this fair to me? One share of GM, two shares of Tandy. Who's got time for this? Sure, the girls are gorgeous, but my wife and kids won't understand my keeping up my spirits instead of the mortgage payments. At least the latest one won't visit or call. Blessed peace! She works for the competition."

Eve's eyebrows rose. "Merrill Lynch?"

"Yes, how did you know?"

"She told me."

"No kidding. Bill might have to watch out for this one. And you, too. I don't wish my wasted hours with these hunters on you."

Eve frowned and accepted Fergueson's sympathetic business pat without a second thought.

A man was bent over the typewriter on Miss Kay's desk. Eve passed his rear and entered her office. It wasn't like Miss Kay to be late. Ten minutes later, she buzzed for her secretary.

Her door opened and closed, and a body crinkled into a leather chair. Frowning at the letter on her desk, she began.

"Dear Mr.—" She looked up at Miss Kay. But there was no Miss Kay. Instead, there was a tall, slim man of twenty-six or seven, pen and notebook in hand.

"Where is Miss Kay?"

"In Florida. There was a call from her mother. I'm Hank Martin. I'll be your secretary for three to six months, until Miss Kay's return."

"Who selected you?" she asked with a touch of indignation.

"Mr. Snell. He was unable to reach you on the weekend. I'm quite competent, I assure you. First in my class at Katherine Gibbs."

"Really. Have you had previous business experience?"

"Seven years in construction."

"Sales?"

"Bricklaying. You know what's happened to the construction industry."

She did indeed, but she was wondering what had happened to W.W.&S. An insistent blink on the PAX demanded attention.

"George—yes! I don't know. How kind of your friend. No, I'm not. Someone else might be, but you know how I love surprises. That's very good of you, George. If he can do the job, then he can keep the job. All right, George."

She cradled the receiver. Unconsciously she moved the chair back to the wall and looked at the man quizzically.

"Wouldn't Sales have been a more sensible entry to Securities?"

"Not for me. I'm not particularly good with people. I like details and prefer working with my hands."

"Mr. Snell tells me he has detailed this position to you as he understands it. Actually, there is a typed list of my requirements somewhere in Miss Kay's files. Find and study them immediately, and I'll inform you of divergences from them as they arise."

"I'll do that. Thank you. I appreciate your granting me this opportunity to work with you."

Eve had never thought of Miss Kay's position as one of opportunity.

"All right, Mr. Martin, your opportunity begins with "Dear Mr. Howell, Your request with consideration in regard to—"

She glanced from letter to ceiling as she spoke, aware of the sound of pen on paper. This would never do. How everyone would laugh! Eve Nelson with an outrageously handsome male secretary! George Snell had obviously gone out of his ivory tower mind.

She sat, hands intertwined under her chin, looking unhappily across his desk at George Snell.

"Are you out to destroy me, George, because if you are, you've made an excellent beginning."

"Eve, I couldn't reach you. It was an emergency, unless you consider even one day without a secretary a lark, in which case, why am I giving you a secretary at all?"

"Does one day equal six months? And you've created the emergency by giving me this—this man! I'll be the butt of every office joke!"

"Don't be sexist, Eve. He's highly qualified, and you do need a secretary immediately. You'll be working 'round the clock. Here, take a look at this."

Her eyes grew large as she read the telex from William Wetcliff Sr. in Tahiti.

"Unbelievable, isn't it? When the silent partner becomes vocal, he does it with neon lights. An office in Tahiti so he can feel close to our operations wasn't enough. No, he's got to come out of retirement at 90! He's loonier than ever, but shrewder, too. Yes, indeed, our dear, old partner Frederick W. Williams has been buying additional company stock for the past year. He's told Bill he now has controlling interest again, and serving senior citizens is at the top of his agenda. I was on the phone with Bill for an hour. We think Ghandi resistance is best. Bill has convinced the old man that publicity at this time of sluggish market activity would depress sales morale and redound against us in the Market. But on the quiet, we'll have to work on office plans to serve seniors in Florida, California, Arizona, and New Mexico. And just when our international operations are in trouble!"

"What an unconscionable misuse of your time."

"Yes, well, it's not exactly my time, and not a total waste." He addressed the woodwork.

Eve understood too well. "I'll quit first."

"Now, Eve, just think what this will mean. Fred wants to appeal to the moneyed retirement crowd. With a handle on all aspects of this venture, guess who would be first in line to be vice-president, Southern area?"

"Bill Wetcliff Jr."

"He's not interested. He can't picture himself dating senior citizens".

"But you can picture me?"

"You're not looking at this properly, Eve. Perhaps it's too early in the morning to digest all this."

"And where will I find the time for two full-time jobs?"

"That's where Hank comes in."

"Surely you could have thought of a woman."

"The only woman I'm allowed to think of is my wife. Hank's father is an old wartime buddy, and when I saw him again at our reunion Saturday—"

"I may not be your buddy, George, but I thought we were friends."

"We are, Eve. If I had a daughter, I couldn't be more concerned about her than I am about you, professionally"

"Don't make this out to be a favor, George."

"I think this assignment will be good for you. I think Hank will be good for you, too."

"Now, just a minute—"

"Professionally, professionally, for heaven's sake. Look, Eve, you're — slipping. Only little things here and there, nothing especially noticeable unless someone is looking, but it could get to that. I don't want it to. I fished you out of our midtown location because you couldn't be ignored. Your volume was stupendous, your appetite for work voracious. You were a somebody, a somebody important to us, so I gave you the title and salary of a somebody, and you performed beyond it, until recently. Something has happened to you, Eve. Maybe it's that thirtieth birthday, maybe it's questioning who the somebody named Eve Nelson really is or who she wants to be. You can't need a vacation, you just had one."

"Slipping! In what way? Wooing five-million-dollar accounts away from the competition? Compacting the internal communications system for a saving of millions? Or are you referring to Igor, who wouldn't recognize good management if it bit him on the nose? When have I slipped? Where?"

"Human beings do slip, Eve. You shouldn't feel threatened for being human."

"Threatened! What are you trying to say, George? Come out and say it!"

"I have said it, Eve. It's nothing as simple as losing your job. You'd have no trouble finding another. It's those doodles at meetings, those occasional memory lapses in spite of Miss Kay, that tightening efficiency I sense whether you're greeting a client or a messenger. It's your manner, Eve. It's different, and it's been troubling me."

"You're imagining, George, and you're expecting perfection. As you say, I'm only human. I may work like the devil, but sometimes I forget. It's never been anything important. And sometimes the work may make me seem unfriendly. Isn't it worth it for what I do for W.W.&S?"

"Yes, but is it worth it for Eve Nelson?"

"We're speaking professionally."

"The line of demarcation——"

"Is very clear," she concluded firmly. "I want a replacement for Mr. Martin."

"I gave my word, Eve, and so did you."

"Under duress."

"Which is what the whole securities business puts us under. Don't think of yourself as saddled with Martin and you won't be. Don't imagine what doesn't exist."

"I must say the same to you, George," she said wryly. She stood up. "If I'm not back in my office in five minutes, a very temperamental and impatient client will accuse me of the heinous crime of forgetting." And she slammed her way out of his office.

Eve Nelson and Hank Martin were looked at curiously and with noticeable obeisance and awe by all at W.W.&S. Eve understood why. They made a strangely compatible duo. Martin was polite, distant, unsmiling, and endlessly working. He took coffee breaks and ate lunch at his desk. Eve found him efficient and adaptable. Contrary to her expectations, however, he did not pretend to be eager to please her. He did his job thoroughly and well, and that was all. Eve was glad. When they spent their first evening together at her apartment, sifting through and collating data on the firm's clientele communications system, she had no fear.

"Amazing. The avant-garde electronic mail system that cost a bundle is only used sporadically, and used least of all by Phil Mott's people, and he suggested it!"

"We rarely use it, either," noted Hank Martin.

"You're right. And why don't we use it?" she wondered aloud.

"Habit and ignorance, probably."

A nervy response, thought Eve, who was nevertheless unable to refute his conclusion.

They sat on the floor surrounded by piles of paper.

"Would you say, then, that the system is impractical, or the people?"

He shrugged. "The point is that the electronic mail system isn't working here."

"So you do whatever is necessary to get the desired results."

"Yes."

"Regardless of the methods used?"

"Maybe."

Eve laughed. She appreciated his frankness and his ethics.

"You know, organizing all this information is more time consuming than I expected, and evaluating it may take forever. We're more likely to celebrate a Silver Anniversary of research before we are able to celebrate the opening of our Southern offices. Would you like a drink?"

"I'd rather not stop now, if you don't mind. I'll have something when I get home." He squinted at a memo. "I can't make this one out."

Eve slid to his side on her living room's Aubusson carpet and bent over the memo with him.

"Fergueson uses speedwriting."

They attempted to sound out the words together, stumbling over letters, laughing over gross and obviously unintended interpretations.

"The speedwriting is understandable. We need a course in Fergueson's handwriting!"

Eve smiled at the impenetrable memo and turned her face toward Hank Martin's. He did not look at her, but put the paper down and picked up another. Eve slid back to her pile.

"Well, this one is legible," he said with relief.

He would accept no food or drink and initiated conversation only about the work at hand. Eve had a fleeting wish for Miss Kay; at least she was human.

"Are you sure you won't have some coffee before you leave? You won't have to bother making it when you get home."

"I don't drink coffee at night."

As Eve sipped her coffee alone, she wondered what Hank Martin did drink at night. It was an odd thing to think about, but Hank Martin was an odd man. But there was greater oddity about him that Eve noticed as the weeks went by. He was at her apartment now each weekend in increasingly business-like attire. His sweater had been succeeded by a vest, which had been succeeded by a jacket, which had been supplemented by a tie. Eve was amused by his attempt to impress the boss. She saw no need in her own apartment to assume office mentality while assuming office work. Beige and black suits were for the office; pastel silk blouses and dresses were for home.

"Aren't you hot, Mr. Martin?"

He made no movement towards the buttons of his jacket.

"I rarely sweat."

"But you do feel heat?"

"It doesn't bother me."

She grabbed his wrist and felt for his pulse.

"Thank God, you're still alive!"

She removed her hand from his. He was looking solemnly around the littered floor.

"Here it is!" he declared triumphantly. "Davis's charts are always dogeared."

"You're rather dogeared yourself," she whispered dramatically, putting out hands to touch him, then thinking better of it. The serious and somber Hank Martin made her feel strangely lighthearted and girlish.

"Mr. Martin, I am not about to bite you, caress you, or seduce you, so you can relax and perform your job in a more human way."

He reddened. "I think my work has been more than satisfactory—superb, if I may say so. I have no cause to question your behavior and you have no cause to question mine," he addressed the wall.

"The quality of your work is more than I had hoped for. I only thought you would be more comfortable if you weren't so serious about every piece of paper and every word I say. Aren't you uncomfortable a little? Come on, now, admit it."

"I feel fine, and we still have a lot to do tonight."

Eve could not resist. She leaned conspiratorially toward him. "You're a good man, Charlie Brown. Aha, you almost smiled."

He bit his lip in acknowledgment and prevention, then cleared his throat.

"You don't have to make fun of me."

"Yes, I do," she said. "You're such a wonder in helping me, I feel I should help you, and acquiring a sense of humor, even at your own expense, is a great asset in business as well as in your private life. Or are you only this way at work?"

"Can't we get on with this?"

"Yes, of course. I'm sorry, Mr. Martin. But I'm breaking for coffee first."

She got up from the floor, turned her back on the living room, and walked shoeless toward the kitchen. Hank Martin looked directly at her, or more correctly at her back, for the first time that evening—at her slim legs, her swaying hips, her bouncy long hair. He drew a handkerchief from his pocket and wiped beneath his collar. There was the sound of water in the sink and her stockinged feet on the kitchen floor. Hank reached out for a low-stacked heel and ran his fingers over the soft glove leather.

Chapter Five

E ve looked at the ticker with dismay. In addition, her mother had reprimanded her severely for working at home with her secretary. Eve had explained he was only harmless Hank Martin, but Mrs. Nelson refused to agree that any man could be "only" or "harmless," and had warned her daughter not to jeopardize her position at W. Worse yet, old Williams was furious at everybody for everything. Eve slumped in her chair. It was all too much. The light flashed on her intercom.

"Yes, Mr. Martin?"

"Another call from Jack in Bora Bora. Will you take it?"

"No, you take it. Handle it, will you?"

Jack Johnston was Williams's assistant, as Hank was hers.

How ridiculous to continue calling him Mr. Martin. But there were his suits and ties and her mother's admonitions.

"Miss Nelson, I told him that since we were responsible for organizing, synthesizing, and analyzing the data, we would not provide it until we had a chance to do so."

"Good for us!" She paused. "I suppose we'd better work on it tonight. Are you free?"

"Whenever you need me, yes."

"Then call The Palace Inn and reserve a small conference room for tonight. We can both get home easily from there."

"But there's no need for the expense."

"Yes, there is, Mr. Hank Martin," she stated firmly.

"I'll make the arrangements immediately, Miss Nelson."

Hank Martin stared at her office door for a moment. She was definite about there being a need for a conference room atmosphere. Could she possibly—No, and yet she had made it quite clear—He was dreaming. He dialed the operator.

There was a brisk breeze blowing, and it lent an appropriately businesslike air to the evening as Eve ascended the hotel steps. This was affected somewhat by a cheery "Eve!" hurled at her from the side of the lobby. Elaine Dawson descended on her, trailed by Bill Wetcliff Jr.

Eve moved a hand to fasten the second button from the top of her V-necked dress. She pressed Wetcliff's hand.

"Bill, why don't we make it a foursome?" asked Elaine.

"That might not suit us all," he suggested.

"Oh, yes, of course." She looked awkwardly from Bill to Eve.

"I'm here on business," Eve explained.

Wetcliff laughed heartily. "In the evening, I don't doubt it."

"It's true."

Wetcliff bowed slightly in her direction. Hank Martin's arrival brought forth a stifled guffaw from Bill that provoked Eve beyond the limits of self-control.

"The boss's son laughing at himself? This will never do. Elaine, you must stimulate the man's ego before his last shred of self-esteem vanishes. Will you do your best? Will you promise?"

Elaine's obvious confusion was matched by the look of amazement on Wetcliff's face.

Hank Martin shook Bill's hand. "I hope you're not minding our business, Mr. Wetcliff."

"Not at all, Mr. Martin."

"Good. Eve and I have a busy night planned."

"Good man, Martin!" He slapped the younger man's shoulder.

Hank turned to his boss. "You see, Eve, he didn't call me Charlie Brown."

"Is that what you are?" asked Wetcliff. "Well, I like you, Chuck. Elaine, do you think of me as Charlie Brown?"

"I don't know. I don't quite understand."

"Well, I've got a whole evening to explain." And he put an arm through hers, saluted the couple with the other, and walked Elaine away.

Eve Nelson faced Hank Martin in anger.

"Mr. Martin, your unspeakable gall is beyond apology."

"I did not intend to apologize. He was laughing at you because you were in a hotel with your lowly secretary, and the only appropriate revenge was to get even. Wasn't that what you tried to do?"

"I'll thank you to allow me the right to defend myself, if and when defense becomes necessary. Your interference confirmed the worst of his stupid assumptions."

Hank Martin opened his mouth to speak, then thought better of it. She gave him her back as she advanced to the elevator. He followed her, and in silence, they rode to the conference room on the third floor.

"Perhaps you'd rather we didn't work tonight, Eve," he offered.

She turned to face him at the door.

"And that's another thing. The name is Miss Nelson. We certainly will work," she stated vehemently. "I get paid to work, and you get paid to work. To work. Not to make gallant speeches and embarrass your immediate superior."

"I understand."

They organized personnel tasks by department. Hank Martin's were clearly executive rather than secretarial.

"We should include Miss Kay's workload," he suggested. "I'm only temporary."

Eve agreed. Miss Kay's work had been increasingly delegated to the secretarial pool. Eve had never needed an assistant before, and but for this workload aberration concocted by old Williams, she wouldn't need one now. In the future, she could manage on her own.

The minutiae of work seemed to stave off the onslaught of exhaustion. It was only when the harmonious machinery of their joint endeavors was stopped by a wayward report that they realized they were tired.

"I'll phone for some beverages. Or would you rather get away from this room for ten minutes?"

Eve looked at her watch. It was 11 o'clock.

"For the night!" she said.

"We haven't finished," he reminded her. "We couldn't have more than an hour's work, and tomorrow is Saturday."

"All right."

She immediately regretted the submissive response. Perhaps he was right, but that wasn't the point. Irrationally, she wished for Miss Kay, who she knew would be, by comparison, a questionable asset in the work at hand. The work had blotted out Elaine Dawson and Bill Wetcliff, but they came to mind as she left the room. They were probably safe in bed, but at this hour, not together. Elaine Dawson could not keep the skin beneath her eyes unlined and keep late hours too. But Eve Nelson's luckless day had still an hour to run, and as she entered the coffee shop, she saw with dismay the couple she had hoped to forget and avoid. Wetcliff waved Eve and Hank toward them.

"Really, we're only down for a few minutes," Eve began.

"Don't tell me that you were denied room service."

"We had to get out of that conference room," Eve declared. "Drinking soda with job descriptions dancing before our eyes was counterproductive."

She despised Wetcliff's too good-natured acceptance of this statement. She would have despised his rejection of it too. Still, the threat of the work waiting upstairs was unable to dissuade Wetcliff from insisting on their company.

"Since it is no part of your purpose tonight to be alone beyond the necessity imposed by your work, you have no reason not to spend your reprieve with us."

Hank held the chair out for Eve, and she sat down, hoping that her detestation of Wetcliff wasn't apparent.

Wetcliff did not choose to talk of work, addressing most of his remarks to Eve, while Elaine Dawson sat wide-eyed and Hank Martin prudently kept quiet and drank his hot chocolate. Eve could not sustain her anger toward Wetcliff. He was too charming, too amusing, and too handsome. But dissatisfaction with him remained.

It surfaced as a dispute over the effects of light in the paintings of Vermeer and the Impressionists. Eve defended the cool, almost palpable light of a Monet. She argued eloquently to Wetcliff's elegant nose and dimpled chin, and she was gratifyingly aware of two other presences at the table, but their existence was shadowy before the man commanding her attention now. They gradually intruded on her mind in the form of a clinking spoon and scraping chair. Then a wonderful idea presented itself to her. She looked quietly now from Hank to Elaine.

"Help me out, one of you," she pleaded.

"This discussion is helping me; I know nothing about the subject." said Hank.

"Me neither," seconded Elaine. "I never thought talk of the lighting in this place would come to this!"

"Bill," said Eve decisively, "I think we owe our colleagues a fuller explanation, with demonstration."

"Our colleagues?"

Eve was delighted at Bill's unease.

"Well, if Elaine weren't a secretary at Merrill Lynch, she could be your assistant at our House. We can each say our piece in front of the paintings and let Hank and Elaine decide which explanation makes more sense."

"Our judgments are subjective."

"Not completely. Shall we give the Metropolitan a try, or do you think your arguments won't convince?"

"I'm game, but I don't think they're open now."

"Oh, you!" She gently, almost coquettishly brushed away the statement with her hand. "The Met's open late Friday evening. Shall we try it then?"

"Very well. May the better light win."

"I'd love it," enthused Elaine, not clarifying exactly to what she was referring.

"All right," said Hank, shrugging off some of his solemnity.

"Then Friday it is. But we've an hour more of work," Eve moaned.

"You're tired," said Hank. "The business won't collapse for want of an hour."

Mrs. Nelson was incredulous. "You've made a date with your secretary!"

"I have not. This is an educational outing, with Bill and me as teachers."

"I'll bet Bill Wetcliff thinks you're dating Hank. Soon, the whole company will think so. And what on earth must Mr. Martin think!"

"Mother, you're getting hysterical. We won't be alone and, believe me, we'll pair off properly before an hour is gone, me with Bill and Hank with Elaine."

"A very pretty plan," said Mrs. Nelson with asperity, "but I doubt if a construction worker turned secretary is likely to seek his own level when the lady boss has done the inviting and when his female peer is the girlfriend of a boss's son."

"He will if Bill pays attention to me and if I make it clear that's what I want."

"Have it your way, Eve. I still think you're better off joining Mensa, but if you can pull this off, you know I'll be the first to applaud."

If.

Chapter Six

"Excuse me, but which of these books do you recommend?" The librarian frowned at the young woman staggering under a pile of books as she plunked them, more or less, onto her desk. Elaine Dawson picked up the volume that had landed in the wastebasket. The librarian glanced at the titles.

"For what purpose?"

"For learning about the work of Monet and Vermeer. I'd like something easy to understand."

From a corner table, a young man watched as the librarian spoke, lifting books and putting them down as the young woman's head bobbed in agreement or shook in uncertainty. He laid the book he was reading print-side down on the table. It was Time-Life's <u>THE WORLD OF VERMEER.</u> As Elaine Dawson turned, two books in hand, he smiled at her from across the room. It was the smile of a happy, relaxed young man, a smile that had never been exposed within the confines of W.W.&S. At first she did not see him and seated herself in the center of the room at a table occupied predominantly by college students, almost hidden by the books piled around them. Hank laughed, receiving the stern gaze of an elderly gentleman reading a newspaper. He watched, fascinated, as she turned pages and took copious notes, turned pages and turned pages. She pushed the books away and propped both hands under her chin.

"You can't give up now," a voice whispered in her ear.
"Mr. Martin!"
The college students glared at her.

"Kids! But they keep at it, and so should you." He wedged half his backside onto her chair. "Now, you haven't begun properly."

"I haven't?" Her eyes opened wide.

"No, you haven't," he said kindly. "Your notes are about Monet and Vermeer, but they're not what we need to know for Friday."

"They're not what we need," she repeated, savoring the "we."

"No, the subject is light in the paintings of Monet and Vermeer, not Monet and Vermeer."

Her "Ah!" evoked an encore of glares from her tablemates, and Hank Martin, taking their books in one arm, uttered a "Come on" and led her, blinking, into the sunlit street.

"It's 11:30. Is it too early for you to eat lunch?"

"Actually, I'm starved."

"Gray-cell work does that to you. But if you don't mind working up a bigger appetite, I thought we'd walk over to The Plaza."

"Oh, I couldn't really."

He looked at her quizzically for a moment before he understood. "We're not going 'Dutch.' Do you pay when you eat with Mr. Wetcliff?"

"No, never. That is, I've only seen him a few times, but no, he wouldn't allow that."

"I wouldn't either."

"Oh, I didn't mean to imply you would. I'm sorry. But it's frightfully expensive there. I'd be happy to eat somewhere else, really I would."

"No, you belong at The Plaza, and I'm taking you there. I don't want you feeling sorry for me. Mr. Wetcliff is ten years my senior. When I'm his age, I'll have a great deal of money too, only I'll have made it on my own."

He was gratified by the wonderment and glow in the face she turned toward him. It reinforced his certainty that Bill Wetcliff was not an emotionally insurmountable obstacle.

Martin's manner with the maitre d' and his firm assurance with the waiter in The Oak Room were impressive. As they settled into Chicken Kiev and Beef Stroganoff, Hank motioned toward the book with his fork.

"Light can do fascinating things, both practical and aesthetic. What do you think of the lighting in here?"

"Oh, it's lovely, so soft and elegant, so romantic."

"But it's too distant a light for reading books. When we get to dessert, I'll have the waiter bring candles so we can read properly."

"But we'll be here forever reading!"

"I guess there is a limit to how much of my company a woman can take, but you needn't worry about that. There is a way to get the information we want in a short amount of time."

"No, no!" Elaine protested. "I could stay in your company forever. You're such a gentleman, and you seem to know exactly what you want in life and how to get it. I respect that."

"Thank you, but respecting someone and enjoying his company, especially forever, aren't quite the same."

"That's not so; I enjoy being with people I respect."

"I'm flattered."

"It's the truth. You must think more highly of yourself or you won't be happy. People will take advantage of you, make a fool of you, and you'll get nowhere no matter how hard you try." It was obvious that Elaine Dawson's experience had taken the floor.

"I'll remember that I'll need help. A man can't will himself to think he's wonderful." He put a hand on hers. "You say all the right things, all the kind things."

She blushed. "The food is delicious," she stumbled.

He took his hand away from hers. "The Stroganoff needs a touch more—um—something. I've made it at least a dozen different ways from the recipes of the gourmet 'greats,' and this does not rank near the top."

"You're a cook! How marvelous, and you're so masculine. I mean—"

He put up a hand. "That's all right. I thought I'd look silly in a white hat too."

They laughed. And sitting there in his navy plaid jacket and blue polka-dot tie, his straight black hair falling casually on his forehead, he looked somehow important as well as handsome.

"What made you want to cook?"

"Auto mechanics. Really! I was always helping my friends fix their jalopies, and one day my mother asked me to fix one of her appliances if I could. She knew I couldn't resist a challenge, so I tried. And would you believe it, I had more trouble with that blender than with the engine on a '55 Buick. Anyway, that got me interested in kitchen appliances and then the food they're used to prepare."

"You could have become a mechanical engineer!"

"I became a construction worker instead. Now, let's see how quickly we can gain an understanding of the construction of light in the works of Monet and Vermeer."

He cleared a space on the table to stack the art books. Then he placed her hands on the top volume and his hands on hers.

"Do you take these books for better or worse?" he intoned solemnly.

"I do," she responded.

As she burst into laughter, Hank's eyes wandered carelessly toward the window that framed them. His laughter halted abruptly, but he managed to keep a semblance of a smile. Glancing in on them were the eyes of a slim woman in a flowered print dress. He lifted one of his hands and waved at Eve Nelson. Elaine waved too, and after a moment of hesitation, Eve did likewise.

"Notice the light," Hank Martin said, his eyes still on the window that no longer presented Eve, "the natural light." His voice trailed off. "Nothing like ours," he resumed with forced pleasure.

"Oh no, Hank, nothing as wonderful as ours!"

They met at the top of the impressive, wide staircase in the entrance hall of the Metropolitan Museum of Art.

"We are taking tours," announced Bill Wetcliff. "Very special, individualized tours."

"Is that what we've decided?"

"Yes, Eve, we have. I'm confident you'll approve of my equitable little plan. It will give us the opportunity to persuade each of our friends to our point of view. We'll spend ten minutes with Vermeer and ten with Monet. Hank and I will begin with Monet, you and Elaine with Vermeer. What say you?"

The term "our friends" did not please Eve. Who were Elaine Dawson and Hank Martin to her? She pictured them hand on hand framed in a Plaza window. Apparently, they were something to each other.

"I think we should allow them to view the paintings with each other and form some preliminary opinions before we interfere. Meanwhile, I'm not convinced that it's hopeless for us to persuade each other."

"We're set in our opinions. Hank and Elaine are still malleable. It's our duty to mold them." There was a twinkle in his eyes. "Honest, kids, no coercion."

Eve refrained from biting her lip. "Malleable, kids." Did Bill consider her ancient?

"Any questions? Good! In twenty minutes, we'll switch for Round Two. Let's go!"

Elaine followed her dutifully, but Eve guessed that her interest lay more with life than art, while Bill's interests lay in both spheres. Only a perceptive woman could get and hold him. She was glad Elaine Dawson and Hank Martin had met.

"How is the Plaza food these days?"

"Hank says it's not so good. He can do better. His chocolate mousse sounds scrumptious. Nothing like it anywhere, he says."

The man's a chef! The office cookies and instant coffee—he had never complained or even commented.

"How lucky for you, or do you mind?"

"Oh, no; I think it's wonderful."

"The cooking or the man?"

Elaine's eyes followed the movement of her feet on the floor. "Both, actually."

"Now just hold that ripply, airy blue water in your heart Eloquent, yes?"

Hank examined the painting face-on, at angles, up close, from several feet away.

"Amazing brushwork and color, Mr. Wetcliff."

"Jesus, man, this is what comes of practically living with Eve. And it's after five; the workday is over. I'm Bill, for Chrissake."

"Just what are you implying is wrong with Eve?" he asked stonily.

"Relax, Hank; I'm not about to disparage your boss. Eve's a first-class businesswoman, accent 'business.'"

Hank's eyes stubbornly held Bill's. "You can accent the 'woman,' too."

Chapter Seven

"**R**ound Two!" announced Bill Wetcliff cheerily.

Elaine's look of adoration destined for Wetcliff lingered for a momentary but significant interval on Hank Martin.

"And to my chagrin," Wetcliff continued," I must admit that Eve was right. I should attempt to persuade her of the merits of Monet's light over Vermeer's before I try to convince Elaine. If I can persuade Eve, I can persuade anyone, so I'm saving you, Elaine, for last. Now we'll see if Eve can withstand my intellect. We'll see you both back here in thirty minutes; I won't pretend to be achieving my goal with Eve in a mere twenty."

"No, Bill, you were right. Our purpose in coming here was to persuade Elaine and Hank, not each other," said Eve, knowing full well what her purpose had been. "Our ideas are set in concrete, remember? Our conversions can wait."

"Purpose amended, waiting period rescinded," declared Wetcliff. "Let's go," and he led Eve away.

Elaine heaved a sigh, then smiled shyly at Hank.

"Didn't we cover the subject pretty well at The Plaza?"

"I guess we did," he agreed. We can explore some of the other galleries?"

"What a lovely idea! Which way shall we go?"

"Would you like to see the Viennese clothes in the Costume Institute?"

"Oh, yes, would you mind?"

"Not at all. It's down the stairs and to your left. The signs couldn't be clearer. I've been meaning to see the medieval bones exhibit for some time. Extremely boring, I hear, but it interests me. I'll direct everyone to the Institute for a quick look and to pick you up."

"But they'll lose their concentration!"

"Not those two, and we mustn't lose ours."

"But—"

Hank kissed her lightly on the cheek. "We'll see you in thirty minutes."

Elaine grimaced after him. She could understand her inability to compete with the worldly Eve Nelson, but medieval bones?

To hell with old Vienna, she thought, as she headed down the stairs toward it.

"Stubborn as ever, Eve."

"Say opinionated."

"Is that better?"

"Much."

Bill Wetcliff laughed. "I suppose that still extends to my skill as an artist."

"Bill, I never said you lacked talent."

"I don't recall your defending my work for the reception area."

"We wouldn't want to give our clients the idea that they can look forward to being financially stripped with us."

"What's wrong with a foretaste of marketplace reality? Anyway, the nude was pink, so the warning wasn't totally dark. It's unfair to center so much attention on my nudes. Don't be like the rest of them, Eve."

His tone and his appeal surprised her, but she did not question them. They were intellectual equals. There was respect residing in that, respect and excitement. Hadn't she suggested this Friday meeting to prove just that to him?

"If your clothed Majas are equally arresting, you are the complete professional."

"Think I could make a living as an artist if they were?"

Eve looked at his broad-shouldered, muscular build and his handsome face.

"We need you at the shop."

"Dad does; the heir apparent must be groomed. The Board does; they can count on my well-timed outlandish suggestions to keep them awake. The staff may; rumors of my sexual prowess make their lives bearable. But you? You zip along beautifully in your work without me."

"Will you feel better if I promise to need you at least once each day?"

"And let me know each time?"

"If you're not busy listening to someone else tell you the same thing."

"Eve!"

"Bill Wetcliff, where are we going? This isn't the way back to Round Three."

"I thought we'd take a little detour to see the Italian drawings. I have quite a collection, you know."

"Don't tell the guards," she warned.

Bill put his arm around her waist to usher her through the door. The large rotunda faced with paintings gave a taste of more in the rooms beyond them that traced the circular shape of the Lehman wing. Bill and Eve passed potted trees and descended the stairs to the drawing collection. They had both been to Venice, and the Canalettos and Guardis stirred memories. Pencil had personalized the Piazza San Marco more than experience had, and the circular journey under the soft lights, the stroll on carpet that told no tales, made it even more so.

"Remember that?" asked Bill, pointing to a particular view of the bay, as though they had been there together and shared that night together.

"I remember," she said, a faint, faraway smile crossing her face.

"You look beautiful that way," he said.

She looked up at him in surprise, then away. *We should spend more time like this.*

With penciled-in pleasures, she thought. They would have to be, delicate prints under soft lights to prevent fading. They couldn't last otherwise; they surely couldn't last.

"I did some pencil sketches in Aspen last winter. Mountains, ski trails, lodges, nothing unusual, quiet little things, but they seemed so exhilarating, so special at the time. Guardis and Canalettos will endure, but Wetcliffs—." He shook his head. "The nudes make a splash for a while, at least. Nudes always get attention."

"I'm not going to feel sorry for you, Bill."

"You should. I have to sink pretty low to be noticed."

"Don't tell Modigliani or Renoir that."

"Outside of the Boardroom, would you know I existed if I didn't have this—this reputation?"

Eve looked at him in amazement. "I think so," she finally said.

"It's nice of you to say."

"It's true. You've got some fine qualities, Bill. You're honest, enthusiastic, talented. How can you doubt yourself so?"

"It's easy when there's no one you respect to tell you otherwise."

"Don't you respect me?"

"Very much," he responded warmly.

She turned toward a Guardi. "The tint adds charm."

The pale pink, blue, and brown wash did indeed.

"It suits you. I'll buy it for you."

"You're crazy, Bill!"

"It blends with your pink sweater and brown skirt. It would look wonderful under your arm."

She laughed appreciatively. "I'm sure the Met is anxious to sell it."

"What a wonderful laugh, what warming colors!"

She tried to suppress a smile and shook her head in disbelief. She bent toward the Guardi.

"You're not very encouraging, Eve," he said in a wounded tone.

"I'm trying to be," she said softly.

"You are? Well!"

"Shush, Bill, keep your voice down."

"Not a chance," he boomed, "unless you have dinner with me next Friday night at The Carroll Inn."

"All right, all right. That guard looks as if he wants you arrested."

"My heart has already been arrested."

"So silly," she said, obviously pleased. "We'd better get back to the others."

Hank Martin leaned dangerously over the rail at the top of the stairs inside the Lehman wing. He could not see his prey, but exclamations first from one then from the other reached his ears. He dared not go down, though he certainly had as much right to be there as they, which, considering their arrangement, was no right at all. He knew that the drawings were faintly lit, and he had neither seen nor heard other people in that sheltered area. Well, what did he care if she demeaned herself by running off with the office Adonis! Women were fools, women bosses not excepted. And good for Wetcliff! Women deserved no better than they were willing to accept. But his lips compressed tightly and his knuckles stood out clearly as his hands grasped the rail. The guard below came into view, and he felt a senseless relief. He saw the couple round the corner for the remaining half of the circular display. He glanced at his watch. They would be late for Round Three. This evening had merely been a ruse to allow them time together. Wetcliff was a crafty operator, all right. Hank conveniently forgot that Eve had suggested the Met. He stood upright and squared his shoulders. This was foolishness. He strode to the exit in the strength of this conviction. Staunchly refusing to pace, when Eve and Bill arrived, much too slowly for the length of rooms they had had to traverse, Hank greeted them brusquely.

"Elaine will think she's been abandoned," he said pointedly. "She wanted to see the costume exhibit. I said we would meet her there."

"This is sabotage, Hank. If her head is too full of costumes to appreciate the virtues of Monet, you will have destroyed the entire purpose of this evening."

"I think not," said Hank dryly.

Wetcliff threw him a sharp glance, while Eve apologized too profusely for their delay, failing to mention its cause. They were all grateful when they entered the diversionary precincts of The Costume Institute. They found Elaine admiring a gold and diamond-encrusted brocade gown of 18th-century Vienna.

"Clothes were so romantic then," she crooned dreamily.

"And stiff, heavy and uncomfortable," reminded Eve.

"They were worth it. What's a little pain if you can look like that?"

"You mean like a dummy stuck in heap of material?" asked Wetcliff.

"You think feminine women look like dummies?"

"There was a twinkle in my eye when I said that. You didn't see it because you were looking at Hank."

Elaine blushed and Hank Martin reddened, but Eve knew that Elaine had done no such thing.

"Since your head is full of costumes now, shall we dispense with our art instruction for the night? You can instruct me on the merits of the costumes you've seen, instead."

"But Bill! We were to be persuaded, and the process isn't finished!" wailed Elaine,

"Actually," said Bill, "it's better this way. You've seen the paintings in each other's company without pressure from either Eve or me. Taste is subjective, and I'm sure you've decided on whose paintings appealed to your taste. Haven't you, Elaine?"

"Definitely Monet," said Elaine.

"You see?"

"Well, I haven't made up my mind," said Hank stubbornly.

"For some people, it takes time," came the sympathetic response. "Come back several times, and you'll be able to make a decision."

"This was not Miss Nelson's intention," retorted Hank, now conveniently recalling the source of this outing.

"Do you mind very much, Eve? I'm rather tired of marching back and forth, and these costumes do look beautiful. Shall we make Elaine our instructress? Shall the teachers learn from their pupil?"

"If Elaine would like."

"I only want to look!"

"And we'll help you. We'll all offer our analyses and learn from one another. That's democracy."

Hank Martin muttered that it was something else, and he went along with the farce for the space of three costumes before he could take no more. And with neither excuse nor apology, he left the field to his superior.

Chapter Eight

Hank Martin tossed in bed most of the night, torturing himself with meaningful looks, imagined and real, that Eve had given Wetcliff: respectful looks, adoring looks, possessive looks. His words had been constantly addressed to her, and she always had responded to them, hadn't she? His eyes had constantly devoured hers, and she had welcomed this, hadn't she? His arms had kept her from walking blindly into a pillar, and her voice had enfolded him, hadn't it? Hank finally fell into an uneasy sleep. He dreamed Eve and Wetcliff were on a Ferris wheel and he was on the ground just below it. As their car bent toward him, he attempted to grab onto its bar and pull himself in, only to fall back. Time and again he tried and was frustrated, and each time Eve and Wetcliff had laughed and waved as they were propelled out of reach. Hank awoke exhausted, sweating profusely. He took a shower, drank three cups of black coffee, and grimly headed for the office.

Eve's secretary-assistant was already behind his desk. "Good morning, Mr. Martin." She swept past him and shut the door on his echoed response. She hung the jacket of her suit on the back of her chair and sat down. Within five minutes, every inch of the desk was covered with account files, transaction slips, and memos. She ran a hand across her forehead as she pressed a button for her man on the Market floor. She gave orders, asked questions, and rapidly scribbled notes. Her activity remained feverish for the balance of the morning. Hank Martin's attempt to serve her coffee was greeted with an irritable "not now." At noon, she had him order her a chicken salad sandwich, and she remained closeted in her office for the remainder of the day.

At 5 o'clock she put down her pen, leaned back in her chair, closed her eyes and wondered why she felt so upset. She had done an enormous amount of work that day, and there was no cause for her nervous stomach and rapid pulse. Maybe she was coming down with something, but she was never ill. The day was over. She would go home and get a long night's sleep. But she did not rise from her chair. She could not. She tried, but her leg muscles felt sluggish, her body unwieldy. Too much sitting, she thought. She leaned back in the chair and closed her eyes again. The day was over. She would be sitting forever over figures, research reports and investment plans. She would spend her life in a large office with semi-masculine furniture, periodic visits from data-minded names in her client stable and periodic excursions to monthly meetings designed to enhance the bottom line. She would devote her life to forwarding the financial interests of people she scarcely knew, might never meet, or couldn't care less about, and her motive was hardly altruistic. She was successfully driving herself through life, but she wasn't happy. It wasn't her fault. She was doing her feeble best. It had got her Bill Wetcliff's attention and a date. But she wasn't quite sure how she had done it. Her intellectual challenge? Her soft sweater? He had found them resistible before. At one sight of Elaine, very resistible. Perhaps the "good life" bored him, and Eve was respite from it. His compliments and praise were indigestible, welcome but unreal. They were too sudden, too unreasonable to last. Just another kind of business. Even Elaine knew that. But unlike Elaine, she also knew that men were not inscrutable, only unreliable. She longed to go home. A light flashed on her desk.

"Good night, Miss Nelson."

"Good night, Hank," she responded without thinking.

Hank Martin stared at the intercom in disbelief. Was he no longer Mr. Martin, then?

Eve was not aware how long she had been sitting at her desk until the phone ringing in the outer office caused her to look at the clock. It was 5:30. She waited until the third unanswered ring.

"Eve Nelson speaking."

"Miss Nelson. Oh, I'm sorry. I thought that—I'm sorry."

The speaker was about to cradle the receiver, but Eve would not allow this.

"Mr. Martin has already left, I'm afraid. Shall I leave him a message, Miss Dawson?"

Her blush was almost audible. "No, thank you. I thought he might be gone, but I had to be sure. I mean—well, there's no point in calling him now. Thank you, anyway."

"You're not angry at him, then. I'm glad."

"Angry? Why should I be angry?"

Eve hesitated, loathe to upset a relationship important to her goal.

"He doesn't seem too fond of costumes," she finally said.

"Why should he be? That's a woman's concern."

Eve refrained from pointing out that currently the world's most adored designers were men, and that Martin's abandoning her at the exhibit might reasonably create in her a tinge of animosity toward him.

"Actually," continued Elaine, "I just got hold of two tickets to a lecture on architecture, and I thought he might want to join me tonight."

Good thinking, thought Eve, but why not artist Wetcliff? Or was it a matter of "a bird in hand," or one that could more easily be brought to hand?

"I'm sure he'll appreciate your thoughtfulness when I tell him in the morning. Enjoy the lecture. Perhaps you can take notes for him and discuss them with him when you see him next."

Elaine seemed doubtful. "I don't know. I'm sure I'll see him, of course. We work so near each other, and it's a small world, as they say," she ended weakly. "But you know," she confided, "I'm not particularly interested in architecture, though I'm sure I could be if Hank explained it all to me."

"I'm sure you could, too. Why don't you be brave? Go to the lecture, take those notes, and astonish and delight Mr. Martin with them. He'll love explaining them to you. Men adore that sort of thing."

Instantly she felt the lie. Outside of themselves and an easy lay, Eve had no idea what men adored.

"Come with me!" exploded Elaine. "Please come! You can take notes for Bill."

"I beg your pardon, but I have no need to take notes for anyone."

The ice was palpable.

"Don't be cross with me. I'm not all that stupid. It's obvious you like him. You should show it more. You're too smart to let him get away. Come to the lecture with me. It's at The New School at 7 o'clock."

"I'm too tired to go anywhere but home."

"You mean executives can give secretaries advice but…"

As Eve listened to the speaker drone on, she wondered why she had come. She had wanted to be alone. She had spent the day working alone, had eaten dinner alone, and had intended to spend the evening alone. Yet here she was with a potential rival with whom she otherwise had nothing in common, half listening to something about the structure of residential buildings. Oddly, she felt alone, the vocal flow reinforcing the flow of emptiness within her. Elaine nudged her and pointed to the words Beaux Arts, which she had underlined on her paper. Eve merely nodded. The Beaux Arts Trio as architect? In the finest sense, yes. The nuanced beauty of their Haydn was touching, alive, personal, real, sensuous. Nothing of the purely sculptured and cold about it. And wasn't architecture sensuous? Hadn't the doyenne of architecture critics Ada Louise Huxtable said so? A jumble of style, music and passion filled her mind. There was some structure, some sense to it all, wasn't there? Almost inperceptibly she shook her head in denial, even as she increased her attention to the speaker.

He was in the midst of discussing the creative design of setbacks when Eve became aware that the woman at her side was discussing something of a different nature with the man sitting behind her. Elaine's chair leaned dangerously, and only the intervention of Eve and Elaine's talk partner kept her from flying backwards. Either the danger or the nasty looks of several distracted members of the audience brought Elaine to propriety. Her whispers ceased, and her writing began anew, not notes, but letters. She penned a dozen to her correspondent in the rear and received as many in return. The speaker had reached a crescendo of urgency about setbacks when a head directly facing the lectern caught Eve's eye. And to her shock and dismay, she recognized it as that of Hank Martin. On her pad, Elaine had just written "I'd love to." Eve whipped the pen from her hand and on the next sheet scribbled, "Hank is in the first row. Don't blow it." Elaine's eyes widened and met Eve's. Under "I'd love to" she added, "but not tonight." Neither woman heard the remainder of the lecture. They were the first to stand at its conclusion, but they needn't have rushed. Hank Martin was waiting for them in the aisle before they had left their row.

"I didn't know you were interested in architecture," he addressed them both, smiling.

"Only Elaine is," declared Eve stiffly.

"I'm trying to learn," said Elaine. She waved her notes.

"Good for you. I'd enjoy comparing them with mine. Over a drink?"

Elaine beamed into the air, the most she dared, to return the wave of the exiting stranger she had spoken and written to for the past hour.

"Shall we go, then?" asked Hank, taking this as Elaine's response. His eyes took in Eve, too.

"I can't really. I must get some sleep."

"I would have thought you'd have gotten some this hour."

Eve smiled. "Not enough."

"If you come with us, I'll promise you more."

She laughed. "Thank you, but—"

"No? Well, it's good to see you laughing. You've been too busy to laugh much these three months. We'll see you home first and—"

"Don't be silly! I'm not a child."

"I insist."

"Good night to you both," Eve said firmly.

"Now, there's a woman who knows her mind," exclaimed Elaine as Eve walked away.

"Let's hope not."

Elaine's eyebrows rose.

"Life's no fun if you're always sure, don't you think?"

Eve had just settled comfortably under the covers when the phone rang.

"Are you all right?"

"Well, of course I'm all right. Hank?"

"Yes. I wanted to make sure you got home safely."

Eve sat bolt upright in bed. "Do you realize, Mr. Martin, that I'm a grown woman and well able to take care of myself?"

"Yes."

"And do you realize that if, through some unlikely scenario, I hadn't gotten home safely, there would be nothing you could do about it?"

"Yes. But you are all right?"

"You wake me to ask me that?"

"I'm sorry, were you sleeping?"

"Well, not quite," she relented. "But you needn't worry. I'll be in the office early tomorrow ready to tackle the complexities of the day."

"I wasn't thinking of tomorrow."

"Then whatever were you thinking of? You've probably left that lovely Elaine Dawson alone in a coffee shop in order to make this ridiculous call. And no woman who looks like Elaine Dawson should be left alone, as any man of sense would know."

"I'm sorry, would you repeat that? I'm afraid I lost your drift."

"Hank Martin, what's gotten into you? I want to go to sleep."

"So do I."

"Then do it. Good night!" She slammed the receiver into its cradle.

Eve tried to resettle herself comfortably in bed, but it was useless. Each new position presented another question, and nowhere was the calm of oblivion to be found. Hank Martin had never seen her home before, had never called, like a good mama, to make sure she had gotten home intact. Of course, she reflected, he had never had the opportunity, apart from their hotel room business meeting the previous week, and he had made no fuss then about her ability to get home alone. He *had* asked to see her home, but that was the routine, gentlemanly thing to ask any woman any evening. How had he phrased it? "Would you like me to see you home?" Hardly personal. Would she like. He gave no indication that he would like. He had taken liberties in addressing her in front of Wetcliff, but that was merely a protective gesture. One should protect a lady from disparagement, and one must protect one's boss. No, there had been nothing personal about Hank Martin's behavior toward her to date. He certainly hadn't treated their work meetings in her apartment as rendezvous. Then why this sudden interest in her welfare? Her mother's fears came to mind. They were utter nonsense. She had the respectful concern of her subordinate and a date with Bill two nights from now. Why couldn't she sleep?

Chapter Nine

"**G**ood morning, Mr. Martin."

"Good morning, Eve."

She shot him a sharp look at this informality as she continued to her office door.

"Your mother called. She would like a return call immediately."

Eve threw her briefcase on the desk. A sleepless night and a call from her mother. This was not a propitious beginning to the day. She sat at her desk and dialed.

"Mother, what's happened?"

"Darling, you must help me. I can't go on any longer. There's three inches of water on the kitchen floor and pails full of water under the pipes in the cabinet. Everything is soaked. I told you I phoned that new plumbing company last week when a small leak developed. Then there was a leak in another spot, and they came, and another, and they refuse to come anymore. They can't find what's wrong. They say contact the manufacturer."

"And a good lawyer. You still retain Dempsey for the shop."

"The law can take forever! What about this swimming pool in my apartment? I can't live like this, Eve, I just can't! Pomeroy and Fritz is on W.W.&S.'s list of recommended stocks. They're my pipe people. Could you contact them for me — I'm relegated to their secretaries — and find out what causes their pipes to leak so I can instruct a plumber and dry out this apartment?"

"You have a warranty. Try some other plumbers and sue P&F for reimbursement. At least one plumber in this city must know his job."

"I don't want the aggravation. I want the facts first, then I'll call another plumber. Please, Eve. I hate to be a burden, but I don't ask much of you. An occasional phone call, lunch once a week..."

"I'll see what I can do, Mother."

"Thank you. Could you get back to me this morning, dearest?"

"I'll try."

Eve sighed heavily. She was not about to use their brokerage arm as a repair intermediary.

"Mr. Martin, get me a list of the best plumbers in the city."

"Certainly. What's the problem?"

"That's what I want the plumber to tell me, or rather, my mother. Her kitchen pipes are leaking for some unfathomable reason."

"I know something about plumbing."

"Mother needs an expert."

"I am an expert."

"Knowing something about plumbing is not what's called for. I'd like that list this morning."

"Don't mistake my modesty for ignorance. If I can't do the job, I'll get somebody who can. I'll be at your mother's apartment after work."

"I shouldn't have asked you. This is personal business. I'll check out the plumbers myself."

"I'll get on it right away and give your mother the information. You've got an appointment in half an hour, and Research has just delivered those papers you requested. I'm bringing them right in."

"You will take care of that plumbing business?" she asked almost absent-mindedly, her thoughts already partially occupied with the papers he had just placed on her desk.

"You needn't worry. Your mother won't complain again to you about it."

Eve glanced up at him as he left the office. She had become increasingly aware of his arrogance and efficiency. She was not offended. She had never been served so well, she thought, as she gave her full attention to the papers.

"Thank goodness," said Mrs. Nelson without preliminaries, as she ushered Hank Martin into the apartment. "What did they say caused the flood?"

"I can't say yet."

"Didn't my daughter call Pomeroy and Fritz?"

"No, but she did ask me to. I thought it better to examine the pipes myself first."

He got down on his knees, flashlight in hand, and peered into the cabinets.

"You thought! You are not paid to think, only to follow orders. Get up this instant before you destroy what's left of my pipes."

"I have a degree in construction engineering. I've never used it, but ... Turn on the water just a little."

She complied. "I don't believe it."

"Good. A little more water, now."

"Construction engineers do not become male secretaries."

"Probably not. Aha!"

"You've found the trouble?"

"Maybe." He turned off the water, took out a Swiss pocketknife, and started scraping and banging.

"You'll break the pipes!"

He got to his feet and turned off the water.

"That wouldn't be hard. How long have you had them?"

"Two years."

"Remarkable they lasted that long. I'll get you a plumber now, and a section of this pipe will get you full reimbursement. Have you got the sales receipt?"

"Yes, right here." She fished it out of a pile of papers impaled on a rod.

"I'll make a copy of it and bring you back the original this evening. I'll pick up the pipe segments the plumber will need, and I'll deal with Pomeroy and Fritz. If this is part of their cost-cutting procedures, they're in for an earnings tumble, and on behalf of W.W.&S., I'm going to tell them so."

"Mr. Martin, I love you."

Hank Martin turned visibly pink. "I hate when people are rooked with shoddy workmanship," he mumbled.

He glanced at his watch. "I'd better hurry back."

"My, yes. Eve must find you indispensable at the office. How wonderful of her to send you here."

"Actually, I sent myself. Goodbye, Mrs. Nelson. I'll be back tonight."

"Sent yourself! Heavens, this must be your lunch hour. I'll bet you haven't eaten yet!"

"I'm not hungry."

"You're not leaving without something in your stomach. You'll have some chicken salad and my own special walnut chiffon cake." She put up a hand to silence him. "You will not budge from this apartment without lunch. Eve will have to wait another hour for your assistance. That's final."

A light was flashing on his intercom as Hank Martin approached his desk.

"Yes, Eve?"

"I typed the Metcalf memo and delivered it myself, Mister Martin. I received two calls for information in your files and a personal call for you from Elaine Dawson. Rather than leave these memos exposed on your cleared desk, they are cluttering mine."

"I'll be right in."

He strode fearlessly toward the barricade behind which Eve Nelson sat. She glared at him, motioned to some papers and cast her eyes on a sheet of figures before her.

"I'll make up the half-hour," he said confidently, addressing the top of her head.

"That's not the point."

"Never expect perfection," he stated matter-of-factly. At the door, he turned toward her. She had risen from her chair with the sudden ramrod exuberance of a furious woman.

"Your mother's expecting us at 6:30. We should avoid the heavy traffic if we leave at 6:00. Since I won't be leaving at 5:00, voila! My debt of half-hour paid in duplicate. I'm making no request for overtime." And he made his exit.

She stormed out of her office after him. "What do you mean—"

"Shush," He looked around them. "People will think we're quarreling."

"We are quarreling."

"Employees are yelled at," he instructed. "Only lovers quarrel."

She slammed herself back into her office. Eve Nelson couldn't remember when she had been so angry. She misdialed three times before getting it right, then tapped her fingers impatiently on the desk.

"Mother! What did you say to Hank Martin? I'm not shouting. He had no right to. You berate me for working with him after business hours and you invite him home? I do care about your heart, but what about my reputation which you claim to be so concerned about? Do your water pipes take precedence over that? I don't care if he said he was King Tut's plumber, and I'm not coming with him tonight. You and Hank and Harry can have your cozy dinner without me. Goodbye."

The horror struck her immediately. She had been cruel. Crazy and cruel. Why had she dragged in Harry? What did he have to do with anything? Her mother was certainly entitled to her life and secrets. Surely, she wasn't jealous of her own mother. Live-in companions were convenient even if kitchen plumbing was beyond them. Perhaps her mother even had what was called a meaningful relationship, but Eve, try though she had in days long past, had always found meaningless a more appropriate description for mere physical coupling. And her mind had never been engaged. But Bill Wetcliff was more than a sexual challenge, wasn't he? Eve groaned. Perhaps meaningful relationships had more meaning when you resisted the temptation to determine what that meaning was. When the phone rang, Eve responded to it before Hank could.

"I'm sorry, darling, I would have mentioned Harry, but I didn't think you'd understand. He's still in Michigan visiting his family. I know you and I love each other and that we wouldn't interfere in each other's lives, but since Hank Martin was so wonderful to me and since I did invite him for dinner... Please say you'll come too, darling."

With her wrongs flooding her mind, Eve could make but one response.

"Forgive me, Mother. I understand. Of course, I'll be there." But as she hung up, Eve realized that she did not understand. On holiday and in her dreams, she had understood everything very well. It would have been frightening not to understand now, but the wood paneling and Put and Call accounts reassured her.

As Hank Martin closed the car door after ushering Eve inside, it struck her that she had never looked at him before. At Mr. Martin, her secretary and assistant, yes, but not at the man. Somehow even at the museum and lecture, his features had taken on business configurations. She snatched a look at his profile as he walked around the front of the car to the driver's side. He was very handsome. She wondered if Elaine Dawson thought so too. Not that it particularly mattered to Elaine Dawson. Certainly it didn't matter to Eve. Her cheeks warmed. But Bill Wetcliff was different. He was unconventional. Brilliant and unconventional. He just happened to be handsome too. A construction engineer as a male secretary wasn't being unconventional enough. It wasn't the occupation, it was the man. Not that she was deeply interested in Wetcliff, she told herself, but at least his motives were clear and above-board. Hank Martin's motives were clear too, if not as open and honest. Eve was his challenge. Oh, there was no doubt. He was working on her as she was working on Bill Wetcliff. American enterprise at work. Yes, it was all clear and admirable in its way, she thought with a marked lack of enthusiasm. One mustn't expect perfection. Hank started the car.

"I didn't mean to get myself invited to dinner."

"I know. You needn't apologize."

"It's hard to refuse your mother."

"I'm aware of that. I hope you like salmon steak."

"It's one of my favorites."

"That explains it. It's not one of mine."

"Good heavens! I never would have suggested it. Your mother asked and—"

Eve smiled at him. "I'm not blaming you. I'm not even blaming Mother."

"I wish I hadn't said anything. You shouldn't have to suffer through a meal because of me."

"Oh, I won't be suffering. The entertainment will take my mind off the food."

And enjoy herself she did.

"Salmon is Eve's favorite color for the bedroom. It complements the dark wood beautifully, don't you think?"

Hank blushed slightly. "I can judge only from your kitchen, Mrs. Nelson, and here, yes, very much so."

"The bedroom effect is remarkable. A queen-size expanse of yellow velvet tufted headboard in a frame of rich mahogany. You must show it to Hank sometime, Eve."

"I'll bring it to the office."

"What colors do you like, Hank?"

"Most colors; I'm not fussy."

"How wonderfully open-minded of you, isn't it, Eve?"

"Undiscriminating."

"And open-minded. I'm so glad you could come."

"Did he have any choice?"

"Eve, really. How many young men would choose dinner with a lonely, old woman?"

"But he didn't. He chose you."

"Unlike my daughter, who's been too busy for our lunches two weeks in a row. You really must come with Eve more often, Hank, or I'm not likely to see her at all."

"He can come instead and tell you all about me. And he would never argue with you."

"Which is why I prefer if you came too, dear."

The entertainment was wearing thin. Eve rose. She looked at her watch.

"It was delicious, Mother—the food, the chat, seeing you after all these days." She bent to kiss Mrs. Nelson and give her a hug. "But I've got to get up early tomorrow, and I've a few hours more of work."

"With Hank?" she asked brightly.

"Alone."

"The food was delicious. Thank you, Mrs. Nelson." Hank clasped her hands.

"Hardly gourmet, but it's kind of you to say."

"I'm never kind about food."

"Oh!" She gave him a coquettish smile and a tilt of her head. "I wish we had more time to talk, but with Eve rushing you off like this—"

"We did speak before and during dinner, Mother."

"My daughter, the economist. Time economy was never meant to apply to mothers," she scolded.

"One of the banes of progress," observed Eve.

"And not the least of them," responded Mrs. Nelson, patting Eve's hands.

Eve appreciated the silence during the drive home. It gave her time to dwell on how Bill Wetcliff would have filled it, how he would have charmed her mother, how the crinkles of annoyance she felt at her mother's behavior that evening would have been flushes of pleasure. Hank was silent also, in the elevator and until she turned the key in her lock.

"Would you like me in earlier tomorrow? There's the Bartlett account to prepare."

"No, I won't be needing it until Monday."

"That's true. Well, goodnight, then."

When Eve closed the door behind her, the stillness struck her strangely. She undressed and put the bath towel within reach of the shower. There was the slap of rushing water on her skin and tomorrow's schedule running through her mind The silence that followed was the usual friendly one.

Two hours of poring over notebooks and files brought a rational conclusion to the day. She nestled comfortably in bed and fell asleep dreaming of supper with Bill Wetcliff at The Carroll Inn.

Chapter Ten

The clouds were up with Eve at 7 o'clock. They followed her to the office and hovered outside her window. Hank Martin was all propriety. Gone were the flippant remarks of yesterday and the aggressive concern. He addressed her as Miss Nelson and was all condescension and efficiency. This enabled Eve to get through the day despite the weather and to indulge herself with occasional lapses of concentration brought on by the clock and the promise of the weekend ahead.

"I'm leaving early, Mr. Martin."

"Where shall I direct emergency calls?"

"Nowhere. There will be no emergencies until Monday. Have a good weekend."

He didn't like her smile, or her jaunty walk, or the way she quietly closed the office door behind her. He swallowed. He would spend the evening making his special chocolate mousse. It would surprise Mrs. Nelson in the morning. If anyone could inform him of Eve's whereabouts, she could.

The powder-pink knit dress was ideal, feminine and romantically whisper-soft. Not too daring, it boasted only a moderately scooped bodice but displayed the length of her arms and the most shapely section of her legs. The candlelight playing on her skin and dress would set off to advantage the wit and candor of her conversation. At least she hoped it would. The Carroll Inn. She couldn't remember hearing of it before. It was just as well. She harbored no preconceptions about it, except for the candlelight. The experience would be fresh. She reached inside the refrigerator for a yogurt to tide her over until 9 o'clock. The Carroll Inn. She thought she was familiar with most restaurants in and near the city.

Why was this one unfamiliar? It would be delightful to be surprised with a new gem of a place, but still ... Out came the Yellow Pages for all points one hour distant by car. But no restaurants, hotels, motels or inns of that name were to be found.

"Operator, I'd like some information."

For the next hour, she covered adjoining states to no avail. She moved further north.

"Thank you, Operator." It was Vermont. With all that moonlight.

Eve was furious. The pleasing prospect of two days with Bill Wetcliff was drowned in an attendant audacity. How could he expect her to spend the weekend in one pink dress? Answer: When you had Bill Wetcliff, you didn't need clothes. Eve kicked the leg of a chair. That conceited macho moron! Her mind counted for something, as he would soon discover.

"This is just another form of business," she told herself. "Treat it as such. You've proven your desirability to Bill on the only level of affection he understands." She jumped to her feet, swung open her bedroom closet, and pulled out a backless dress. She tossed the bra back into the drawer. "And reinforce it. And then we'll see who is the victor and who the victim." And she slammed the drawer shut with a finality that rocked it on its hinges.

Hank Martin grimly considered the morning. No, not Mrs. Nelson's effusive thanks for the mousse. What did he care for that? But her ignorance of her daughter's whereabouts, that daughter's absence from her apartment, and Bill Wetcliff's absence from his were food for somber thought. He had not been ashamed, since no one would know, to phone all rail and airlines to determine how and to where they had fled. Apparently, they had gone by car and could be anywhere. Just as he acknowledged the hopelessness of discovering their destination, desperation opened a possible route. He was soon dialing the private garage near Wetcliff's apartment.

The parking attendant regretted being unable to help, but since Mr. Wetcliff was off somewhere in Vermont for the weekend, he suggested putting business matters on hold until Monday. Hank Martin spent the afternoon on the phone with Vermont. His eventual success in his search did not gratify him. What could he do? Eve Nelson was a grown woman entitled to choose her lifestyle and her men. Even so, if she were his sister or his wife… But she was neither. He had no call on her affections, but he could not stifle his own. He could only suffer. He could admit the truth and suffer. But desire dimpled the truth. On several occasions, she had called him Hank, had praised his work, and focused her wit upon him in a casual, friendly style. If those expressions had been of no significance to her, why had she uttered them? Why had he developed a fondness and a hope? With the logic of a man in love, he determined the truth was not clear and that imminent resolution of the perplexity was essential. He would not allow that it was too late. That simply could not be. Elaine Dawson would be available and eager. He clenched his teeth.

"Elaine, your voice is just the tonic I need. I'm surrounded by papers that I promised myself I wouldn't take home. Please see me tonight. I've got to get away—with you."

"Oh, Hank, I wish I could, but I'm busy tonight. I can make it tomorrow."

"I'll be a dissipated wreck by tomorrow. If I'm alone, I won't be able to keep myself from work, and there's no one else I care to ask."

"But I can't disappoint Jim."

"I'll bet he's disappointed you in some way at least once. Just the thought of you has kept me going. Picture candlelight and wine, a swim before dinner, the romantic Vermont scenery."

"I've never been to Vermont," she said wistfully.

"Come with me now!"

"I'll tell Jim I've got laryngitis."

"You're wonderful. Can you be ready by 5 o'clock?"

"Sure. What's your favorite color?"

"Any color you wear."

"You're sweet. See you at five."

Hank replaced the receiver with both relief and disbelief. She would come. But he was astonished at the stream of romantic slush within him. He shook his head to clear it, the while hoping that enough bilge remained to see him through the weekend. This was war.

The car turned onto a winding drive off the highway. Pink, white, and orange flowering bushes hugged the road. In the distance, elevated above a tumble of trees, lay The Carroll Inn.

"It's good to see you again, Mr. Wetcliff," barked the parking attendant.

Bill Wetcliff pressed a bill into his hand.

"It will be even better if you don't say so next time," he whispered.

The Honeymoon Suite was lavishly appointed with silks, satins and brocades. Chandeliers illumined each room, including the bathroom, where crystal swans were the faucets and mirrors reflected the oversized pink tile tub reached by broad, white marble stairs. The French windows opened onto a balcony overlooking a profusion of honeysuckle and rose bushes, whose mingled fragrances offered a natural headiness that Eve especially appreciated at this time. Bill Wetcliff ruined the effect by approaching her with assurance and attempting to take her in his arms.

"This will have to wait, Bill," she said gently, pushing him away.

He looked around him. "Too much competition. Is it safe for me to suggest a stroll, or will it mean I have to wait even longer?"

"A man like you can be assured of getting what he deserves," Eve said sweetly.

Elaine stewed. For a man in dire need of her, Hank Martin seemed to find the road more interesting than her company.

Her companion seemed to realize that more was expected of him. "I've never been there before, but I've heard it's very special. Bill Wetcliff has been known to go there, and there can't be a higher recommendation than that."

"He's nothing," she said.

"He's fickle, but he's talented and rich," Hank continued doggedly.

"You'll be rich someday."

"Not many women would be willing to wait that long."

"I'd wait."

"And Bill Wetcliff has a way about him, don't you think?"

"Oh, pooh Bill Wetcliff!"

"But he's too slick, too devious for you. He'd be a devil of a man to handle."

"I can be slick and devious too, you know. I'm not as simple as I seem. I don't want to talk about Bill Wetcliff anymore."

Hank pecked her cheek. "Not a word about Barnacle Bill for the rest of the weekend."

"I wish you'd picked another place."

Hank was all concern for Elaine from the Inn door on. He was a gentleman at heart, and he was pleased that his purpose here could be best accomplished by playing the gentleman with a vengeance. The first challenge to the gentleman's honor was not many minutes in coming.

"Not available? I requested the Honeymoon Suite."

"So we noted," said the manager, fingering a piece of paper. "But we also noted that it was engaged, and that only on the off chance of a cancellation could we offer it to you. We guaranteed you available accommodations. Do you wish to accept them?"

Hank looked uncertain.

"I'm afraid we will reluctantly have to lose your patronage if you refuse either of the other accommodations we offered." The manager closed his book with finality.

Hank took Elaine's hands in his. "I know you're disappointed, honey, but would you mind very much if we took the Silver Suite?"

"As long as we're together," she answered bravely.

At The Carroll Inn, where "rooms" were unheard of, the suites bore plaques rather than numbers to indicate their identities. From his earlier telephone conversation, Hank knew all about the Silver Suite. He knew it had silver-flocked wallpaper, chandeliers, mirrors, and that it was next door to the Honeymoon Suite.

"Thank you," he told the bellboy, as he handed him a month's tuition.

"Anytime," the young man beamed.

"God, I hope not," thought Hank, as he bowed his lady into the suite.

The evening began with cocktails on the terrace at the table Eve had chosen. A hardy breeze was blowing, and Eve's ruffled hair gave her an aura of wild allure.

Wetcliff positioned his chair beyond the draft from the constantly opening dining room door. He took his cue from Eve and said little as she smiled at him, pressed his hand, and looked out into the darkening foliage. When he rose to lead her in to dinner, she resisted.

"Dinner here would be so delightful. The air gives me such a sense of freedom," she exulted. "And we'll be alone," she whispered.

Observing the exodus from Nature, he understood why. The breeze had become a decided wind, which now fingered Eve's hair violently.

"When I'm with you, there is no one else, even if hundreds surround us."

"What did you say?"

"I said I'd be alone with you wherever we are," Bill shouted, battling the wind.

"Alone with who?"

"With you! With you!"

"I'm glad I'm with you, too!" And Eve bent forward to kiss him lightly on the lips.

"We can't talk out here. Let's go inside."

"How wonderful! I'd love to walk out here. We'll develop wonderful appetites."

What in the name of Beelzebub was she trying to do? wondered Wetcliff. Her hair swirled madly, her face suffused with color, her eyes danced. This Eve Nelson was a devil. He was thrilled at the nighttime prospect but dismayed at the immediate one. He couldn't deny her; she'd think him a milksop. She led him into the garden, ecstatically holding her face out to the wind and chatting happily about God knows what. Wetcliff couldn't hear a word. Leaves showed their undersides, and petals tore away from flowers. When they returned to their table after what seemed to him an interminable engagement with belligerent Nature, his voice was in shreds. The waiter beckoned them from inside.

Eve whispered conspiratorially to her companion throughout the meal. His communicative eyes, his large noble hands, the rugged manliness of his cracked voice, all drew praise from her. Wetcliff had regained his wits enough for Eve to suggest a swim before dessert. Bill Wetcliff believed in continuity, at mealtime as well as in other aspects of his life, and this business of eating-walking-eating-swimming-eating in the space of an hour did not conform to his habits or his ideas of health. Eve persisted. The pool would be empty at mealtime. They would have it to themselves. Perhaps they could dispense with the backstroke and the sidestroke and initiate several new ones? Bill's eyebrows rose. Coffee and pastries were put on hold, and arm-in-arm they rode the elevator to their suite for their swimwear. No sooner had the elevator door shut them inside than Bill grabbed her and closed his mouth on hers. She was breathless when he released her, less from pleasure or shock than from a familiar disappointment, a shattering of a secret hope and childish illusion that what is important takes time to acquire, that gratification that is grabbed does not grow.

"I like it," said Bill as she pulled a bathing suit with peaches and cream undulating lines from the drawer. "But if you hadn't known this was a weekend jaunt, you would have brought nothing. I would have preferred that." He unzipped her dress, and as she bent slightly to slip out of it, her breast, unencumbered by a bra, moved appealingly forward. Standing behind her, he placed his hands firmly on her waist and moved them up to massage her full breasts. His lips lingered on each large nipple, and as his hands slid quickly downward, Eve gently pushed him away.

"Not during dinner," she said. "It's bad for the heart." Her panties were off and her bathing suit on before her half-slip dropped to the floor.

"If you're my dinner, it's all right," Bill protested.

"You mean dessert. The midnight raid on the refrigerator."

"More than dessert. And swimming in the middle of a meal is not exactly designed to prolong life. You see what I'm willing to do to please you? Fortunately, the indoor pool is heated."

"Oh, I did so want to swim outdoors."

"Well, at least I'll die happy."

The cold water was not conducive to frolicking, and after a few perfunctory laps, they left the pool.

"Now for some hot, hot coffee and dessert," said Wetcliff, briskly toweling himself dry.

Eve's eyes shone with unnatural light. "Let's pick dessert! There's a blueberry patch beyond the hedges."

"Where it belongs. I refuse to work up either a sweat or goose pimples over blueberries. The waiter can bring them fresh and clean from the kitchen. We do want him to earn his tip, don't we?"

"He's earned it already. I doubt if he's ever served as prolonged a meal as ours."

"We have no berry basket," he offered lamely.

She held up a room towel and sprinted down the garden path. What could he do? He followed. When he caught up with her, she was facing the towering bushes with dismay.

"No problem," croaked Wetcliff. He flexed his muscles, stood erect, all 6'2" of him, and waded through the underbrush. He jumped for berries, throwing the booty into the towel Eve held hammock fashion.

"Move in closer."

"Who knows what I'd be stepping into." She looked askance at the tangle of undergrowth.

"That's my adventurous girl," he chided as he continued to throw her the berries.

"We've got a blanket's worth now," he said, stomping out of the greenery. "Too bad they're not strawberries."

"You'll have no need of an aphrodisiac tonight," she responded.

"Any night," he croaked, appearing wounded.

The waiter was unruffled by their attire, but registered surprise at their bounty.

"Wash and serve them with mounds of whipped cream," instructed Wetcliff.

"Yes, sir." The waiter hesitated. "Would you prefer cornstarch or baking soda?"

"We don't want them in pastry."

"I understand, sir, but we've only one blueberry patch, and to keep the guests from stripping the bushes, well, we have this sign. Perhaps you couldn't see it in the fading light. The earth surrounding the bushes is planted with poison ivy. We use ladders, and gloves, of course."

"Poison ivy!" Wetcliff shot to his feet.

"I recommend the cornstarch," said the waiter.

Wetcliff would not look at the blueberries. They sat in a covered bowl on the dresser next to a heap of whipped cream in a bowl of ice. Eve had brushed the cornstarch from his toes to his thighs, and he sat up in bed, morosely surveying the sight.

"I can't believe I could have been so stupid."

"I'm to blame for not seeing the sign. I'd do anything now to make amends for my carelessness." She caressed his face, and he clenched his teeth in frustration.

"The entire blame is mine. I should have led the way. I'm a dolt, an idiot, a first-class fool." His shredded voice broke.

"At least you're first class," she said soothingly. She handed him a glass. "Just gargle again."

"Damn my throat," he barked hoarsely. "I can't even take a little wind."

"I came with a wonderful man who's not going to let a little poison ivy and hoarseness keep him down for more than one night." She ran her hands down his arms. "He's too determined." She massaged his chest. "Too virile." Her hands mussed his hair. "Too—"

He pulled her toward him and kissed her violently on the mouth.

"Tomorrow," he rasped. "I'll make it all worthwhile to you tomorrow."

She pulled slowly away from him, turned back the cover on the newly arrived adjoining bed, and blew him a kiss. She felt it was all worthwhile already.

Chapter Eleven

Elaine Dawson was ecstatic about the suite and the view from the terrace. After a champagne toast, Hank Martin urged a champagne bath upon her in the tub that seemed like an oasis carved out of a mountain of marble and tile. As Elaine settled in for a luxurious soak, Hank walked onto the terrace. He saw Eve walking in the garden. He could not greet her without betraying his feelings. Anger, embarrassment, and jealousy welled within him. They would be impossible to hide. That way, profit did not lie. But he longed to see her face aflame, hear her voice break, watch her eyes avert his, in short to see reflected the shame of discovery that he anticipated. This desire was so strong that it overcame his fear that his own feelings would disgrace him, so descending the steep terrace steps he approached her. He came from behind as if to pass her on the path, and as he began to do so, a seemingly casual glance and double take, accomplished with the smoothness of necessity, achieved the meeting. Eve's reaction was one of shock and thinly veiled anger.

"Mr. Martin! What are you doing here?"

"This place had a reputation, and we thought we'd see if it was justified."

"Have you just arrived?"

"Yes. My friend is in the tub, so I thought I'd take a stroll."

Eve reddened. "Explanations are unnecessary."

Her eyes lowered as he underwent her sharp gaze, for he knew that last comment was meant to apply equally to herself.

"Enjoy the weekend, Mr. Martin. You probably will if you avoid drafts in the garden and blueberries."

With misgivings, he watched her walk away. Essentially, she had said goodbye. Accidental meetings would be suspect. Worse, she was ashamed of nothing. Defiance was in her voice, independence in her stance. Why did he love her so?

"Hank Martin here! What rotten luck," thought Eve crossly. It would be ridiculous to think he had followed her. His manner toward her had never been personal. Hadn't she told herself so many times? It had been gentlemanly and business-directed, from work at her apartment to her mother's plumbing. He had come with someone and would be too occupied to interfere with her activities, and interference was certainly not his purpose. But he would see Bill, and she did not want him to. Hank had nothing to fear from her sight of his lady friend, but she had much to fear from his seeing her with one of his superiors. Not that he would talk and embarrass her with the liaison, but that he would share her secret. Theirs was a business intimacy, and she perceived his knowledge of her life outside the office as an invasion of her privacy. What specifically she was afraid of she could not say, only that she feared and resented Hank Martin's appearance at The Carroll Inn. Keeping Bill and Hank apart would be impossible unless Bill remained in the suite until departure the next day. As Eve entered the lobby and saw him bounding down the stairs wearing a face-consuming smile, she realized this would be impossible. Fleetingly, she thought of going elsewhere, but immediately rejected that possibility. She would not run. Anyway, she was curious to see the woman Hank Martin had brought there. Bill put an arm through hers and led her outdoors.

"You're looking at the man you came with!"

"I'm so glad. I expect a lot from that man."

"And you should," he beamed proudly.

" Perhaps a watercolor of the garden or the view from our terrace."

He squeezed her hand. "You've been wonderful, Eve, so warm, so understanding. Is it because your eyes are so generously blue and your hair waves so beautifully around your face, or is it your determined air, those high cheekbones and your softly rounded nostrils?"

Eve turned her face away and pressed her lips together to keep from being convulsed with laughter. Bill turned her face back to his, took her in his arms, and kissed her in his smoldering style. With his lips sucking deep inside her mouth and his tongue slowly circling hers, she felt a sickening throbbing coursing through her body, sickening because although he had undeniably stimulated her body, she was starkly aware that the stimulation ended there.

Hank Martin returned to his suite with a dozen roses. They would be his substitute for affection and attention, neither of which he was in the mood to give Elaine. The woman deserved something. The transfer of her interest from him to Wetcliff would be thwarted by Wetcliff, he felt sure, just as Eve had disabused him of her interest in him. Only a fool would go from Eve to Elaine, he thought. Unfortunately, jealousy required an object. He kissed a wide-eyed and glowing Elaine as she sniffed the roses before he dashed into the bathroom. He showered absentmindedly. Removal of his competition would not make Eve care for him. Still, it would remove a potent distraction. He was toweling dry when he realized that the water was still running. The sound emanated from the other side of the wall. In the bathroom of the Honeymoon Suite, either Bill or Eve was showering. The slow luxury of a bath would not suit the impetuous Bill Wetcliff. Hank grinned. In an hour of darkness, hope! He picked up the ivory-handled back brush and began banging on it for attention. He paused, then slowly banged out eight letters. With a towel around his waist, he made a quick exit from the bathroom, grabbed pencil and paper from the desk, and began to write.

"Hank, what was that dreadful noise in there?"

"A neighborly message. Someone next door was banging out numbers on the shower wall."

"Good heavens, are we next door to a nut or a secret agent? Hank, what's the matter?"

"This is the matter," said a grim-faced Hank, as he snatched the paper from the desk and thrust it under her eyes. He had placed a letter under each number, and the resulting communication was "I love you."

"Do you love him? Did you come with me to make him jealous?" Hank demanded.

"Who? I don't love anybody. There is no one else. This is crazy! Someone is playing games. It has nothing to do with us."

Hank dialed the front desk. "You may be right. Hello, yes, Silver Suite. I'd like the name of the party next door."

"You shouldn't involve yourself. We could be dealing with a madman. The manager can—"

"Yes. Thank you. No, you needn't ring him."

Hank replaced the receiver with deliberation and looked past Elaine to the terrace chairs.

"His name is Bill Wetcliff," he said quietly.

"No—oh, no, that couldn't be. We had only one—. It just couldn't be!"

"But you see, it is," he continued, subdued. And the compliment and desire coupled with a rival's certainty worked to make it seem that it was.

"Would you like to speak to him alone?" suggested Hank.

"Certainly not. I'm here with you. His love is none of my affair."

Hank saw the illusion of power glitter in her eyes. "Then he's too late! The fool has lost! Or you never loved him at all. His looks, his wealth meant nothing more to you than amusement. How irresistible he must think he is!"

Elaine was silent.

"By the time I'm 65, I expect to be as rich as Bill Wetcliff. Meanwhile, poverty doesn't frighten me. Even if my business investments lower my standard of living, even if I'm on the verge of qualifying for Welfare, I won't mind, because it will all come right in the end."

Elaine gave attention to the contents of a drawer.

"You're angry with me," he said. "I blackened the name of a friend. That was rotten of me. I'm sorry."

"No, really, I'm not angry with you at all," she said, distance in her voice. "I just can't decide which blouse looks better with the chiffon skirt. Which do you prefer?" She held them up for his inspection.

The Carroll Inn was elegant but small, and there was no avoiding other diners unless one ate in one's suite. And why do that? And so, as couples casually filled the dining room, two of them were placed, not so casually, if the truth be known, at adjoining tables. They met in the foyer. There were awkward greetings, staccato good wishes filled with unavoidable intonations of surprise, and grateful farewells as they were escorted to their tables. The seating of Martin-Dawson within earshot of Nelson-Wetcliff brought forth light hand waves and disconcerting laughter. Wetcliff motioned Eve to rise. She motioned him to stay. He motioned an exchange of seats. She indicated they were to remain seated. Wetcliff faced Elaine, and Martin faced Eve, and they would endure the situation. And if Eve judged rightly, Elaine would be a powerful ally to giving Eve's behavior toward Wetcliff a sanction of believability it would otherwise lack. She leaned forward to whisper to Wetcliff, unnecessarily pushing a lock of hair off his forehead. He made menu suggestions. She responded with another whisper and a hand on his cheek. He finally leaned forward.

"Your secretary will have this all over the office. You've got to live with that man from 9 to 5. For heaven's sake, control yourself."

Eve pulled back in obvious anger.

Wetcliff tried again. "I don't want you hurt on my account."

Elaine's face was aglow, and Hank Martin remarked on it. Of course, her beauty was caused by Wetcliff's refusal to cozy up to Eve in Elaine's presence. Hank whispered compliments to his tablemate while straining to hear Eve's voice.

He was grateful when she stopped invading Wetcliff's space. And as they both began a meal of "hanging back," verbally and affectionately, Hank and Elaine simultaneously began an hour of theater. Wetcliff was in a lip-biting mood without being able to indulge in it. He knew that Eve was offended, and Elaine was enjoying herself exorbitantly, ordinarily a cause for suspicion when the enjoyment was with a man other than himself, but Hank Martin's words might justify such pleasure. What did a woman like Elaine Dawson know of clever lines and subtle wiles? But Eve Nelson knew, and her respect for Hank Martin plummeted. This resourceful man was really like any other. A "different face for a different place" philosophy did not appeal to Eve. Each person was a single whole, a pooling of all facets of his behavior, and a fake in the bedroom could prove as much a fake in the boardroom if the situation warranted it. Could this apply to Bill Wetcliff as well? No, the whole of him was well-known. That knowledge was protection, putting his colleagues on their guard, making deception, however unlikely, actually impossible. Hank Martin could not be trusted. She was aware of his game-playing, most notably with her mother, but somehow in the flower and greenery decked Carroll Inn, it took on a sinister appearance. Music on the terrace drifted in with dessert. It was chandelier music, suited to the ballroom and suggesting to the diners the appropriate activity to follow.

Hank prevailed upon Elaine to sample the fruits of the bar. She was not averse to sipping and listening to his praise of her, or rather catching snatches of it as she followed, through the open French doors, the progress of Eve and Bill dancing on the flagstone terrace. She was grateful when Hank ventured the fox trot. It made him look the least foolish on the dance floor, he said. Her minimal interest in this statement was masked by a smile. Hank eliminated the need for talk by holding Elaine so close that he afforded her only the opportunity to breathe. A few whispered words sufficed to make him look the attentive romantic. By contrast, Wetcliff held Eve like a gentleman. Overt passion was not for public eyes, and so he told Eve.

"This is why they are both secretaries."

"They lack education. I'm surprised your example didn't impress Elaine. Is that why you stopped seeing her?"

"She's too common."

"Commoners, properly trained, can challenge the nobility. Henry Higgins showed what can be done with promising material."

"I prefer promising material of the highest order," he said, gazing steadfastly into her eyes.

"You have no idea what she is promising."

"I have considerable imagination."

He held her a fraction closer. She was well aware of fractions; she dealt with them daily. The fox trot segued into a cha-cha. Hank Martin performed well. No extraneous hand motions or fancy footwork marred the clean simplicity of his steps. The contrast between his dignified cha-cha and his lascivious fox trot interested Eve, so when the trot returned, she urged Wetcliff to save a suffocating Elaine and instruct, by demonstration, a needy Hank Martin. He reluctantly agreed, and Eve walked slowly to a bench.

"Miss Nelson," came the expected voice behind her.

Eve turned, smiling. "Mr. Martin."

He indicated the band. "Shall we?"

She looked amused. "If you trot, perhaps; if you play the fox as with Miss Dawson, definitely not."

"We shall trot, of course," he said solemnly. And she allowed him to take her hand and lead her back to the dance floor. He held her at as respectable a distance as one can and still continue to dance together. At one point, another couple backed into their clasp, and so loose was it that their togetherness was momentarily broken.

He had said "of course," she thought. He was displaying proper behavior to his boss. He maintained a steady stream of conversation, or conversation it would have been had she contributed, but his chatter partially obscured the beauty of one of her favorite songs, a meltingly lovely ballad.

The man had no feeling, no taste, but as his superior, she should have expected none. He had said little to Elaine, but his gross embrace of that lady had been thoroughly repulsive. Apparently, he could do nothing right. His work flashed through her mind. Well, perhaps "nothing" was too extreme. Hank Martin led her back to Bill Wetcliff.

"What did you think of our mid-section twist?" Bill asked proudly.

Hank looked at Eve. "I don't believe we noticed."

Eve felt a warmth suffuse her face.

Wetcliff, interpreting it to his own advantage, could not avoid a triumphant "That's all right. It was just a little something I improvised to show Elaine what could be done. She'll explain it to you, Hank."

Bill reclaimed Eve for the mambo. She couldn't understand why Hank Martin's inconsequential "of course" should rankle so.

Hank watched anxiously as Bill Wetcliff pecked Eve's cheek and left the room. He was relieved to see him turn right to the elevators rather than left to the Men's Room. Then he had left it in his suite, the vitamin E he, in an unguarded moment in the office, had admitted to Hank he took to intensify his virility. Hank waited several minutes before suggesting to Elaine that she needed a wrap to ward off the air-conditioned chill, and then, most ungallantly, failing to suggest that he would return to the suite to get one for her. He saw her to the elevator, alerted the well-tipped bellboy, and with the elevator door barely shut, took the stairs two at a time to the floor above. Seconds later, he was in the bathroom banging out his message. If all went well, the bellboy would detain Elaine with lengthy pleas that she allow him to be of assistance. Hank rushed to the door Elaine would soon open and flattened himself behind it. When she entered, he made a noiseless exit and dashed down the stairs. With the bellboy delaying a returning Wetcliff in an uncooperative elevator, Hank would have a few precious minutes to talk to Eve. He arrived at the dance floor breathless.

"May I sit down?" he gasped.

"Good heavens, yes. What have you been doing!" She flushed. "I shouldn't have asked."

"I can't answer anyway," he responded, breathing heavily. "Where's Bill?"

"He went back to the suite for something."

"Geritol?"

She laughed. "That he doesn't need."

"I didn't mean to pry," he lied.

"That's all right," she lied back. "I don't even remember what you asked."

"I'm glad. Then you certainly won't remember other questions I asked that irritated you, like 'Did you get home all right' and 'When shall we leave for dinner with your mother.' Or 'I hope you're not minding our business, Mr. Wetcliff.'"

That last especially burned her cheeks. She could not prevent it. She recalled the meeting in the hotel with partners reversed, with Wetcliff making an outrageous assumption as she and Martin anticipated a night of dreary business for the firm. Martin's defense had been as good as agreement with Wetcliff's assumption, and the rush of anger she had felt toward Martin returned.

"I remember nothing unpleasant, Mr. Martin, unless I am reminded, and since you wish to please me, I assume, you will not wish to mention such things again."

"Will you remember this weekend?"

"Parts of it. Not this one."

"What can I do that you will remember?"

She thought a moment. "Nothing. Do nothing, and I will remember it with pleasure."

"Now who is interfering?" he scolded.

"Oh, I didn't mean that. Do whatever you wish with your life."

"But is Elaine out of Bill's life?"

"It would seem so."

"Then where are they?"

"Your concern for details goes beyond the office."

"Does that make us equals?"

"Must we be equals? We each have our places and our individuality, which leads us to those places and sustains us in them. We're equal in that, but such equality precludes our being equal in any other way."

"But our tastes are similar," he pursued.

"I don't think so."

That crushing rejoinder was about to be appealed when Wetcliff and Elaine came toward them. Each whisked the partner away without a parting word. Elaine hustled Hank into the lobby.

"He won't admit it!" she cried. "He insists I banged the message to him—just now! I hadn't entered the suite yet, but he was leaving his and insisted I was leaving too, and that I had just declared that I loved him! It was humiliating!"

Hank shrugged. "Don Juan is ashamed to admit that he's fallen hard."

Yes, thought Elaine, that could be. Bill was either toying with her or ashamed to admit his feelings. So ashamed that in tracking her flight with Hank, he had had to provide himself with an alibi—Eve. Fitting the facts to her temperament, she felt a rare security, and observing Hank's intense gaze, she felt a bogus power.

Bill Wetcliff felt much the same, but the rarity of fraud from the opposite sex left him open to it. Elaine and Eve merely reaffirmed his opinion of himself, an expected and indeed essential occurrence. His beliefs and behavior were frozen in time.

It was a magical night somewhere in the world for some, but for neither the male nor female components of our two couples. They were too busy to appreciate it if it occurred and too busy planning to allow it to occur. Wetcliff's anxiety was especially acute, for he expected to juggle two conquests in close quarters. Adulation would come. He was dancing cheek to cheek with Eve. Whispering bona fide nothings in her ear, he anticipated the night with excitement. But he was not truly a creative man, and the predictability of his behavior could not escape a clever woman.

As he held Eve close, his heart beating fast, she almost mouthed his desire that they return to their suite. No sooner had they done so than he swept her into his arms.

"I adore you," he croaked hoarsely.

"Darling, perhaps you should gargle with salt water. The effect of that dreadful wind won't go away."

"I don't need salt water, I need—"

"A throat lozenge. Every time you speak, I blame myself for keeping you in the wind."

"I feel fine, but words are insufficient to empty my heart. I'll say nothing except this." And he lifted her and carried her to the bed.

"The terrace!" she cried. "It's so much more romantic on the terrace." And she held out her arms for another lift.

He carried her to the terrace door and attempted to kick it open. With both hands occupied, only Eve could easily unlock the door, but she seemed too busy cooing into his ear to notice his problem. Placing her on her feet for a moment was the alternative solution, but the Tarzan image would be lost.

"Eve, would you turn the knob, please."

She affected not to hear, and he struggled with the door a bit longer before repeating the request and getting compliance.

"It's never looked so beautiful," she said, addressing the moon as Wetcliff pulled her close. She violently pulled away.

"A mosquito! Oh, let's go inside!" She held out her arms to him again.

He carried her inside with determination. At least his mind was determined, but his legs wobbled a bit, and to a woman less starstruck than he presumed Eve was, it would have seemed that he dumped rather than placed her on the bed. He puffed a few breaths before nervously laughing them away. For him, the moment had arrived. Not, however, for Eve. She kept up a stream of impassioned chatter his voice could not cope with, and a combination of hands and voice warded off his intentions with subtle reminders that speechless, breathless men who stumble into poison ivy require a longer lead time to promote their amorous designs.

Wetcliff waxed as eloquently as his voice would allow. From his memory, he withdrew the most passionate lines of poetry, drama, and psychology. His words conveyed him into such a paroxysm of delight that he found himself on his knees before her. He scratched the back of his neck and continued his eloquence.

"Oh, dear," said Eve. "I'm afraid mosquitoes are not a romantic breed. I'll get the calamine lotion."

Wetcliff moaned morosely. More than the weekend had been lost. Eve's solicitous words only served to depress him more. He urged her to go for a stroll and, seeing that was really what he wanted, she obliged.

As Eve wandered, she wondered what she really wanted. It wasn't to teach that male chauvinist a lesson he was incapable of learning. She looked back at the muted lights behind the shades of the hotel suites. And suddenly, or so it seemed, silhouetted on a shade of the Honeymoon Suite, were two forms intertwined, a movie-still now progressing to slow, passionate motion. Hank's voice spoke to her from the darkness.

"We're out for our exercise, they're in for theirs."

The growing darkness masked the flush on Eve's face.

"You're lucky, Eve Nelson. You haven't hurt yourself yet, but you came close. Office affairs can be deadly. It would be foolish to clip your rise at W.W.&S. Snell's all for you, and you're in line for the next prime opening. You're a realistic woman. Don't blow your life now."

"Pardon me if I don't thank you, Mr. Martin. My life is not dependent on W.W.&S. or your advice. For a man who treats his date so cavalierly, sharing her with the boss's son, you are certainly the ultimate realist. I congratulate you on taking your own advice."

"Don't be stubborn, Eve. You know I'm right. I'm taking a separate suite for Elaine."

"Most generous of you and, once more, very realistic. Are you going to reserve a separate suite for me too, or is kowtowing to two honchos simultaneously unproductive?"

"That was unkind. May I walk with you?"

"Shouldn't you be busying yourself getting that suite for Elaine?"

"I can't leave you alone in the dark."

"This is what comes of associating with my mother."

His heart skipped. She was surely smiling.

"Wait for me. We'll talk some more, and I'll walk you back to your suite in half an hour. That should give them enough time."

"The mathematics of passion," laughed Eve.

Hank Martin sprinted toward the hotel. He felt like dancing in the lobby.

Chapter Twelve

The twosome strolled the grounds in silence. On a bench here, under a tree there, were couples supplementing the invigoration of the cool night air with each other. Eve cast a sidelong glance at Hank. His hands were in his pockets, his eyes alternating between the view straight ahead and the ground. Occasionally he kicked rocks or twigs from the pathway. He was a talented man, thought Eve, a talented subordinate, and any amorous predilections for her he might have, and she had no reason to believe he had any, were of less importance to him than his career.

Half an hour had elapsed in what seemed to Eve like five minutes, and Hank escorted her to the Honeymoon Suite. Light was faintly visible under the door. Eve hesitated. Hank took the key from her hand and unlocked the door. Bill Wetcliff saw Eve framed in the doorway and rushed with arms opened wide to embrace her. Hank quickly stepped in front of Eve, knocked the extended arms to the right, and laid a single, well-placed blow to the Wetcliff chin. From a shadowed corner Elaine ran to the man as he stumbled to the floor.

"Oh, Bill, Bill," she wailed. "That was cruel and inhuman!" she hurled at Hank savagely, and then in tones thick with innocence, "I only came by for a chat with Eve."

Eve was unable to stifle a guffaw. Poor Elaine! Favorable prospects always turned against her.

Eve was a solicitous roommate, as she plied Wetcliff with sympathy and liquor enough to get him to sleep through the night. As he lay snoring lightly, the telephone rang. It was Elaine hesitantly inquiring after Wetcliff.

"I'm afraid that he won't be in condition for you again tonight. He finished a bottle of scotch. It will take a tub of coffee to sober him up in the morning."

"Oh, I'm so sorry, Eve. Hurting you that way was dreadful of him, but you do understand. Even strong men can be cowards when it comes to breaking hearts. I'll be right in for him. It's pointless for you to have to look at him all night. He's upset you enough."

"But we couldn't possibly drag him into the hall, and if we ask for help, we'll feel required to explain. And if you and I switch suites, there will be talk. Our company is such a prestigious firm, and Bill is so well-known here that, well, frankly, my reputation would be impaired. I would hate to have my promotion jeopardized by rumor of a rejection, even of the extra-curricular type."

"Oh, no! That would be horridly unfair. Stay with him the night. Bill owes you that much. Are you sure he won't be needing the coffee soon?"

"After what he drank and the way he's snoring, he won't need it until tomorrow evening. But I'll call you in the morning, and we'll administer it together."

"Eve—what can I say?"

"Thank you and good night are as appropriate as anything."

"Thank you, thank you, dear Eve, and good night."

"Good night, you foolish woman," said Eve to the cradled receiver.

Eve showered and put on a dressing gown. It was all bows and lace on scooped chiffon.

"Will this do?" she addressed a snoring Wetcliff. She whirled around before his unseeing eyes. "Well, I don't think much of your taste either."

She tossed the train at him and swept to the terrace door. Peace. The crickets, the swaying leafy darkness, and an almost imperceptible breeze smoothed away pre-occupations, dissolving all desire for the clever pose, the witty remark. It was a moment when one was vulnerable to the truth, when one's fluid nature and the planted variety could commune and even coalesce. There was a rustling at her elbow, and she turned sharply to the adjacent terrace.

"Mr. Martin."

"Miss Nelson."

She cast her eyes back on the darkened nature before her, but she was alert to the intrusion.

"The air is good tonight." He paused, allowing the breeze of inspiration to push him relentlessly on. "It looks as if we are the only two enjoying it at this hour."

No figures broke the darkness on terraces within their view, and Eve nodded her agreement. Her remaining beside him, an inch of metal grillwork away, encouraged him.

"You seem relaxed," he pursued.

"I always relax on weekends," she responded doggedly.

"How do you manage it? My mind is always so full of plans."

Restlessly she readjusted her stance. She had no wish to instruct him.

"I manage. It's attitude."

"Is your attitude contagious? I'd be grateful to catch it."

She faced him. "You have caught my office attitude, and I appreciate that. But I would like to leave something for you to generate yourself." She turned her attention once more to the darkness.

The veins stood out on his forehead, but the darkness would have swallowed the sight even if she had been looking at him. She stood a minute longer gazing into the night, but it had been ruined for her.

"Good night, Mr. Martin," she said, with a casual, absent-minded glance in his direction.

"If I can be of any help—"

Her abrupt thank you made his uselessness clear to him. What was not clear to him was that a glance behind her had revealed that Wetcliff was stirring. She opened a bottle of scotch and poured some into a glass of water. She put it to his lips and murmured consoling words as he sipped.

By morning, when Elaine phoned, he remained deep in alcoholic stupor. With a satisfied glance at Wetcliff, Eve admitted the waiter with breakfast. Elaine was at his heels.

"I won't allow myself to believe it's finally happened," said Elaine, flushing eagerly. "How could it? So rich, attractive, intelligent. How could he want me?"

Eve said nothing.

"But why should good things happen only to other people?" she asked defensively.

Eve nodded. They shouldn't, she thought. They should happen to women who throw themselves to cannibals, who sacrifice themselves because they are afraid not to, afraid that in a world of gorgers, one survives by committing suicide. To give so much for so little merits reward. And sometimes, just to indicate that it can happen, there is indeed justification for fools. She did not think this was the time.

"He says he loves me. I so want to trust him. What do you think?" Elaine asked eagerly.

"I will not guess, and neither should you. You should know. You *can* know. A true love is never completely hidden. A love so secret that its object is deprived of the pleasurable knowledge of its existence is not love."

"He followed me here and banged his love for me on the bathroom wall."

"He followed you?"

"Yes. When he found out I'd accepted Hank's invitation for the weekend, he took you. Oh, I'm sorry, Eve. It was beastly of him, but surely that's a sign of love. And poor Hank, who needed me so desperately ... Oh, I know I've been awful to him. But what else can Bill's behavior signify but love?"

"May I ask when Hank asked you here?"

"Saturday afternoon, yesterday. He said he was wild for me, that the work was driving him crazy. Oh, no, Eve. I don't mean he was blaming you. I'm putting this very badly. I don't know how Bill found out, but thanks to a bit of luck, I'm off the back burner. I wish I knew if it were for keeps."

"There are advantages to saying 'I love you.'"

"He already had them." She blushed. "What reason could he have, then, for a lie?"

"Did he look you in the eyes when he expressed his love?"

"That was rather hard with a wall between us. The bathroom wall," she repeated, in answer to Eve's puzzled look. "He banged 'I love you' on the shower wall. Hank is very sensitive to such things. He caught on immediately and told me. Of course, I'd heard the sound. Then, later, when I went back to the suite, Bill referred to it." "To banging on the bathroom wall."

"Yes. Of course, he didn't repeat those words exactly when we spent—uh, time together last night, but he was so busy—I mean, well, you know."

"He said he banged those words on the wall?" insisted Eve.

"I don't remember exactly how he phrased it. But there was banging, and I certainly wasn't responsible for it."

Eve's lips tightened. She had seen Hank Martin sprinting up the stairs. His idea of humor did not amuse her. He had quickly wearied of Elaine and imagined a clever way to be rid of her. Before this weekend, she had thought well of him. She regretted seeing a side of him that had no bearing on his job. It demeaned him in her eyes and could not help but affect her attitude toward him at work. But what, after all, was an attitude? Would it change her typing instructions to him or the form of her dictation, or the length of his lunch hour? Any feeling of revulsion toward him would not surface. The details of the 9 to 5 existence would prevent it, even if her emotions could not. Her emotions. Given the world in which they were nurtured, they necessarily tended toward the negative, when she was conscious of them. Remembered dreams didn't count. Of what practical use were they? She became aware that Elaine was looking at her. To what had she been requested to respond?

"Thank you, Eve." Elaine grasped her hands for a moment, her eyes shining with unspent tears. "I *do* know. There *is* nothing to be said. My heart, my mind, my entire being tells me that he loves me.

I'm so afraid—but I know it's true. You've been wonderful. When he proposes, it will seem like the most natural thing in the world."

"Not for Bill," Eve thought, but she only said, "Are you sure you've gotten over Hank?"

"Oh, yes! Frankly, he's a bit dull, but he paid so much attention to me I couldn't hurt his feelings." She sighed. "But of course, I did. I hope he forgives me. He says he does."

"Men do say things," mused Eve. And suddenly a wild idea entered her brain. Elaine, Fortune's fool, like Romeo, deserved a better fate. She aimed to please, and she had earned her dream. And Bill Wetcliff had sown enough oats.

"Since you have made your decision, I can reveal the joyous news to you. I had to be sure that you clearly wanted Bill. Marriage is probably the most awesome and frightening relationship. For the sake of happiness for both of you, I had to be sure, but now I can tell you. Bill proposed to you last night."

Elaine's mouth fell open.

"And I accepted for you."

This was too much for Elaine, who fell back into the chair from which she had risen.

"He thought I was you, you see, and besotted with liquor as he was, he was as wonderfully eloquent as you know he can be when he begged you to marry him, to save him from skirted opportunists, to muss his hair and kiss his nose, to have candlelit dinners in Paris one night and in Rome the next, to have you waited on hand and foot at your homes in St. Moritz, London, and Palm Beach. If the effort of speech hadn't exhausted him, and if he hadn't fallen asleep, he would have gone on until dawn, but he paused to ask you to be his wife, and I didn't have the heart to say no. Thank goodness you want him too! You've both gained the joy, and I've avoided the embarrassment of explanation. You won't tell him it was I, will you? He would be mortified. A man like Bill, constantly pursued by women and set on avoiding marriage would be devastated if he knew that when he finally succumbed, he had addressed the wrong woman."

Elaine's eyes stared incredulously into Eve's. "Are you sure he proposed to me?"

"Do you doubt that he would?"

"Oh, I can't believe it; I mean I *can* believe it, but this is crazy…"

"Romantic," Eve substituted. "I wish you had been there to hear it, but you will be hearing such things for years, I'm sure." The male object of their conversation stirred. "I'll go now," said Eve, rising. "There's plenty of coffee for you and Bill. And make sure he gets something solid into his stomach. I'll take a stroll and be back for my luggage. Hank will drive me home before lunch. You two can have the rest of the day here as you should, without worry or complication." She patted Elaine's shoulder, but that young woman's thank you was aborted by a yawn from Wetcliff.

Eve retreated immediately, without remorse. She understood Wetcliff's character and knew he would not deny the proposal. How could he doubt the gushing certainty of a transparent female? Design was not in Elaine's nature, except for the most elementary. Deceit was beyond her intellectual range. Bill would not doubt her word, and while he was frantically scrounging for a method to extricate himself from the attachment, he would allow her delusion to remain. A marriage proposal to such a one as Elaine, and especially under the circumstances she might relate, would be repugnant to him. Her simplicity, amusing as a toy, would repel the husband in him, if such there was. But he was a gentleman and would make the rejection her choice rather than his. Elaine could expect a vile, though virile, lover. She would feel both the joy and the pain and be instructed in the future to choose more sensibly.

Eve almost turned down another path when she saw Hank, but recalled she had to prevail upon him for a lift home. The thought gave her slight uneasiness. She could flee in a taxi, but the expense and the cowardice that would connote were abhorrent to her. When she made a decision, she did not flinch from carrying it out. She greeted Hank immediately and asked him directly.

She longed to avoid Bill Wetcliff and equally longed to observe his behavior as the fiancé of Elaine Dawson. Eve determined to wait and observe, not because she allowed herself to succumb to this emotional temptation, but because she wished to clearly ascertain that the matter had, for her, been successfully concluded and would not smudge over into the business life they shared. So, it was not mere accident that she saw them walking arm in arm, hers tightly grasping his, and upon displaying surprise by their nuptial news, she wished them joy in life. Of Wetcliff, abashed but brave, the words that popped into her head were "stout fellow." He weakly apologized for not taking her home, appreciated her sportsmanship, and in general delighted her with his game but bewildered acquiescence to the situation. Hank shook hands with the newly betrothed, wished them well, and took Eve away with a precision and economy that seemed to bear out a quality that Elaine had found repugnant in him, but it so perfectly suited the occasion, so well contrasted with Wetcliff's manner, that Eve required effort to contain the desire to giggle and clap her hands. She had been very wicked and regretted it not at all.

Hank said little during the long drive home. He seemed preoccupied with the road and his thoughts, and Eve did not intervene. When they stopped for lunch and gas, he was equally quiet, attending to his plate, the spoon in his coffee cup and the pattern in the wallpaper. When he began to speak, it was of juggling client service with the demands of old Fred Williams. Eve was glad to hear it. It meant that despite his unwelcome knowledge of a corner of her private life, he would keep it to himself and get back to work.

Eve had barely shut the apartment door when her phone rang. On the other end was an outraged mother. She had been horrified, mortified, and frightened nearly to death. It wasn't the weekend, but the man she so strenuously objected to.

"Never, never would I interfere with your pleasures, but Bill Wetcliff will destroy your career. An affair with a fellow worker is dangerous enough, but with a boss's son, it is madness."

Eve could not calm her mother. Her fears were too great, and the histories Eve herself had heard of office passion turned deadly prevented her from denying the veracity of her mother's words. The fact that she and Wetcliff were not a pair and that no danger was to be anticipated did not wash with Mrs. Nelson.

"You've done worse. You've made a fool of him. Do you think he'll remain blind to that? Your friends will decamp faster than Indian Summer. When Bill creates a breeze, Eve, Snell will desert you if it becomes a storm. And don't expect embarrassment to keep Bill from it. He need not use the truth to ruin you. How often is that used to achieve ends these days? You'll be blacklisted in the entire investment community. You'll lose everything."

"Not everything, Mother, not my self-respect. My career is nothing without it."

"Your self-respect? Was it self-respect that caused you to go away with a womanizer? Self-respect to torture him with the pain of carnivorous insects and poisonous plants? Self-respect to trick him into a marriage commitment for which he is totally unsuited? Do tell me of your fabled self-respect. You've put me in such agony, I'm desperate for a fairy tale."

Eve was stunned into silence. After an almost palpable interval, during which her mother stubbornly refused to hang up, she said, "I'm sorry, truly sorry for everything. I don't seem to understand myself anymore. I wish I weren't such a tremendous disappointment to you, Mother."

Mrs. Nelson softened. "You're not a disappointment to me, darling. What a ridiculous thought! I'm very proud of you. I only want you to be happy. Perhaps Bill won't find out. These vain men, however bright they are otherwise, never doubt their appeal. You may be safe. But avoid him at the office and be circumspect with Hank. One can't be too cautious—after this."

"Hank Martin? How can you think I'd be anything but circumspect with him?"

"I can't think it, but I had hoped. Well, if there's no deep bond, he isn't worth losing your position for at W.W.&S. Pretend he's Miss Kay."

"I'll do that. She'll be back in a month, and he'll be gone. Don't worry about it, Mother. Enjoy your own life."

Mrs. Nelson sighed. "I'd love to, but the shallowness of yours keeps diluting mine. Sleep well, darling, and don't be angry at your old mother. Lunch this Wednesday?"

"Of course. Don't forget the sale on Rivington Street. I'll expect to hear all about it."

Eve prepared for the evening ablutions in a state of unease. She turned on the radio, but nothing would do. The rock music was garish and disconcerting, the Latin music was too unabashedly romantic, the folk music wail was depressing, and the uninhibited cheer of a Mozart divertissement was decidedly out of accord with her mood. The order of Bach was nowhere to be found. She would have to await the morning activities at the office to simulate them. She lay awake in bed for a substantial length of time. One might not have everything, but one had to have something, and she had chosen revenge over self-esteem. Perhaps she had chosen revenge because she lacked self-esteem, because she resented her failing. "Projection" psychiatrists called it. Bill Wetcliff led a satisfying life despite his thwarted artistic pretensions, which he had turned to profitable psychological and public-relations use. He had "something." On a continuing basis, what did she have? She fell into an anxious sleep pondering this.

The office seemed as usual the next morning. Eve did not see Bill Wetcliff, and Hank Martin was already at work typing when she arrived. It was only at lunchtime when her office door, unguarded by the usually vigilant Martin, swung open that she realized that routine was on the verge of drastic change.

Chapter Thirteen

————— ❧ —————

"I'm picking you off one by one," exclaimed a tall, gangly, gravel-voiced man of 101 with about a dozen hairs on his head. He struck a dramatic pose in the doorway.

Eve, a sandwich in one hand and a pencil in the other, put down both. The weekend and a bad night had made her cross and self-destructive.

"Wouldn't picking us out be wiser? If you pick us off, you'll be racing from office to office Keystone Cops fashion running the entire show yourself. But your figure suggests that you may have been practicing just such maneuvers in Tahiti." She rose and walked around to the front of the desk, right hand extended. "How do you do, Mr. Williams? Would you like a sandwich?"

"By crackers, you're a new one!" exclaimed the old man, refusing the hand.

Eve chose to interpret his words literally. "I've been with W.W.&S for ten years." She motioned toward the desk. "It's tuna."

"Fish enough in Tahiti. Ever been there?"

"No."

The old man cackled appreciatively. "Snell said he'd never had the pleasure, Jennings said it must be paradise, and Bordon said he's heard it's very picturesque. And you say 'No.' I like that, but impertinence with me won't do," he said, cavalierly ignoring his own. "Use it on anyone else you please, and if it expedites my expansion plans, I'll thank you for it."

Eve recalled what she had heard about the fabled Williams, and as he spoke, she poured him a cup of tea. He merely nodded acceptance.

"I've never trusted women. I'm told that today I should, that all their contemptible qualities have finally found a useful outlet in business. But I don't know. You're a mercurial and contradictory lot. I can't hold the wind."

With stories of his five marriages in mind, Eve said, "Experience can mislead us. We must always look beyond ourselves to understand ourselves and others."

"That's a pretty gust," he said. "I voted nay when Snell put you in charge of my babies, but then I didn't have the clout to make it stick. Now that I'm majority stockholder again, I can do as I please. I expect to be followed and obeyed. Can you manage both?"

"Perhaps. Please explain further."

"Wind, wind! I don't have to explain anything before its time, or even after."

"You're intent on creating a bit of a breeze yourself. Shall we try to blow together?"

He gazed at her with interest. Finally, he said, "Snell's out if you give me a Northeaster."

"I will give no such thing."

"Glad to hear it. They left the Ark two by two, remember. Pull all your office files on the branch planning. I'm a hard copy person."

"Of course, Mr. Williams." Eve began scribbling on a pad.

"Now!" he ordered.

She walked to a cabinet and pulled a ten-inch stack of folders. The intercom lit, and the old man leaned over her desk.

"Williams here. Get back to work, she's busy!" he barked into the instrument.

"I don't take pleasure calls," asserted Eve.

"If it's so danged important, he'll march in here and talk to you in person. Good exercise, too. Sloppy body, sloppy thinking."

Eve's eyes rested briefly on the uneaten tuna, and she looked questioningly at Williams.

"Blast the tuna," he said, and pulled a package of Oreo creams from his pocket, offering her the second one.

An air of nervousness pervaded Williams, Wetcliff, and Snell. At times it billowed into anxiety. Gallagher had too many problem accounts, Davies had allowed a condescending letter to a client to pass over his signature, and Smith had misplaced his Montblanc pen.

Williams called for full-scale meetings, impromptu only in the immediacy of their timing. All involved in in-house transactions, customer service, and publicity were called to account for their activity and, on occasion, their inactivity.

"Good lord, Fred," said Wetcliff Sr., "you just got here. There's time."

Williams cast his eyes down on his person. "Do I look like I've got time?"

Hank Martin performed as errand boy, and, indeed, executives as well as secretaries were pressed into the service of Frederick Williams. The securities business, usually a regulated tizzy, approached bald frenzy, and only Williams regretted the fall of night. It was when an astute underling pulled up the blinds in the conference room and the hour could not be denied that the old chief bowed to the propriety of closing shop for the day, two hours past the usual time, three hours for some. He waved them off with a "Tomorrow, tomorrow. Go home." The principals off, word spread rapidly to those inconsequential talents who made the firm work. Williams was pleased by their orderly removal from the premises. Nodding approval at the backs of their heads, he could not see the dazed expressions or hear the whispered trepidation. It would not have mattered to him if he could. The feigned backslapping and handshakes of his two partners, he accepted as mere formality. The senior partner back from the dead would not have been welcome in his day either. He roamed the offices for an hour more, poking in drawers and cabinets, running his fingers along the woodwork. And when Security let him out, he smiled broadly, either the crooked smile of a satisfied old man or the mischievous smile of a young scamp, one could not tell which.

Eve was awakened from a sleep of exhaustion by the ringing of the telephone. She noted that it was midnight as she reached for the receiver. Wetcliff Sr.'s cultured voice was unmistakable, as was his urgent tone.

"Eve, we've got to stop Fred. George, Bill and I have been breaking our heads over this for hours. You're important to our plans. You must meet us for breakfast, shall we say 6 o'clock at Joe's Café?"

"Shouldn't we wait to see what—"

"Good heavens, no! Fred will destroy us all. You don't understand him as we do."

"But why?"

There was a scuffling with the receiver, and Bill Jr. was speaking.

"Eve, Dad's right. We need your help. Please meet with us."

Eve smiled at the expected persuasive powers of the son, and it kept her from responding for an instant.

"At 6 o'clock," she finally said, and rang off.

Snell, her mentor, had not spoken. Was his agreement with Bill Sr. reluctant, or was the former junior partner merely being appropriately placed? She did not question further. Sleep was more welcome than intrigue now, and she sought it with the certainty that its preciousness would be enhanced by its paucity in the time ahead.

"Good morning," said Eve drolly. She shook the rain from her hair and eased out of her raincoat.

Wetcliff Sr. dispensed with the salutation and greeted her with an imperative.

"We must not wait," he insisted. "Fred is not your cautious one thing-at-a time executive. When he acts, expect an avalanche. He'll have us dousing fires all over the place, and he'll love it. The old devil is no more of an executive than Inspector Clouseau is a detective. At his best, Fred is a first-class catalyst for change, at his worst a trouble-maker of grandiose proportions."

"A menace, all right." Snell lit his pipe.

"He couldn't stop innovating. He went on past the point of useful return, insisting, bullying, firing. That slump we had in the '80s was pure Williams."

"Singlehandedly brought W.W.&S. to its knees," observed Snell between puffs.

"We were saved by a pair of defective skis. He recuperated in Tahiti. When he came back, he was a minority shareholder. We borrowed up to our foreheads to swing that event. And Fred, after a farewell speech no one there will ever forget—"

"Infamous."

"—swore off big business and big cities and retired to Bora Bora. Now he's back to 'do unto us,' and it's going to be with a vengeance, believe me. He's had nothing to do but plot for twenty years."

"And ride the surf. He said he's very good," added Snell.

"Someone should have tampered with his surfboard."

"He's a remarkable man," said Snell, rousing himself somewhat. "Let's not downgrade his talents."

"No one who knows Fred would do that. We've got to survive them. Don't think the gifts you sent him at Christmas have made you immune to his hammer."

"I was thinking no such thing, Bill. Fred was responsible for the initial success of W.W.&S. and deserved appreciation and remembrance."

"He won't deal so kindly with us, George. The years haven't softened him."

"I'm not denying that. That's why we're here."

"We've got to attack before Fred does and focus on one area, so we can concentrate our ammunition. He'd love us to divide so he can conquer. If you're with us, Eve, you'll move into Bill's position, and he'll make president."

The V.P. slot. Being as innovative but more circumspect than his son Bill, Eve could expect to wield an influence beyond his in that position. She looked thoughtful but said nothing.

"Fred wants us to go international," continued the senior Wetcliff, "to actively trade stocks on the major world exchanges, and eventually to do so to the exclusion of anything else. And for senior citizens, yet! The fact that we have few international stock specialists, would lose most of our present clientele, would be offering seniors less than a diversified portfolio, and would go bankrupt in the midst of the effort is of no consequence to Fred. He's never forgiven us for taking over, and he's out to break us and this firm, even if it breaks him too."

"It's all that Tahiti sun," observed Snell.

"Fred is adamant, stubborn, viciously so, and as healthy as the Statue of Liberty. He has only one weak spot—women. He detests them, probably because he is continually persuaded by them to do outlandish things."

"He has tendencies of his own in that direction."

"Which women accentuate," said Wetcliff, somewhat out of patience with George.

"Women were his thing years ago. He's 90 years old, for Pete's sake."

"Fred is living years ago," responded Wetcliff caustically, "and Eve is eminently suitable for the job." He looked at his son for confirmation and received it.

Eve blushed and blanched. "What job?" she asked icily.

"A high-minded one, of course. We're running an investment firm, not a brothel. You're to get Fred to invest his own funds so heavily on a trial balloon with a seemingly superb foreign investment we've researched that he bankrupts himself in the process. If he's forced to sell his shares of this firm, his power over us will be gone."

"What could be easier?" asked Snell dryly, evoking a curt glance from Wetcliff Sr.

"It is an honor that I dream not of," responded Eve. Bill Jr. laughed. He knew she was quoting Juliet's response of parental urging of marriage to wealthy Paris. Snell smiled, connecting only with Eve's sarcasm, but Wetcliff Sr., impervious to literature, replied that the aforementioned reward would underscore the honor and his and Snell's gratitude for her assumption of it.

Snell turned his face away, requiring Eve to float on her own. She was appalled at this attempt to bribe her into high intrigue, amazed at the power they confidently expected her to wield over old Williams, but ultimately amused at the outlandish proposal. Coming from the elegantly proper Bill Sr., his personal life aside, it was doubly amusing and unexpected.

He responded to her hesitation. "Eve, you are our best hope, the company messiah."

"How will you expect me to proceed, should I agree to your proposal?"

"That, Eve, is totally up to you. We trust that the incentive will bring forth all your innate faculties—"

"—of deceit?"

They protested.

"Mr. Williams will be expecting that," she continued. "He told me he distrusts women. Wouldn't deceit from male quarters be more surprising and successful?"

"We lack that special persuasive power that has always worked so well on him."

"In business?"

"No, but there's your element of surprise. Female associates didn't exist in his day."

"We couldn't think of what the hell else to do," blurted Snell, "but drag you into it and make it worth your while."

"George! Excuse me, Eve, but we weren't as crass as that."

She thought to inquire into the extent of their crassness, but refrained. They were desperate. Fred Williams knew them well, and if he was as clever as they believed, he could predict how they would think and act, probably even anticipating their using her against him, but he could not predict how she would behave. It was pointless to denigrate the morality of her bosses or make herself seem less the lady. In the struggle to exist, morality was often a victim.

"I will forget you made this offer to me."

"You've been an asset to this firm. We'd hate to lose you," continued Senior smoothly.

"Does he speak for you, George?"

Snell fiddled with his napkin and said nothing.

"Bill?"

"This company must survive," said Junior, stabbing the tablecloth with his fork.

"Fred Williams expects me to do what he tells me to. If I don't, I'm out, and he's made it quite clear that I'd be out—" she looked meaningfully at each of them, "with company." She pushed her chair back. "Thank you for the coffee, gentlemen," she said, the filled but untouched cup at her elbow, "and a good day to you all."

It was so early, it looked like Saturday on Wall Street. As Eve mounted the steps to Williams, Wetcliff, and Snell the stillness was almost palpable. Frederick Willard Williams stood, arms akimbo, in the doorway.

"I'm not impressed," he stated flatly.

"But I am. Did you spend the night rifling all the cabinets?"

"I did not."

"You should have. You'll never know what goes on, otherwise."

"I can't trust anyone, eh, except you, of course."

"Including me. But if you're willing to risk my coffee and some home-baked croissants, join me."

He followed her to the elevator and up to her office and watched silently, his fingers on chin and mouth, as she made and poured the coffee.

"Haven't you figured me out yet?" she asked, placing a plate of croissants at his elbow.

"Well, you've made and poured the coffee, like a good girl, but you haven't watered the plants. Where are they?"

"They deplete the oxygen, and I'm rather partial to breathing."

"You're not concerned about your secretary's respiration?"

"My secretary is not concerned about it. The plant in her office is hers."

"Mr. Whatshisname seems too complex to be the daisy type."

"But Miss Kay is not. Mr. Martin is her temporary replacement."

"So now women eat the bread, and the men catch the crumbs."

"That's not an accurate generalization, and you know it."

"You don't know me well enough to know what I know. Is Miss Kay on leave lecturing at Oxford?"

"She's in Florida caring for her mother. St. Petersburg, where a favorite activity is waiting for the Social Security checks, talking about them, and cashing them. W.W.&S. should be a hit there."

The old man's eyes narrowed. "You know we'll be expanding in Palm Beach, so don't get snippy with me, Miss."

"We'll be expanding there if the research survey determines it's economically feasible."

"It will be."

"Or we'll make it feasible?"

"That's right."

They ate in silence, Williams casting long, intimidating looks at Eve, and Eve, stomach slightly aflutter, stoutly withstanding them, but barely able to contain her amusement at the childish behavior of her superior.

Fred Williams downed the last of his croissant. "You bake well."

"Mr. Martin baked them. I've never tasted any better."

"Mr. Martin is a wonder. Does he do windows?"

"Possibly. He does bricklaying very well, I hear, and general construction. He's been very helpful in formulating layout designs for the branches you envision."

"Has he now? I was impressed with some of those, so the man can design spaces and croissants. And who knows what other designs he's got in mind." He chuckled. "The American dream! Now I'll be off. I've got some file rifling to do, and I want to have my Dracula mask on to scare the tin-pack leadership trio.

Fortunately, women can't lead, but they never stop trying." And with this civility, he left the room.

Fred Williams banged the gavel three times. Actually, he banged a hammer, the significance of which was not lost on the assemblage. Anyway, meetings at Williams, Wetcliff, and Snell were never banged to order, but called to order in the civilized manner of adults, first because the firm had cultivated a quiet image, and second because employees came to comparative order upon entering the conference room. Casting preliminaries aside, the CEO and major stockholder got right to the point.

"You've all been a great consolation to me these past twenty years. When a man is forced into retirement and his accessories take over, talented men both, I grant you, well, it takes the man out of a man. You've all kept me going, and I thank you for it. Reading the research I've commissioned done on you has been like reading romantic novels, biographies, and how-to-do-it books rolled into one. Yes, indeed, I've had the pleasure of getting to know you very well. I've always admired anything new, so I expected the younger members of the staff to be especially dear to me, but our older members have you kids licked there. Not in business, of course. And no one, old or young, has come close to challenging my corner on the creativity market. If someone had, I wouldn't be here now, but, as Dorothy Parker would have said, here we all are, aren't we? I've kept you late today, just as you will keep yourselves late in the future to achieve our new goals. We are going international, and we're doing it now. Letters will be sent to all our clients announcing our new services and requesting that they indicate which investment firm they want to handle their American stock and bond accounts beginning the first of the month. Despite my decrepit exterior, I can handle the business, as my former partners well know and as you, from Williams mythology, probably know by now, too. But my knack for client relations has never been widely appreciated, especially by the clients, whom I do not have the privilege of knowing as intimately as I do all of you.

"For the vital task of retaining our clients and encouraging them to accumulate bulging foreign portfolios, softer talents than mine are needed, but in a shrewd shell. Therefore, I have made Eve Nelson senior vice-president, client services. I am allowing her to continue personally servicing the accounts of select clients in addition to doing an awesome job in her new position. All other positions in our reconstituted company will not be filled. We're going to avoid the too-many-cooks syndrome. But each employee of this firm, when given a task to do, will be informed of the position under which the task falls and perform it as if the position were his. Failure to do so will not be allowed. In other non-highfalutin words, you will do a crackerjack job each time or be fired."

"What salary schedule will we follow?" came a voice from down-table.

"The one you've already got, you dimwit. Do you think we can change salary schedules for every job you do every day?" barked Williams. "We're all in this together. One man's success is every man's success. Uh, pardon me, ladies. If we get too persnickety about titles and pay at the outset, this enterprise will be dead at the outset, and I can't believe that any of you has a particular relish for death."

Fred Williams was neither surprised nor affronted when, at the conclusion of his tongue-lashing, Eve Nelson motioned him aside.

"One double-crossing female less. Did it never occur to you to do me the courtesy of asking?"

"I'm not into that social stuff, and you might have said no."
"You're too good to lose, even if you are a woman, and you're the only important staff person I can't rattle a skeleton at, so it's threats for them and honey for you. But my method doesn't affect the fact that you're in a growth position."

"Following your orders, I'll make more enemies in a short time than most make in a lifetime, and when I leave your employ, those enemies, by then comfortably ensconced in competing firms, will shred my career."

"I'm giving you full authority in this position, but," Williams shrugged, "if you don't think you can handle me…"

Eve smiled. What ambitious businesswoman could resist this challenge? She could. Easily. Five years earlier, even two years earlier, she could not have, but she had stopped running long enough to realize that at the top of the hill was another hill and another beyond that one, and that she would never stop running, never have anything tangible or permanent or important. Her dreams had become more frequent and more easily remembered, and with alarming regularity interrupted her breakfast and marched boldly into her office at the most inconvenient times. They were the dreams of a woman who wanted to walk through life, absorbing the view with enjoyment with a kindred soul in pants. So, she smiled at Fred Williams, knowing he would take it as acceptance of his proposal, and indeed meaning it as acceptance, because she didn't care, because the frustration of a stunted private life made her reckless of a business life that led nowhere. Her wild vengeance over the weekend had been cathartic. This more dangerous playing with position might be more so. She accepted the Williams proposition because it was madness. And if it destroyed the paper world she had created and for which she was appreciated, then maybe she would be left with something for herself, even if it was only pain.

Chapter Fourteen

Williams was a relentless taskmaster, but the scarcity of smiles these days at W.W.&S. did not adversely affect Eve, who rarely smiled at work and who was now too busy to have the time for dreams. The CEO and major stockholder seemed to walk on cat's feet, and to relish the embarrassing moments he constantly inflicted on staff who stole mere minutes from their day to chat or breathe. Eve seemed to do neither, and, except for that first day, Williams accorded her the courtesy of knocking before he entered her office. Formal announcements of his imminent arrival were prohibited, and a variety of sound codes, changed weekly, were developed to confound the seemingly omniscient tyrant. Rumblings of personnel departures rose and subsided. No one Williams wanted to remain could afford to leave. Unleashed, his arsenal of information could prove deadly. Certain intimations, casually dropped, instantly cured wanderlust. It was easy to determine those so persuaded. They worked through the lunch hour and almost through the dinner hour, too. The investment house was running on fear. Williams was not an office man. He was constantly poking around and making inquiries in everybody else's. No one dared to suggest the existence of the intercom. Williams wanted more than it could give. He was in and out of Eve's office at least half a dozen times a day. Having determined to allow the intrusions to wash over her, even as she swam with them, she was not upset. She calmly replied to all the chief's inquiries as he barked them at her.

"We've lost 25% of our clients. What the hell are you doing about it?" She told him.

"That damned reporter is ridiculing us in print, on the radio, and on three television programs a day. Who the hell does he think he is?" Eve told him.

He always left her office growling, and she was never able to resist a smile as he made his exit. She knew he was pleased. Strangely, so was she. He bullied, bossed, and exaggerated, but she liked him, perhaps because he ultimately approved of most of her suggestions and actions, perhaps because he insisted on a closetful of facts before budging from a preconceived idea or formulating an unexpected one.

It had been six weeks since the company's metamorphosis and since the Wetciffs and Snell had met with Eve over breakfast. Apart from significant looks when their paths crossed occasionally in the halls, they made no reference to that meeting. Eve had no idea whether the trio was pursuing the plot to oust Williams from the catbird seat, and the trio had no idea whether Eve was laying foundations to undermine such a plot. Though Williams treated Eve as mercilessly as others in public (and only slightly less so in private), the trio had begun to worry. Eve had made no effort at chit-chat of any kind. All this could merely be caution, but the woman seemed unflappable. Eve Nelson never appeared thrown by Williams' manner or accusations. This was commendable, but suspicious. Despite their experiences with the old man in the old days, *they* were thrown, and it was inconceivable that any mortal, especially a woman, would not be thrown, too. They could not fathom that their goals were not hers, that the investment firm no longer regulated her breathing.

Bill Jr. understood something else, or thought he did, and it drove his elders to the verge of panic. He realized that a woman of achievement like Eve would not take kindly to personal rejection, sudden and undeserved, seconds from success with him. He had not taken kindly to it, although he had extricated himself calmly and cleverly from Elaine Dawson, but women, he believed, had long memories, and Eve's reluctance to commit herself to their constructive conspiracy could have been born of feelings beyond business.

With the blessing of his father and Snell, he determined to renew social ties with Eve. Office romances, frowned on always to varying degrees, were positively dangerous in the Williams reign, but in that danger lay advantage.

Young Bill caught up with Eve at the corner of Wall and Church streets. She wondered why it had taken him so many weeks. She understood him well.

"You haven't aged at all," he began.

She had to laugh but said nothing.

"Old Williams has the army mobilized and all passes canceled. But I've missed seeing you. How have you been managing?"

"Acceptably. I'm still on payroll."

"And will stay there; I'm convinced of it. Fred needs you. You're the only one who can manage both the office and him. If he were fifty years younger, I'd be very upset."

She smiled into the traffic. "Aren't you?"

"You mean Dad's little conspiracy? Of course not. It will come to nothing. Fred has a royal flush, and not even a beautiful, talented woman can change that hand. But you can change mine. I've got all the cards I want, but somehow, they don't stack up well. I guess I'm getting older and less effective at games. That fiasco with Elaine—" He shook his head. "How did that ever happen? But it did, and I let you slip away, or rather," he gave a half-laugh, "you graciously stepped away. Not only have I gotten older, I've become a fool."

His hands were cast disconsolately in his pockets. She patted the closest arm. "Don't torture yourself. You're not any more of a fool than most men."

"Thanks for the sympathy, but then, I don't deserve any, do I?"

Their feet reached the sidewalk at Fifth Avenue and Fortieth Streets.

"Walking is a wonderful release for tension, but you're already eight blocks out of your way."

"Not at all. I've moved. But what tension are you under? You rarely take this hefty hike home. You said things were going well."

"Questions, questions. My turn. Where are you living, and why did you move? That's a conversational ploy, not a romantic catechism."

"I wish it weren't a ploy. But I'm living in paradise because I wearied of my slum. And that's a romantic ploy, not a romantic catechism."

"You're not going to follow me home." Dismay crept into her voice.

"Not at all." And he tipped an imaginary hat and began to cross the street.

"Don't be silly, Bill." But he was already dodging traffic. "Silly, senseless, juvenile," Eve muttered as Bill paralleled her walk home. Men were vain, impractical creatures, and it was useless to advise them. Nevertheless, in her head, she did. Perhaps he heard her, because on her nth frustrating look to her right, he was gone. She was relieved. After work, she wanted relaxation, not Bill Wetcliff. The realization startled her. But why the surprise? Hadn't she been telling herself all along that he had been merely a challenge to be enjoyed and punished as an example? But to whom? Who would know besides herself? Bill thought that what she wanted was to reform him, to attain him on her own terms. He was tall, handsome, and wealthy—most women's ideal. But if he required so much analysis, he wasn't hers. If one had to think a man's qualifications through, he wasn't an object of love. Working out an acquisition's suitability took place from 9 to 5. After hours, she wanted love.

"I do want everything," she thought, "but love is everything—as long as we can both make a living." Eve was ever practical. Moving on "automatic," she returned the doorman's greeting, pressed the button for the elevator, and put the key in the lock of her door. The lock rebelled, and she rattled the door several times to achieve compliance, but in vain. She was speechless when the door of the apartment adjoining hers opened and Bill Wetcliff stepped out offering assistance.

"What on earth!" she gasped.

"So much quieter than my last neighborhood," he said, opening the door easily. "Ideally quiet, if you'll allow me to open the door for you daily and eliminate what little racket there is."

She hadn't meant to merely slam the door in his face. He deserved something more, something unique, but she couldn't think what. She had not closed the door on W.W.&S. for the day. Oh, no. It would seep through the wall. It would blow through the window if she opened it. Her inner sanctum had become a prison. She shook with rage. She began pacing the floor to relieve the emotion. And a strange thing happened. She began to laugh. It was a smile at first, then a giggle, a guffaw, and finally a real laugh, open-mouthed and full. She laughed at her foolish sensibility, her anger, at the entire W.W.&S, comedy, at her life. Finally, she plunked down on the sofa exhausted, and sat there examining the crack on the opposite wall, searching for the infinitesimal stain on the club chair, until the doorbell rang. With effort, she persuaded herself to respond to it.

"He's just another human being," she told herself, "more or less."

With no inner purpose at all, except to be strong, she marched with determination to the door and, addressing no words to it at all, opened it smartly.

"Mother!" she exclaimed.

"Hello, dear," said Mrs. Nelson, sweeping past her daughter and hurling her jacket onto the sofa and herself into a chair. "Don't tell me I'm a nuisance, you're very busy, and you're expecting somebody. You're not expecting anybody, are you?" she asked hopefully, Eve's need overriding her own.

"No, no one," came the bewildered response.

"Thank God. I'm very depressed."

"Mother, what is it?" cried her daughter.

"You'll say it serves me right. A foolish old woman taking up with trash and expecting another Maury Nelson. A stupid, senile, old woman, desperate for companionship and picking up garbage. The demented old fool, it serves her right, that's what you'll say."

"I'll say no such thing," Eve said firmly.

"Well, I will. Harry's left me."

"Oh, Mother, I'm so sorry."

Mrs. Nelson gazed into her daughter's eyes. "I really believe you are. He wasn't much, but I liked him. We seemed to get on so well, and then—" She flung her arms out, unable to continue.

Eve embraced her mother. Raising false hope was not in her character; neither was denigrating an object of love.

"I took such good care of him. No more stained cuffs or moth-eaten collars." She sniffled. "And I cured his bursitis in one week with the same remedy that worked on your father. Meals—you would have thought he was dining in a hotel! Maybe that's what he did think, so why not trade in one waitress and maid for another? That ungrateful skunk, that cowardly moron! Leaving me a note in the morning to say he was going home to Michigan to marry an old family friend. Sick old fool! Does he think she'll take care of him the way I did? He won't find it so easy to pick up and leave after he marries again, unless he leaves in a casket, the imbecile. This is what I get for allowing him to go home to visit, and this is the appreciation, the gratitude I deserve. I should have reconciled myself to loneliness when your father died. I thought I had. There was the business and you. It wasn't enough. Dan and Phyllis saw fit to marry foreigners like Harry and move to their home states to bring up my grandchildren away from me, so what could I do? I've always had to keep busy. I should have worked for The Red Cross."

"They never would have allowed you to take charge." Eve kissed her mother's cheek.

"That would have been their mistake."

"Isn't Seymour chafing to leave? You could run the shop yourself. Or marry one of your customers, it is a men's shop, after all, and have him run the shop while you run him."

Margaret Nelson waved the thought away. "There's no one suitable; Seymour's looked for me. Anyway, I'd never allow a husband of mine to take over my business. Can you imagine if I had done that with Harry?"

"That was why you refused to marry him. You thought he wanted to get involved in the business."

"At our age, marriage isn't necessary."

"I guess Harry thought it was."

"I knew you'd criticize me."

"I'm not criticizing. A way of life is a matter of temperament. And you're in good company. Frederick Williams wouldn't buckle to marriage again or to subordination."

"Which is why he's making life so difficult at W.W.&S. Thank you, dear."

Eve laughed. "Really, Mother, he's a good sort, just different. If he can cope at 90, you can cope at 55."

"Can you at 30?"

Eve sighed. She knew where this would lead.

"Don't you think it's time we spoke about this openly, honestly, and fearlessly?"

"Brandy, Mother?"

"Absolutely not. I have the urge to prepare dinner for us, and then we're going to talk."

Eve bit her lip. Good Samaritans were not always rewarded.

Chapter Fifteen

E ve paid little heed to the triple knock on her door. It was the courtesy knock of the never-announced, constantly visiting Williams. She glanced up at him as she continued writing on the small, uncrowded segment of her desk. The light scratching of her pen on the paper was all the sound to be heard.

Finally, "Old bag's waiting for you downstairs. Says she's your mother."

This earned a comet eyeflash rebuke from Eve, who continued writing.

"Not bad packaging, though," he amended.

Her half smile was not lost; he had been waiting for it.

"I'll be with her in a few minutes," she murmured.

"You don't expect me to tell her that, do you?" rasped the old man.

"Certainly not," responded Eve.

"Palm Beach response still improving?"

"Another eighty-two clients clamoring for the convenience of that sunshine branch."

He grunted approval.

She rose from her chair. "The full Florida report will be ready by the end of the day." She smiled and left the office.

"No frills, that woman, none," said Williams with satisfaction.

He stood there for a minute after she had left before turning and leaving himself. In the hall, he winced. Bill Wetcliff Jr. always provoked that reaction. His presence provoked it, the sound of his voice provoked it, even the mention of his name provoked it. Fred Williams had made vague attempts to analyze this reaction and had concluded that playboys of the Western world were simply not to his liking, but he did not delve beneath this. Having determined that he did not like the man, he considered the reason of little consequence. He could not forget him, however.

"Too bad he's the son of the company co-founder," Williams had often muttered. "His ideas aren't bad, but are they good enough for me to retain a man I don't like?" Time would tell. Williams had never held nepotism sacred.

The halls of Personnel were empty. Williams scowled. He himself rarely ate lunch. Not what you would call a meal, anyway, at least not before closing time. Still, it gave him satisfaction to stroll the empty corridors. This was all his, quietly and obediently his, and when those two-legged, lazy noisemakers returned, they would be his, too, for as long as he wanted them.

Standing undecided in the quiet of the second floor was a young woman.

"What do you want?" barked Williams.

"I'm looking for Personnel."

"So am I. Drat them all! If a crisis occurred between 12 and 1 o'clock, the cat would have to take care of it. We'd better get a cat!" He fingered the nearest desk intercom. After pressing several buttons, he gave up in disgust.

"Damn!" he roared. "Want a job?"

"Yes, I do. I—"

"Follow me," he barked, walking quickly into one of the offices. "Where do you work now?"

"Merrill Lynch."

"Why are you leaving?"

"For better opportunity."

Williams snorted. "What's wrong with the opportunity at Merrill Lynch?"

"I'll never get anywhere there."

"Never get anywhere here if you arrive at lunchtime!"

"But there is no other time."

"Yes, yes, I know. Stupid statement, stupid response. Why the hell should I care why you want to work here. Can you type?"

"Yes, at—"

"Take shorthand?"

"Yes, at—"

"Sit down!" He thrust a pad and pen at her. "Take this down. 'Dear Miss Gorty, your typing is poor, your spelling execrable, you smile too much, and you wear patterned stockings. You're fired.' Sign it F.W. Williams and type it."

He strummed his fingers on the desk as she typed and twirled the paper out of the machine almost before her hands left the keys.

"Let me see." He looked. "You're hired. Leave Miss Gorty's termination notice on the desk. Report here tomorrow at 9 sharp."

"Salary?" she began.

"Of course you'll get a salary," he snapped. "Better look through the files to acquaint yourself with things before Gorty gets back."

So it was that at 9 o'clock the following morning, Eve Nelson found herself sharing the doorway to Williams, Wetcliff, and Snell with Elaine Dawson.

"Mr. Williams hired me yesterday," said Elaine in response to Eve's astonished "Good morning."

A half turn revealed the entrance of William Wetcliff Jr., whose offer of a lift to work Eve had refused, insisting she preferred to enjoy the morning traffic in a bus. She held the "Open" button in the elevator long enough to see his reaction to the newcomer, whose warmth and sparkle toward him was more suited to an evening than a morning greeting. The door closed on a stammering, visibly shocked Bill Wetcliff. Eve would keep more than an elevator door between them, between her and a fool, who had too little sense to guarantee the separation of his social and his business life. She grimaced. She had been guilty temporarily of the same. As for Elaine Dawson, it was hard to dislike a woman she pitied.

The elevator door opened to reveal a sour-faced Fred Williams, arms crossed, feet apart planted firmly in the parquet.

"My office, now!" he commanded Eve.

He took a chair facing hers, ignoring the chair behind the barrier of his imperial desk.

"That Florida report will not do."

"I can change the report, if you like, but that will not change the facts: Our clients and potential clients there have little interest in going international. They are mainly retirees, not yuppies. Palm Beach does not a Florida make. We'll make out gangbusters if we stick to the traditional mix, but if we go completely international, we will lose our client base. Large cracks have already started appearing in that. The California report is almost ready, and it isn't much better."

"But I want to go international. That's where the future is, and the past too, for that matter. Stock investments abroad have gone up five times in the last fifteen years, and they have only doubled in this country. The dollar will be weak for at least a decade. Our clients will make a fortune with us."

"Most of our clients are conservative investors, and W.W.&S. has the enviable reputation of being conservative and sharp. Even our risk investors take comfort in that. Destroy that perception and you destroy this company."

"It was your job to educate our clients to the benefits of investing internationally, and you've failed."

"You have seen and approved all the ad layouts, the brochures, the broker mailings, the glowing letter signed by the venerable yours truly that was mailed to all clients, but you refuse to see the fact that neither your aggressive determination nor your paper wisdom and charm have changed the bottom line: If we go international, we go broke."

"Those stupid investors don't know what's good for them."

"Apparently, we don't know what's good for us."

"It's a matter of principle."

"Or stubbornness."

"Principle! I'm as positive as it's humanly possible to be that I'm right!"

"Do you want this company to continue in existence or do you want to be right?"

"I want both."

"Well, you can't have both. Make up your mind which it will be. I must know whether to send clients that mailing about the transfer of their domestic accounts to Merrill Lynch and UBS or whether to write my resume."

"Those should have been mailed last week! I won't tolerate insubordination!"

"Reconsider, Fred. I don't want you to lose everything. We can slowly increase the international commitment. If it's successful, good advertising will make it catch fire. We can become international experts, but we can't jump into deep water at the start."

"I haven't much time."

"You'll live forever; you thrive on change and challenge. I'm not so sure about the rest of us. This company bears your name. When people think 'Fred Williams,' I want them to think 'clever, calculated risk,' not 'disaster.' May I leave now?"

"This office, yes."

Eve had just placed the jacket of her suit around the back of her chair when Fred Williams loomed lanky in the doorway.

"Paper wisdom and charm," he repeated. "That was very unkind." And he smartly gave her his back and left.

Chapter Sixteen

Hank, pleading urgency, had persuaded Eve to have a business dinner with him.

"Are you with them?" he asked flatly.

"What are you talking about? With whom?"

"No, of course, you're not, or you wouldn't be insulting the Chief. Then again, you two get on that way, and you wouldn't want him to suspect you by changing now."

"For Pete's sake, make sense, Hank."

He sat down, relieved. "I guess you're all right, then. I was dining out last night, and I heard them on the other side of the partition - Senior, Junior, and Snell. They're sabotaging the Chief's plan. They read from altered copies of that notice you're going to send all clients about shifting their domestic stock accounts elsewhere. Our 'responsible foreign' investing has become 'aggressive foreign' investing, and they've suggested a 'small, caring firm offering personalized service' as preferable to a brokerage monolith, though they were forced to mention those we contracted with. Can you guess the 'caring' firm they're pushing?"

"Give me a chance to digest what you're saying! Good lord!"

"It's Thompson & Company."

"Thompson! They're on the verge of bankruptcy!"

"A quick infusion of cash will avoid bankruptcy, and good management will soon make Thompson green again. Old Thompson's style never entered the twentieth century, let alone the twenty-first. When the next insider trading results are available, guess what percentage of Williams, Wetcliff, & Snell it will reveal Wetcliff and Snell own?"

"They've sold their W.W.&S. stock and used the proceeds to buy out Thompson! But Thompson is privately owned. There will be no public disclosure of stock trading into Thompson, only out of W.W.&S.! When our clients see that Management has no confidence in its own company – the company will be dead. We must tell Fred."

"Yes, but that could be the final death blow to this company. Two younger company lords who do not have the reputation of having any loose marbles will say that stockholder notice met with the old man's approval. The Chief's denial won't wash. Being colorful, old, and eccentric is only a step away from being bananas in the minds of many. Our clients will run like hell—to Thompson, Merrill Lynch. UBS—anywhere they'll feel safe. If we could only postpone that mailing."

"I just told Fred that if the mailing goes out, I go too. He'll think about it."

"Did he say he would?"

"You know he never admits to thinking about anything."

Hank nodded. "He'll think. He doesn't want to lose you. We'll have to discuss this over dinner."

"Don't force yourself," she thought somewhat angrily.

"Did you dine alone last night?" she said quickly. "If not, your companion could be a witness to what was said."

"I'd rather leave her out of this."

"Of course," said Eve coldly, wondering how the survival of the firm old Fred Williams had founded could be of lesser importance than the survival of a Hank Williams liaison.

Eve began slicing her roast beef. "You're not wild about Fred."

"I don't like his ideas, but he's crisp and clear about them, and he's no backstabber. This is his company, and if he wants to ruin it, that's his privilege."

"And what about the hundreds of jobs that would be lost, Hank, including your own?"

"Life is changing, and I welcome it."

"You don't have a family to support."

"Good people will find jobs. The others are in the wrong profession."

"Harsh judgment."

"Realistic, but I'm generalizing. Eve, are you afraid of thwarting the conspiracy against Fred?"

"No."

"Then let's save the company for him to ruin."

"The first part, yes. I'll fight him like the devil on the second part. What should we do now, Hank?"

"Wetcliff and Snell are like partners without portfolio, but they won't want that known until they have switched the client accounts out of W.W.&S. Insider trading figures won't be out for another month. There could be a leak, of course. A rumor floating about, shall we say? And a copy of the doctored letter they intend to send out in place of ours."

"Good old Henry in Mailing." Eve shook her head. He's probably got a job waiting for him at Thompson. But with thousands of clients, don't those bozos realize that only one has to contact Fred or me for the deception to become known? Calling Fred senile or berserk won't wash away the fact that their letter was unauthorized by him."

"So instead of calling him bananas, they'll call him a menace—a serious danger to the company and the company's accounts. And how sane do his ideas for W.W.&S. seem to us who like him? To those *few* of us? His colorful ways and nasty disposition will be attested to by most of our staff and will not inspire confidence in investors, who look to us for reassuring conservatism and sense. The evil trio will come off as saviors, acting in the best interests of investors and bypassing propriety because of the urgency of the situation."

"So Fred loses either way."

"Unless we can discredit the Wetcliffs and Snell."

"Fred has gotten bios on everyone in the company. He may have just what he needs—we need—to topple those saints."

Hank frowned. "What if they're clean?"

"What if the moon is made of green cheese?"

"I thought it was. So you think everyone has something to be ashamed of?"

"Oh, yes, even you and I. If you don't ask about my indiscretions, I won't ask about yours."

Hank laughed. "In the plural?"

"In the plural. We're certainly aware of one apiece in the recent past."

"Eve, we're talking about behavior that would adversely affect the operation of the company or that indicates qualities at odds with those needed by a company."

"They're not mutually exclusive."

"The Chief won't appreciate the quality that made us delay telling him about these developments."

She shrugged. "We were afraid he would act hastily and give them ammunition to use against him."

"Fear is not a constructive quality."

"Well, I like that! You were the one who suggested we discuss it before approaching Fred with the news."

"Ah, but now I see the error of that decision. I accept the criticism and learn from it. Wonderful quality."

"You're impossible, Hank."

"I hope not, and neither is overcoming fear, but it requires persistent effort, and I know I'll need help to keep from backsliding. I've got to continue doing things I'm afraid to do. Like asking you to dinner."

Eve flushed. "We've just had dinner. Was that such a fearful event?"

"It was a business event. Will you have a non-business dinner with me tomorrow night?"

Eve looked off at the other diners and flushed more deeply. "The company may be toppling about our heads by tomorrow night." She stood up abruptly. "Fred won't appreciate seeing us at this hour, but we'll be spared castigation if we tell him about his dear former partners before morning."

Fred Williams was not a sleeper. After five and a half hours, his muscles wearied of the restrictions of bed, and he read, raided the refrigerator, or watched television, sometimes all three at the same time. He had scoffed at the alleged soporific qualities of waterbeds. Their use was sacrilegious, anyway. Pretending to sleep on the water was akin to pretending to walk on water. How could a man sleep while perpetrating a fraud?

The phone rang.

"What damn fool would ring me after midnight?"

He padded over to the phone. "You're a fool! Who are you?" he barked into the receiver.

"It's Eve. Hank and I are downstairs. We must talk to you."

"Talk."

"May we come up?"

"No. What is it?"

"W.W.&S. is history after this morning's mailing."

"Who says?"

"Your former partners."

"Up!" He buzzed them into the lobby.

He greeted them at the door in his red plaid robe.

"Sit down and get to the point."

"George and Bill Sr. have sold all their shares in W.W.&S. and bought out Thompson & Company. The mailing to the shareholders explains all, basically that with their experience and record, they will turn Thompson around, and with your experience and record, you will destroy W.W.&S." Eve handed him an envelope with five pages of print and graphics.

Fred Williams flipped through them.

"Damn them!" Then he held up the money section of that morning's WALL STREET JOURNAL and read the headline: "SENIORS EXIT W.W.&S." He growled the opening sentences: "The door is open at W.W.&S., but senior stockholders started walking out when senior Fred Williams walked back in. Once the partner who called the shots, the colorful and eccentric Williams has come out of retirement to, as one insider put it, remake the company in his image by taking back the reins and charging full speed ahead to the 18th century."

"Damn fool! I only founded the company in 1948." He read on: "He wants the company to specialize in international investing, we were told. William refused to be interviewed for this article but says he will talk to the media when he is ready. With only two international specialists at W.W.&S., he is apparently not ready."

"And now that tripe will be followed up with this perverted mailing. Do those turncoats think our stockholders will go with them?"

"Well, the seniors are going, and Thompson has as good a chance as any other company of getting them; with Wetcliff and Snell there probably a better chance."

"Who asked you, Martin?" Williams grabbed a pen and pad from the end table, wrote, and shoved the scribblings at Eve.

She read: "Elaine: 1. Buy me 2,525,000 shares of W.W.&S. at the opening bell, 2. Call Publicity Department meeting with me at 10 AM today, 3. Arrange a photo shoot for me ASAP with European, Latin American, and Asian backgrounds."

Hank peeked over Eve's shoulder.

"Elaine?!" they both exclaimed.

"Elaine Dawson, my new secretary, and assistant. Sacked Gorty."

"But she's after our young enemy Bill Jr.!"

"An artist of sorts, isn't he? Bring him aboard too."

"But-"

"I'm going to be the new poster boy for W.W.&S. International. And those initials become all W's next week. A senior courting seniors." His arms reached for the ceiling as he said rhapsodically, "The future is NOW, whether you're 9 or 90, and it's overseas!" He grinned broadly. "I ought to be in pictures!" He ambled to the door, opened it, and waved them to exit. "Don't even think about it for a minute. Pictures, not Bellevue. See you at 10AM."

Eve and Hank worked their way to the bottom of a pot of coffee rather than sleep. They agreed that the cantankerous Williams could be made into a colorful poster boy for the firm, but how? Eve pulled out her cell phone and dialed.

"Hi, Bill. Sleeping at 4 A.M? A young man like you? Even Fred Williams is up, almost dancing in the street, but I persuaded him that his garish red robe would attract too much attention. Said he wanted attention. Do you, my artist friend and neighbor? You could head Publicity, as well as make president at W. Make your own way, be your own man. You'll still be your father's only son. It's a risk, but Fred is taking an even bigger one. He wants you."

Silence.

"Events are moving fast. You can move with them or be left behind."

"Where are you?"

"Vinny's Café."

"Give me twenty minutes."

"You didn't mention me," said Hank.

"You'll mention you when he arrives."

It looked like a football huddle, with three heads bent conspiratorially over the center of the table. As they fanned back, illustrations took center stage, illustrations of Fred Williams smiling up at palm trees ("PALMY DAYS AND GOLDEN RAYS. WARMTH & SECURITY. GO INTERNATIONAL."), Fred Williams scratching his head over a plate of food, the French Alps looming in the distance ("PUT NEW THINGS ON YOUR PLATE AND EAT HEARTY. GO INTERNATIONAL."), Fred Williams caught in the middle of multi-directional Rome traffic ("THEY KNOW WHERE THEY ARE GOING AND HOW TO GET THERE, AND THEY WILL STOP FOR YOU. GO INTERNATIONAL. GO W.W.&S., SPECIALISTS IN GROUND FLOOR INTERNATIONAL DEVELOPMENT. INVESTMENTS FOR TODAY AND TOMORROW. THE COMPANY YOU'VE TRUSTED HAS JUST GOTTEN BETTER. LET US KEEP YOU SECURE AND GROWING. WE KNOW HOW.")

Bill Wetcliff's eyes glowed. "This is just a sample, of course. We've got some good men in Publicity. I'm known there as 'The Naked and the Nude, but they'll see what I can do, what we can do together. I told Dad I didn't want to cut and run."

Smiles all around.

"But do you really think that we can convince Fred to make overseas investment a large part of the package without scrapping our full-service investment goals? He's a stubborn man."

"But not a fool, Bill. When he has time to think things through, he'll bend if this is only a trial, but he won't wait long for results. He doesn't think he has much time. Says neither parent made it past 95." Eve sighed. "That means we don't have much time despite our ages, either."

"Business is always in a fast lane, Eve," said Bill, "and if you can put up with Fred for a short time, I can put up with Elaine. We've got a common goal."

"Yes," agreed Eve. "In a few hours, we will start in earnest. Meanwhile, I definitely need sleep."

"I drove you here; I'll drive you home," stated Hank, looking at Bill with a touch of defiance.

"Bill moved next door. He'll drive me," said Eve.

A deflated Hank watched as a silent, but smirking Bill took Eve's arm and escorted her to his car.

As she fastened her seat belt, Eve acknowledged that Mr. Martin was now Hank, but a business Hank, she calmly assured herself. Suddenly she realized that Miss Kay would shortly be returning from Florida, and Hank Martin would have no reason to be even that.

Chapter Seventeen

Margaret Nelson read THE WALL STREET JOURNAL article with alarm. A small but significant portion of her nest egg was in W.W.&S., and if the company went under her lifestyle was in jeopardy of changing. Eve had tried to allay her fears in the months since Williams' return, but she had met the old coot, and he had impressed her as death sustained by Geritol. Now, it seemed, the company would depart before he did. Her phone calls to Eve had proved fruitless. Finally, she left a message: "I read the article in the JOURNAL. What are you doing about Williams? I insist on knowing. My life savings are at stake." A little exaggeration never hurt. She paced the living room floor. Generous Harry was gone, Eve might lose her job, and the supermarket screamed "inflation," despite expert pronouncements to the contrary. What was a woman to do, a lonely, unattached, non-working woman living carefully on her late husband's pension and social security? The successful clothing store didn't count. It couldn't go on forever. Her lease was up next year, and there had been ominous rumblings of a huge increase on the next one. The cross-country buying trips were tiring, and the store manager was due for a raise. The economy was precarious, and a buyer might not be willing to pay what the store was really worth. She had tried to change Eve's life—Hank had, after her initial dismay, seemed promising. Now she had begun to think that her own life was due for an overhaul first. She didn't have as much time as Eve, though more than old Williams. Williams! Why didn't he go back to Bora Bora, or wherever, and stop creating more problems than life usually created for mere mortals? She was fed up with the financial uncertainly. Eve's response to her phone call could take forever, and she didn't intend to wait.

The faces down the length of the Boardroom table looked pale and unhappy. Fred Williams was adamant, as when was he not, as he finished lecturing Hadley from Research.

"Now Eve, you and your secretary work up a weekly investment program for senior citizens, diversified, but with a big chunk overseas. Make sure Publicity has it in ten days." He held up his hands. "No arguments. Weekly will be painless for them. Twenty dollars, two hundred dollars. You know their incomes." His high pitch became a baritone. "For the price of your daily coffee and cake at Starbucks, the world is yours!" He laughed two octaves higher. "Picture me in Publicity!"

"Must we?" came a loud whisper from the down table.

"I heard that, and yes, you must. Keep you on your toes, knowing I'll be checking on you daily. Bill, with that creep gone to Thompson, you're our new point man in Publicity. All right, all right, department head, department head, for Pete's sake. Titles!" he muttered. "Elaine, you're liaison to point — department head — Wetcliff. Dismissed!"

Fred grabbed Elaine's hand and practically pulled her into his office. "Now, you listen to me. In the next forty-eight hours, you become an expert in the art of publicizing investments. Take these for starters." He piled three books and a dozen investment publications on her lap.

She looked up at him in amazement.

"That's an order. Publicity is not Bill's bag. You're a mere secretary, but I think you're a quick study. There's a lot at stake for you. Don't muff this."

She looked at her lap and was visibly upset. "I know, my job."

"Not your job, you fool. Him! He likes smarts, not dumb blondes."

She visibly brightened. "And I can dye my hair, too!"

"Not yet, too obvious. Go!"

Fred Williams looked at the sun, bravely trying to outrun the clouds. "A lot is at stake for me, too," he mumbled.

Margaret Nelson would not sit down." I want an answer, and I want it now. What are you doing to save this company, my investment in it, and my daughter's job?"

"Her job's not in jeopardy."

"If this company is, then her job is."

"So it's a job, is it, not a career? I'm glad to hear it. We're experts here. We'll take care of business. You can go back to your knitting and mahjong. Good day, Mrs. Nelson."

"You're talking to a businesswoman, not your wife."

"And you're talking to this company's CEO and major stockholder, not your husband."

"My husband's dead."

"Not surprising. I don't have a wife."

"Not surprising."

They both burst into laughter.

"Please sit down, Mrs. Nelson."

Taken aback by the "please," she sat.

"I'd like to get to know you better."

"What!" She was alarmed.

Fred Williams laughed heartily. "Not that way, I assure you. We're too much alike. But we have common interests. We're both concerned about this company and Eve, and I think you can be a big help in both departments. Ever been to Paris, London, Tokyo, Tahiti, and the Caribbean? Your payoff for a paper adventure. Sell the business; you're tired of it, anyway."

"Did Eve tell you that I —"

"Sell the business, you old fool. You're past running around for anything but pleasure. And don't you deserve it?"

"What are you blabbering —"

"Be my poster girl. Travel with me on billboards and magazines around the country. Women live longer than men.

It would look odd seeing a senior male hoofing it around the world solo."

"Your international investment publicity, is that it? Well, since women do indeed live longer than men, why not just a poster girl? Drop the man."

"Very witty, my dear, but not wise. Remember your investment and your daughter's job."

"But why me? Any woman or, considering your reputation, women would do."

"I've mellowed, and I want you."

"Do you always get what you—"

"I like you, in a business way. You needn't worry. We can keep the W.W.& S. success in the family." He opened the door to his private lounge. Go in. Pour yourself whatever you like, have some munchies, take a nap, and sleep on it. I'll knock in half an hour. Gives you plenty of time to think and say yes."

"I can't just—"

"Yes, you can."

"Don't you ever let people finish their sentences?"

"Sometimes. When I don't know where they're headed or when I'm sure they'll say yes. Remember, this is a good deal, a super deal, actually. What have you gone to lose? Think about that." And he shambled out of the room.

Eve had to make time for lunch with her mother; there was no way out of it. She feared her mother's questions, knowing that secrecy was paramount while setting up investment programs, and the ad campaign was feverishly in progress. So she was shocked to hear her mother reveal her insider status as she sat in the corner booth of a near-empty restaurant, with the discussion of Eve's marital status nowhere in sight.

"He's using me, of course, but this will be my contribution to the company's success and maybe just what I personally need. I've had it with the store and with men."

"Yes," mused Eve. "But don't discount the 'men' part."

"What men can I meet? Fred Williams is going to monopolize all the male roles. You certainly don't think I would go for that decrepit geezer, even with his millions. And he made it very clear that I was not his idea of dessert. He wasn't a diplomat or gentleman about it, either."

"But when he left you in his lounge, he said he'd knock when he returned, and he did. He always barges into rooms and offices, except for mine. He knocks."

Mrs. Nelson gave a low whistle. "Guess I'm pretty important, huh?"

Fred turned the pages of the latest campaign report stacked on his desk.

"We're doing well. Of the 22% who exited when I made my debut six months ago, 5% have returned, and we have 15% new clients. Bill's done an amazing job at Publicity, and you've been a fabulous liaison between us, Eve."

"You always said your idea would work, but don't forget it's 20% international, not the whole ship."

"I'll settle for that 20% now becoming 100% of our current net worth in the future. I've come to appreciate domestic growth, too. I very much appreciate it. Your mother and I have gotten on amazingly well on the international front." He chuckled lightly. "She makes me laugh. Good woman, though, good woman. And you and I have worked well together, haven't we?"

Now it was Eve's turn to chuckle. "You make me laugh – often! Good man, though, good man."

"Yes, well, I was hoping you'd say that. It's hard to change at this time in my life, even if I wanted to. Not that I want to." He straightened his slightly bent shoulders to stand a full six feet tall. "I've had a lot of fun this way. Walking through opaque walls and stupid regulations and personal privilege. It's been a challenge; it's been liberating, and it's kept me young." He looked up from the stack of papers he had been shuffling and talking to. His clear blue eyes met Eve's. "Not as young as I'd like to be at this moment." His eyes reverted to the paper stack. "Your mother and I understand each other, and I think we could stand each other for the rest of our lives. It can't be that long for me, and except for a few pet charities I intend to endow well, the bulk of my estate goes nowhere. What I'm saying very badly is –" He cleared his throat. "I've asked your mother if there was room for one more in your family, and she said yes. Without your approval, it means nothing, but we've gotten on so well, I was hoping, actually praying hard, that you'd think we were a match, if not made in heaven, at least made in an investment that could last five years. I'm only asking for five years; I won't last longer. What do you say?"

Eve, who would have been speechless had she been asked to speak at the start of this presentation, now found a voice.

"If this will make you both happy, there isn't a reason in the world for me to refuse."

Fred Williams kissed her lightly on the cheek.

"Thank you, dear. You won't regret it." And he shuffled exuberantly from the room.

Fifteen minutes later, Margaret Nelson burst into Eve's office.

"Oh, darling, darling, God bless you! The last of my worries is gone! He's really sweet, and his growl is delightful! What a match! What a coup! What a wedding! Oh, I'm sorry, sweetheart; it's up to you, of course. Something small and intimate, perhaps. Whatever you want, now and forever! And wait till you see the ring he's picked out for you!"

Chapter Eighteen

E ve was aghast. "Me? He wants to marry me? Are you both insane? I thought he wanted to marry you!"

"Eve, I'm too old for him. He wants to die feeling young. It's only for five years."

Eve slumped back in her chair.

"But you've got to get married, dear."

"Why?"

"Because you must. This nonsense of staying single and having affairs is for wispy, unstable types, not for responsible, well-anchored people with self-respect and knowledge of their value. I want grandchildren."

Eve's head shot back.

"Well, maybe *after* Fred. You've always been practical. Why stop now? You can live the kind of life you've always dreamed of starting almost immediately, and in full, unfettered, even foolish style, if you want to, after five years. You'll never get a better offer, and there are no worthwhile candidates for marriage in view."

"I thought you were keen on Hank Martin for me."

"Well, I'm flexible. At first, I thought he was beneath you, though male secretaries do manage marriage with their female bosses in the movies. The viewer is left to assume that this works out well. But this is real life, dear. Still, when he fixed my plumbing, I did have second thoughts. With a supportive wife who is a business genius, a talented man with a knowledge of the construction business could blossom into a successful entrepreneur, one who could well support a wife, children, and mother-in-law, if necessary. And there was no one else. But now... You don't want him anyway."

"And Bill Wetcliff?"

"Eve, you know that Bill is too in love with himself to be a good husband. Oh, he's stabilized some with this new position, but he'll always have a roving eye."

"Fred's eye got a lot of exercise and follow-up."

"You slow down at ninety. I doubt if he does any kind of exercise. I'm only fifty-five, and I think that Harry was Mr. Last. I can't put up with much insecurity and aggravation anymore. At least think about it until tomorrow morning."

"But those twenty-four hours of happiness will make my refusal hurt him even more."

"How often is it in our power to make a person truly happy? Why shortchange the man with only one day? He's been good to you. You're a senior vice-president, your salary's been tripled, and he makes you laugh."

"What if he lives to be a hundred?"

"Sign a prenup, only until 95. Five years of happiness is better than none. I'll bet he goes for it."

"I was only kidding, Mother. All right. I'll consider it. I don't suppose much harm can be done in twenty-four hours."

"Oh, darling, I love you, I love you! Don't forget a single word I said." And she sailed out of the office.

It was barely noon, but the day was shot as far as Eve was concerned. Marry Fred Williams? It was unthinkable! But she was getting older, worse yet, feeling older, and there was no man in sight for the traditional, practical female. If Fred Williams was a relic, so was she, not of as far distant a past, but a relic nonetheless. She paced the floor relentlessly, finally collapsing onto the brown leather sofa. She had to clear her mind, meticulously follow a crowded agenda of work, and reapproach the problem after 5 o'clock. She knew what the problem was — not whether to accept Fred Williams' proposal, but how to ease out of her acceptance with as much grace and as little pain to him as possible. She would not break for lunch. A Mars bar and coffee would get her through the day. She pressed a button on her desk.

"Hank, a pot of coffee, please."

Three minutes later, the door was opened.

"Surprise!"

Holding a pot of coffee was Miss Kay, sporting a very attractive Florida tan.

"Miss Kay!" She willed her beating heart to return to its proper place. "Welcome home!" She ran around the desk to embrace her. "But Hank-"

"Was just wonderful. Spent the entire morning helping me readjust. Bet you missed having me to confide in. Men have never been able to make the cut. But he's a great guy. Out to lunch now, but he'll return to finish out the day. I'll work with him and be super-prepared to start for real tomorrow. Oh, it's so good to be back! There's a limit to how much of my mother and Florida sunshine I can take! Is there anything else I can get you?"

Eve Nelson stood there looking lost.

Hank Martin kicked an empty bag of potato chips onto the grass. Central Park was a mecca to the lunchtime crowd. Business suits on park benches. The leaves were still on the trees, with red flashes of early autumn. He walked up the stone overpass and leaned over, staring into the still, blue water. W.W.&S. had been a short intermission in his life, just as he had planned. He'd ask Eve for that coveted recommendation and be on his way. That was all he would ask her for, all he had meant to ask her for six months ago. No point in asking for what he would never get, what a novice in finance wasn't worthy of getting, anyway. He could ask for another position at the company. He laughed, remembering Fred Williams' depiction of him as a secretary. An honorable job, but not for a man who wanted to marry his boss. And Bill Wetcliff would waste no time in bedding, if not wedding, the cool, calm, intriguing Eve Nelson. Probably already had. They'd gone up to The Carroll Inn together, hadn't they? True, he'd gone there with Elaine, but that didn't count. He laughed again. Well, maybe it did to Eve, if she cared for him at all, in any way, for any reason. He sighed deeply. Maybe jealousy wasn't out.

Elaine had started working again on Bill. Gotten a lot of business savvy, too, judging from her contributions to Publicity meetings, which he and Eve had been required to attend. Bill had become somewhat in awe of her pronouncements, as he had been of Eve's. Bad news for Eve, if she cared. Good news for him, if he wanted her on the rebound. Hang in there, Elaine, he thought. But he was leaving. Had to, didn't he?

A piece of bread flew from near his left arm into the water.

"I know you're not supposed to feed the ducks, but nobody has asked the ducks how they feel about this." The rugged face turned toward him.

"Mr. Wetcliff! How are you?"

"Struggling," said Wetcliff Sr. "I see you also need to head uptown to get away."

Hank ignored the second statement and addressed himself to the first. "Still trying to straighten out Thompson's balance sheet?"

"A few unexpected surprises there. Still at W.W.&S.?"

"Until 4 o'clock today. Miss Kay is back."

"I was impressed with your work there."

"I didn't know you noticed."

"I always look ahead. I saw Thompson down the road and the need for brains, youth, and energy. I saw you, Hank. The unobtrusive, low-key, efficient idea man. My son never quite filled that bill. Come by tomorrow morning. I have a proposition that I think will interest you." He threw another breadcrumb into the water. "Cast your bread, son. Shall we say 9 o'clock?"

"9 o'clock." Hank shook his hand.

The older man strode off, and Hank watched him disappear into a surging crowd on the tree-lined path ahead. If he could help make Thompson fly, his career was made. Eve would understand a career move, and she would certainly notice him at Thompson. But he wouldn't reveal W's new strategies. Wetcliff Sr. hadn't said he would have to.

"Hank, you're naïve," he mumbled. "But you're also unemployed." He took a circuitous path out of the park and hailed a taxi back to his predecessor/successor – and Eve.

On the way into W headquarters, he saw Bill Jr. and Elaine on their way out.

"Late lunch," explained Bill. "Sorry you're leaving, Hank. But you don't have to, you know. We could find you something here."

"Thanks, but I'll manage." Something!

"If it doesn't work out..." Bill shook his hand, clapped him on the back, and strode off with Elaine. "So you think that Fred and Margaret should have the Alps behind them on that shot?" His voice faded off.

Relying on Elaine, thought Hank. Well, Bill could do worse. Hank entered the elevator, pushed the button, and waited. When the door opened, he was face to face with Eve Nelson.

"Hank! I was hoping we could have a little chat."

"By all means. Come into my office," and he beckoned her into the elevator. The door closed.

"I'm sure we could find you something here; you don't have to leave."

"You should have those words embossed on stationery. Bill's echo. I don't need a handout, just a recommendation."

"Absolutely!"

"So, you won't have difficulty finding something to say about me?"

"Of course not. Your work was superb."

"About me, not my work. You know, me, the person."

"You know you're a wonderful person, hardworking, organized, creative, thoughtful."

"I was kind of hoping that the 'thoughtful' would come first. It personalizes me."

Eve reached for the floor button as she said, "You've always been a person to me."

Hank put his hand over the button. "A person you would like in a non-business way?"

Eve's cheeks glowed red, even in the dimly lit elevator.

"I've always considered you a friend."

"Like Miss Kay, or..."

She turned away. "We've worked so closely together; it's only natural to think softly of each other if we respect each other."

"But I don't respect you."

"What do you mean?"

"Oh, I admire your perseverance, your will to succeed, your career success, but I can't respect a woman who won't allow herself to fall in love with me when she wants to."

"How dare you tell me what I want!"

"I dare because I'm leaving. I've seen you pull back when you thought you were being too open, too friendly with me. And I've pulled back too, but I don't have to anymore."

"There's decorum in business. Working together so closely, at night, alone in my apartment... What would you have had me do?"

"For starters, marry me."

She reached for the elevator button, but he blocked it again.

"All right! If you want to know the truth, we're too different. I'm practical, and you're romantic. Oh, I could feel all that romantic twaddle burning your brain when you should have been concentrating solely on the work. You didn't have to say anything; I knew what you were thinking."

"Are you free for dinner?"

"Haven't you heard what I've been saying? The answer is no!"

"Why are you so worked up about it? Can't you give a dying man his last request—a dinner instead of a recommendation."

Eve turned away from him. Her lower lip was trembling. The silence burned Hank Martin as Eve's words had not. He pressed a button. The elevator door opened. Hank made his exit without a further word without looking back.

Eve considered a transfer to their Florida office. But a V.P. had to be in New York. And there was no safety from marital requests with seniors either, as Fred well demonstrated. She gazed at the sky from her bedroom window and turned on her side for the thousandth time that night. Hank was lucky. He would be elsewhere soon at an upwardly mobile job where he could forget her. For her an upwardly mobile job probably didn't exist. She had no place to go but down. Down—or out. She had been questioning her goals and her purpose in life with no satisfying answers. At thirty-one, she had done what she set out to do, and there was only blank space ahead. Marrying Fred Williams was not an option. Even her mother had called him an old geezer, an impossible man. And he was old enough to be her grandfather. There was no time to hire a shrink or consult a psychologist. She had to know what she wanted now, and she had to tell Fred Williams that and more tomorrow morning. She fell into a troubled sleep but was jolted awake by the telephone. She reached for the receiver, then let her hand fall to her side. It was one of three pertinent people, and she had nothing to say to any of them. Her answering machine came on. And then –

"I know you're in there. Pick up. You've got a reprieve."

Eve reached for the phone. "Fred! What do you mean?"

"I've been thinking. I don't want you to do what your mother and I think is best for you. I want you to want it, too. Maybe we should date for a while."

Eve held the receiver in front of her face and stared at it.

"See how we get on. I do lots of things—snorkeling, swimming, parachuting, tennis, golf. I'm a pretty active guy. I'm afraid I don't have much patience for theater or concerts, all that sedentary stuff, but I do dance. How about dinner and dancing tomorrow night, for starters?"

Eve sighed audibly.

"Good! I'll pick you up at 7 o'clock. Make sure you leave the office by 5 o'clock. No overtime, please. Sorry to have gotten you up at this hour, but I was troubled. I don't want you to be unhappy." The phone clicked his goodbye.

Eve lay very still. The fluffy clouds beyond the window looked soft and friendly. They shifted slightly into furrows and creases and parted for two patches of blue, completing a portrait of the craggy face and soulful eyes of Fred Williams.

Chapter Nineteen

The e-mail message was very clear: "Reservations confirmed for the three of us at The Four Continents, tonight at 7 o'clock. Be there without fail. Mother."

Margaret Nelson knew what she was doing. Eve would be settled once and for all so that she could concentrate on herself. Her life had been entwined with Eve's for thirty-one years, and it was frightening to contemplate losing the purpose of her life. How would she manage without a daughter to nag and advise? But the time had come for Mama to take center stage. That time came, eventually, to every mother. She either ignored it and stood in its glare, sweating and uncomfortable in her unplanned debut, or threw caution and preparation to the wind and, with a "what the hell!" ad-libbed the first routine that occurred to her, reveling in the freedom and the surprise, the newness, and the inner urge. Fred Williams was the first routine that occurred to her, a darn good liberation routine for her and one of limited prison duration for Eve. Eve could do worse, but hardly better, assuming one ignored the façade, which one certainly should. But a mother's guiding hand was needed to pull this off, to get Eve settled so that Mama could get on with her life. The cushion that was her son-in-law would make her efforts, if not failsafe, at least cost-free, if necessary. She had done much for Eve, much that had not been wanted, true, but much nevertheless. She wasn't asking for much in return, and the benefit to Eve was undeniable. Eve had never been a romantic, giddy girl as she had been. Fred was Mr. Perfect for her. "You've got mail" flashed on her screen.

"Butt out, Mama. It's dinner for two tonight. You prefer hamburgers anyway. Buy one—somewhere else! Fred."

Margaret Nelson was stunned, then pleased, then hurt. Eve didn't need her anymore.

Hank looked calmly at the provocative murals in Café des Artiste. Facing George and Bill Sr, the impact of colorful nudes was lost on him. The mailing he had recommended to former and current, but dissatisfied W.W.&S. clients had brought astounding results. The respect for Snell and Wetcliff's business acumen far outweighed the disgust for their personal predilections, although one former W client had written: "Your ex-wife's in Europe, her malicious comments an ocean away, and I've read that you're between mistresses, but please don't get carried away with my money. I'm counting on you, as my family has in the past. Keep your pants on until you're fully organized and zipping Thompson and my account toward success. Remember your priorities—me and the rest of the faithful—and don't get sidetracked by a pretty face. Been there, done that, all of that. Good luck to us both! Eagerly awaiting your first quarterly report." It was signed "Still Married, But Looking."

Bill laughed, and then looked intensely at Hank. "You've worked closely with Eve. You understand how her mind works. What would she advise Fred to do next?"

"You've both worked with her for years. You should know better than I do."

"I can't believe she's changed her nature. She's a great one for pity, and that's a weakness, but she's ambitious, and that's a strength. Overall, she's a conservative professional who'll soon get disenchanted with Fred's counterproductive ways if her mother is removed from the scene. Another object of Eve's pity, a very controlling object, who's apparently having a ball working with Fred on those travel commercials. I've heard they fight like hell, but that's part of the attraction. At one point, you were close to Mrs. Nelson and got on very well with her, Hank."

"What are you saying?"

"Thompson isn't reviving fast enough. We need more cash flow. The quickest way is to get more management fees, more clients. Enough of W's clients haven't jumped ship. That Crazy and his cockeyed commercials have got them mesmerized, made them think that maybe, just maybe, he's onto something. It's all a hoax, of course. The same old company, same old research staff, and analysts."

"That was our ship, remember?" George Snell stared hard at the senior Wetcliff. "Did very well until Fred came and scared the clients and the press. Probably still doing well, only the window dressing has changed. People may be getting used to that. It's the bottom line the clients and the financial world care about." He pointed to the letter still on the table. "Look at that letter our sex-crazed friend wrote. And your son is a major part of the problem. Those watercolors of Fred and Margaret Nelson cavorting around the world are darn appealing. Even my wife, who knows what this is doing to us, can't resist cutting them out of FORTUNE, NEWSWEEK, TRAVEL & LEISURE and displaying them on the refrigerator door. 'Hint, hint,' she says. Worst of all, she actually sent for their investment literature. Says that if an old goat like Fred Williams can make time for both business and travel, so can I."

"But he only travels on paper," said Hank.

"Go tell that to half the world that's fallen for that old reprobate's tricks!"

"Calm down, George. You know, we can do the same thing, water down the effect of his ad campaign."

"Great! So we'll be the Avis to his Hertz! No, we need something different. Not every old couple, or young, for that matter, wants to travel. Some want to build a country home, or buy one and have the money to fix it up."

Both men turned to look at Hank Martin.

Bill Wetcliff turned his palms out on the table. "Why not? If my son can use his art to entice people to roam the world, why can't Hank persuade the homebodies to invest with us. Oil, not watercolor solid, substantial, lasting forever."

"What's wrong with photographs?"

"Wake up, Hank. We're in a creative age. People want the feel of the place, not the actual place. They want rapport, dreams, but solid dreams. Any artists on staff, George?"

George turned to Hank. "Look into this. They have to be first-rate artists, at least as good as Junior. Otherwise, we'll have the expense of hiring out."

Wetcliff nodded, pleased. "Bill has certainly turned a liability into an asset. May make president if the buzz is correct. Showing his old dad that he can manage on his own."

"But you can't! Get him back!"

"What!"

"You heard me, Bill. Get that turncoat back. Let Fred look for an artist people can respond to! We can give him what Fred can give him. And more. We can get him back on speaking terms with his father. You can change your will back, make his mother happy."

"But W is back in the success column. We're still struggling."

"Isn't a challenge what young people want?" George was irate.

He turned to Hank. "Get him back."

"It's enough if Hank gets Margaret Nelson out of those ads. That old curmudgeon flying alone will kill the campaign."

"We'll do that, too." George Snell turned to Hank. "You know Margaret Nelson. Appeal to whatever in her will persuade her to drop out of those ads. And get us Junior. He's more likely to listen to someone his own age."

"His father may be here, but he's feeling powerful and independent there. And Margaret Nelson will oblige her daughter, not me."

"Get Eve over here, too. She's got an eye for Junior. A little persuasion and she'll join us. And Bill's staying at W may be more than proving that he's his own man. Eve's an attractive woman. Get these key people, and we may be able to deflate Mr. Bora Bora's bag."

"But George, what if Fred tries to buy off Hank?"

George narrowed his eyes at Hank. "Can you be bought, son?"

Hank remembered the category Fred had, with clear malice aforethought, put him in—secretary.

"No, sir."

"I thought not. Then you and Junior can fight over Eve on our turf. More convenient for you, Hank. Anyway, you wouldn't want to leave her there."

Wetcliff shook his head to clear it but still looked in shock.

"I guess you haven't heard. There are distinct advantages to having a current wife—they read the society pages and gossip columns. Fred Williams and Eve Nelson were seen at Macombo's last night, dining and dancing."

"For business, it could only be business for her!" erupted Hank.

George Snell leaned back comfortably in his chair. "Not with what she was wearing."

The waitress hovered briefly with platters of turkey and chicken and salads exploding with tropical color. Hank stared at his plate. Was he more secure here with these barracudas than with "something" at W.W.&W.? Was Eve?

Margaret Nelson, through two cups of coffee, looked at the picture of her gorgeous daughter. She was having second thoughts, actually thirds. Eve could do better than Fred Williams. Not financially, never financially, but was money, at least that much money, everything? Her daughter had never been gorgeous before, but here at the Macombo, with a plunging neckline, black spaghetti straps, dramatic eyes, and flowing hair, she looked like every man's dream. She was getting older. Dreams didn't last forever. Why waste her on someone with one foot out of this world? Why deny her a Prince Charming? She thought of an earlier favorite. Hank might be rich someday, but "might" wasn't a sure thing. She could persuade Eve to dive into the social scene—charity benefits, society balls—representing the company, of course.

She could meet an eligible politician, businessman, never-married, between marriages, even widowed, but he would have to be relatively young. Eve deserved a good life, a happy life, a young life. Fred Williams could live to one hundred and spend years challenging a prenup with an age limit of 95. And even five years of his bossiness was unfair for a mother to inflict on a daughter for mere monetary gain. What's more, he would be a solid, impenetrable wall between her and Eve. He was starting already. It would cut her life short and make it impossible to guide Eve. It was unthinkable. She would sacrifice her own independence. How could she subject her daughter to five or ten years of hell? She would admit she was wrong, beg Eve's forgiveness, and urge her to continue almost as before, with the addition of the charity motif. Eve would be so relieved and grateful. After all, isn't this what mothers are for?

Chapter Twenty

H ank Martin aimlessly turned the pages of the magazine. He looked at his watch. He had been sitting in the lobby for two hours. The concierge was shooting ominous glances his way. Where was Eve? When he had phoned, Miss Kay had said that she had appointments until 5 o'clock, after which she was going for a swim. She wasn't in the rooftop pool, and a call to Mrs. Nelson had gone unanswered. Fred Williams had been out of the office all day. This didn't look good. If she had married him, no bait would draw her from W, and Mama and Bill would be unpersuadable. Elaine was no Eve. Junior needed the brainy one to look good, to be productive, and to be an asset to Thompson & Co. He rose from the sofa, stretched, and was about to exit before he was arrested for suspicious loitering when the elevator door opened to reveal a chic navy-blue suit, a ruffled white blouse, sensible walking shoes, and the pulled back, chignoned hair of Margaret Nelson.

"Mrs. Nelson! It's important that I speak to Eve. I won't keep her long. Why hasn't she returned my calls?"

"Probably for the same reason she hasn't returned mine. She's gone, I have no idea where, and I'm worried."

"So am I."

"Are you willing to talk to me?"

"Very much so."

"Well, don't get too excited. I wouldn't be an easy mother-in-law to deal with. You were thinking mother-in-law, weren't you?"

"No."

"Well! Follow me." And she rattled the keys to Eve's apartment.

Fortified with bourbon and brandy, Mrs. Nelson plopped onto Eve's endless, curving, powder blue sofa.

"An explanation, young man. Why are you here?"

"I'm here to raid W.W.&W. of the team of Nelson and Nelson. Not for insider information, but for brain power."

"Eve's brain power, yes, but what grey matter do you detect in me? Is Thompson interested in opening a men's store? Or are you merely flattering the producer of the prize bull?"

"If you can work with Fred Williams, you can do anything. You're wonderful in those senior-travel ads, but we're hoping that you're tired enough of traveling and of Fred to want to settle into some colorful and informative cozy home ads."

"Fred traveling the world alone would look peculiar and unsettling, neither of which appeals to seniors, though it would appeal to me. But it's poor business sense to leave a lucrative position because of whim or personality. You ought to know that."

"Yes, Mrs. Nelson, but without Bill's creative advertising ideas to work with, W.W.&W. could nosedive as sharply as it rose."

"Bill heads Publicity and is about to make president. He's at W to stay."

"He's leaving. He's had a more appealing offer than president at W."

"Impossible! What is it?"

"I've promised not to say, but Wetcliff Sr. and George Snell are fond of you and Eve and wouldn't want you caught in the downdraft."

Mrs. Nelson snorted. "Fonder of their wallets and their sanity than of other human beings."

"Don't denigrate sanity, Mrs. Nelson. It comes in quite handy away from the office—if there's any sanity left after 5 P.M."

"Big bucks and entertainment—oh, Fred can be very entertaining when you're not the object of his jibes and if you take them as the ravings of a madman—help you retain enough sanity to do very nicely, thank you, after 5 P.M. You say you and our kind former partners want to save Eve and me from a sinking ship, but you haven't proven that it's sinking. Now, what's this secret plum that will drive Junior into Thompson's arms?"

"I can't say."

"You're bluffing. Is Thompson doing so badly that the former outcast has become indispensable to acquiring clients?"

Hank stared solemnly out the window and then at Margaret Nelson. "Bill Wetcliff Jr. is leaving. He's coming to Thompson. I'm sorry you don't believe me. There's nothing more I can say." He rose and headed for the door. "At least tell Eve what I said. I hope she's all right."

Hank took the stairs instead of the elevator. Maybe the movement of his feet would have an energetic effect on his brain. He wasn't used to bluffing, but he was desperate. Even competition with Junior was better than leaving Eve in the clutches of Fred Williams. And if what Senior and Snell had said was true, only Junior could pry the Nelsons free from W and Fred. And probably only Eve's appeal could pry Junior free from the same. He was working both ends against the middle, and it wasn't his nature to do so. What on earth could cause a high-flying Bill Jr. to abandon W.W.&W? The air was invigorating. He wanted to walk the four miles home and tell his chauffer to slowly follow him in the car. But there was no chauffer, only the four-year-old Chevy in front of the luxury building that was the home of the woman he yearned for. He unlocked the door and heaved himself into the driver's seat. He paused. His hand went to his chin. He got out of the car, locked it, and walked away. He was making up tricks of a new trade as he went along. He had to. A hard walk home and the emotional exhaustion of the day would have the immediate result of a full night's sleep, after a stop to phone Margaret Nelson and Bill Jr.—her with a message designed to remove her from Eve's apartment and him with a message designed to get him immediately to that apartment. No one would be there, but there would be something for Bill to wonder about as he looked out his window—Hank's car.

Hank was in the process of pouring the bourbon and soda when the doorbell rang. He moaned. He had not yet reached the genteel buzzer-from-a-lobby stage that allowed a person a minute or two to prepare to greet a guest. His current maintenance level was strictly doorbell.

"Yes?" he addressed the door.

"May I speak to you?"

It was Eve. She seemed out of breath as if she had walked five flights instead of taken the elevator, which was highly unlikely. She accepted the bourbon he had poured for himself.

"Are you all right?" He led her to his worn, brown sofa and fluffed a pillow behind her.

"No, I'm not all right. Please give them back, Hank. You're bright. Create your own plans. This is killing Fred. You don't want a murder on your conscience."

"Murder! What are you talking about? What plans?"

"The latest office and advertising plans for the South and Southwest. Arizona, Florida, Georgia, and the Carolinas. Oh, you know. Don't look so shocked. You're not a good liar. You were seen hurrying out of the building yesterday. I don't care how you got in or who you bribed. Just give me the papers, Hank. Don't give them to Bill and George. Please, Hank, please!"

Hank was stunned. "So this is what you think of me? I don't have the papers."

Eve seemed to sink deeply into the sofa, enveloped by the brown, her tan sweater absorbed into it.

"Eve, I tell you, I haven't got the papers. And I wasn't at the building yesterday. I haven't been there since I left last month."

"But you were seen.'

"By whom?"

"Elaine and Miss Kay."

"They're insane! Look, you're welcome to look around my apartment. Come to Thompson and look there all you like.

I've stolen nothing from W, and, judging from the meeting I had with Bill and George today, neither have they. We don't care about your plans. We're developing our own."

Eve's cell phone was insistent.

"Yes? Florida, mother. Checking out our offices and my sanity. What? Of course not, and neither do you. What! Yes, I heard you. Later, Mother."

"If what you told Mother is true, what you've done is unforgivable, Hank. Bill was the legs behind this program. We've no one else capable of taking over. We got you started. We deserved better from you."

Hank knew what she really meant: "I got you started. I deserved better from you." He stood there, shocked and helpless, as Eve headed for the door. "But I can't allow you to succeed." And she was gone.

Hank poured himself another bourbon. It would help him float into oblivion, away from the sting of Eve's words. He could never think clearly tonight, anyway. Time enough tomorrow to sort through this mess of relationships, personal and business. He threw himself heavily into his favorite armchair, drink in hand. And the doorbell rang. She was back! He sprinted to the door, clutching the bourbon, and opened it to a powerful punch in the face. He reeled, the glass shattering on the floor. Bill Jr. pushed past him.

"Where is she?" He made the rounds of the apartment before Hank could get to his feet.

"If you mean Eve, I have no idea." Hank rotated his chin, glad it wasn't broken.

"Oh, you have an idea, all right. Your car is parked in front of our building, and her car is not in the garage. She drove you home. Don't try making yourself too much at home with Eve, little man. She's no fool. I don't know what drivel you told her, but she won't be fooled for long. You can't have both her and Thompson."

"I know that, Bill." Hank threw some ice cubes in a towel and applied them to his chin. "But you can."

"What are you talking about?"

"Eve is coming to Thompson. Your dad, George, and I would like you to come, too. I'm willing to deploy my charms towards business ends if you join us—as advertising director, president, whatever you like. Eve's interest in me is a rebound from you. Elaine seems to be your interest these days, and bright ladies like Eve don't take kindly to being shunted aside by secretaries. At this point, I'm more interested in making my career successful than my love life."

"She'd never leave W."

"Fred's coming on strong, dining, and dancing. I hear marriage is next. He needs her, he wants her, and Thompson is her high-level escape. Then it will be you and Fred. Do you fancy working so closely with that nut job without Eve's intervention?"

Bill sat down heavily. "Where's Eve?"

"Persuading her mother to join us, too. She's proven that she's a big advertising plus, and especially with your ads..."

Bill sat quietly for a few moments.

"You know, it all actually makes sense. I have to think about this."

"Why? Your father's here, Eve is coming, family harmony and romance beckon, and the element of surprise will push our end of the seesaw up and Fred's down. All's fair in business, love, and war. You know that."

"Dad will let me call the creative shots?"

"Absolutely. He needs you. We all need you."

"I'll call him when I get home."

"Do that."

Bill rose and walked slowly to the door. He paused, his hand on the doorknob.

"So Eve's really coming over."

Hank nodded solemnly at what he happily realized was a statement, not a question.

"Sorry about the chin."

"Perfectly understandable."

Hank closed the door and looked with dismay at the floor. He had become quite adept at lying, so adept that he badly needed the last of his best bourbon seeping through the floorboards and around shards of glass. He was developing a serious headache. Eve would never leave W with an unsolved theft. And certainly not to come to a business suspected of perpetrating it. If she didn't say "yes" to Thompson, and soon, her mother and Junior would discover the ruse and not only remain with Fred but become implacable enemies of Thompson. He hadn't liked Eve's words or the look in her eyes when she left. Not more than half an hour had elapsed since her departure, but he would have to act quickly. It was 7 o'clock. He dialed and let the phone ring. Elaine didn't pick up. She was probably on her way to meet the advertising king for, ostensibly, a business dinner. He knew how she worked; she was as transparent as cellophane. He dialed again.

"Miss Kay! Hi! How are you? Good. I haven't seen you for a month, but I've heard that you've seen me—at W. Had I been there, I would certainly have said hello. Do you recall when that was? Really! Are you positive that the back you saw was mine? I see. No, of course, you wouldn't make it up, but someone else might. Yes, of course, I understand. Mr. Williams was merely verifying the manner of my walk. You had better things to do than study it the day we met. You're absolutely correct. No reason at all to impugn the business motives of W's majority stockholder, president, and CEO. Thanks for your time and help. Oh, yes, Miss Kay, you've been very helpful. Goodbye."

Wasn't old age supposed to soften sourpusses, make them kinder, gentler, and more flexible? Not if the sands in your glass were running out and you wanted to marry your Client Services V.P. He'd put Hank down in front of Eve. He couldn't stop the clock, but he could stop Hank. Somehow, he knew what Hank wanted. Not surprising, really. Hank was, after all, a poor actor, or maybe Fred thought of how he would behave if he were sixty years younger. And he was trying to make Elaine indispensable to a macho but insecure Junior. Hank dialed again.

"Hi, Eve. Meet me tomorrow for breakfast. My place. I'll have the plans." Another lie. At this point, so what?

She would hear the message when she got home. Tonight he would create a new, more exciting plan than the one Fred had envisioned. He wouldn't be sleeping, and knowing Eve, neither would she. Hank was uneasy about her parting threat and whether she would get to it before he presented his case in the morning.

Chapter Twenty-One

Fred Williams never slept well. Sleeping was a waste of time, now especially. In old age, he was tired of sleep, as well as odd numbers and odd people. He sought even-tempered, reliable people, but they had to be interesting and if they were women, attractive. Eve would be his even-numbered sixth wife, a calming, intelligent, enjoyable companion. Wild he didn't need. He'd had wild. Anyway, he was wild enough for both of them. But she wanted to get to the bottom of that theft. She was determined to get proof that Hank was the thief. She hadn't said that she didn't believe him; in fact, she seemed to. But she wanted proof nonetheless. If none emerged, Hank would have her sympathy. It wasn't safe to have a handsome young man, who had already worked closely with Eve, win her sympathy. The way he always looked at her... No, Hank Martin had to exit the picture completely and for good. It was best all around. Hank couldn't offer Eve the security he could, or the excitement, either. He had better rest, even if he couldn't sleep. He got into bed and lay quite still. He wasn't comfortable. He turned on his right side, on his left side, assumed a fetal position, sat bolt upright, and groaned. He got up and rolled back the mattress from the foot of the bed. The trouble was Florida. The other evenly spaced envelopes were about equal in weight, but Florida was bulging with paper instructions and wooden layouts. He put Florida on an end table, hoping he would remember where it was. He got back into bed. Why didn't more people live in Georgia?

The clock and the phone woke Fred Williams at the same time. "Pain!" he growled as he lifted the receiver. Neither his face nor his voice could have changed more quickly had they been rubber.

"Good morning, my dear. What a delightful voice to awaken to!" He listened, smiling, the smile slowly fading. "I wish you wouldn't. The damage either has or has not been done. But there's a matter I must see you about at breakfast. It can't wait. Well, then, see him at lunch. The Four Continents at 8 o'clock. Why not? Of course, they'll be open. Very important. Wonderful. At 8 o'clock, then." As the receiver met its cradle, he growled again. "You idiot! Of course. The Four Continents isn't open for breakfast!" He fumbled for his eyeglasses and his phonebook. He dialed, tapping his fingers impatiently on the night table.

"Gorgio, Fred Williams. Sorry to get you up so early." He was all sweetness and charm. "This is urgent. I need a huge favor. Open The Continents for breakfast for me this morning. I know that, but I'll die an early death if you don't. Earlier. don't be funny. No, lunch will be too late. I won't tell anyone; there won't be a precedent. All right, all right. I'm renting the place from 8 to 9 o'clock this morning. Yes, the whole restaurant." He listened, tapping his left slipper. "Damn the cost! I don't care who cooks! Fine with me; you won't hear me complaining about your pancakes. It's only breakfast, for Pete's sake! What can be urgent? What can be life or death? Guess. God bless you! At eight."

He hung up, shaking. A bath would relax him. He had to get hold of himself, be commanding, but flexible; strong, but gentle; light-hearted, but serious; straightforward, but charming. But when had he been charming? Or flexible, or light-hearted, for that matter? Never! How was he to start now, to continue being someone else for the next three, five, ten years? Until he had met Eve, he hadn't wanted to be someone else, had reveled in being the mischievous, ornery Fred Williams he had been comfortable with since birth. But he had acted in school productions. The knack would return. It had to.

He would be the same obstreperous Fred Williams still to everyone else. One exception to the Williams rule, one beautiful, life-giving exception that would make his remaining years a special, shining joy that he could take with him wherever he was going. He had persuaded Gorgio. Now he had to persuade Eve Nelson. The tub was full, and he stepped in.

Young Bill Wetcliff sipped his coffee slowly as he eyed the Chrysler Building, majestic, regal in the morning light. He wished he had a "What if..." machine for Fred Williams. He knew what the old devil had done, had to have done. Hank couldn't possibly have stolen the office plans. It wasn't in his character. Not that it was in Fred's. But wining, dining, dancing like a young buck with a beautiful woman young enough to be his granddaughter, well, that would set the conniving wheels turning. He would never get away with it. Eve would find out, was determined to find out. Her sense of fair play demanded it. What if she turned him down—a pretty obvious conclusion even without the office plan fiasco? What if she sashayed over to Thompson? What if he did the same? What if she stayed out of pity? What if he did the same? What scenario would be the most rewarding for him? He was a favored commodity at both companies, a very gratifying situation, but futures turned on the head of a pin, and he had to know what to do, and now.

Eve held the receiver as she scoured her phone book for the number she had last used when she turned twenty-one.

"Hi, Jenine. Eve Nelson, remember me? Yes, I'm afraid I have been rather prominent in the news lately. Glad you liked it. An update of an old dress. Yes, I know he is, and I know I can't. I need a very detailed reading. No, I don't want your ad-libbed astrological judgment. Wrong! I have no idea what to do—do I?"

Fred was dressed to the nines. He looked like a tall, elegant relic of another age, though he was dressed, handsomely dressed, for this one.

The finest dark blue linen suit ever made, the most impeccable white on a blue polka-dot silk tie, the pure white Egyptian shirt with the long line of buttonhole lace, the thinning white wisps of hair with streaks of black slicked back and gelled down. It was the best he could do, given the insufficient time for a facelift or a magician.

"Park here, Joseph. Set your pocket watch for one hour. Pick me up then, or when you hear me screaming like a banshee in pain or embarrassment in a running exit from the Continents." Fred Williams glanced at his watch. It was 7:45. Friend Gorgio was at the door, smiling, a chef's hat tilted cockily on his head. Fred forced a smile back, twisting the fingers on his left hand, on his right hand, intertwining both hands and twisting again.

"Don't be nervous," whispered Gorgio into the deafening silence. Fred followed him to a table set for the gods. The intricately etched glassware, in a rainbow of pastels, glittered from the cut crystal of the Austrian chandelier overhead. The dishes must have graced the table of Louis XIV. The white linen napkins tied in rainbows of silk were ready to clap to bosom, lap, or lips. The silver gleamed a bright, intricate French presence, and the flowers that separated, surrounded and highlighted each silver, glass, and linen set spread a pink and orange sheen of dawn and haunting honey-suckle fragrance over all. Fred Williams swallowed hard and shot a pathetic, frightened look at his friend. Gorgio put his arm around Fred's shoulder.

"If I can cook, then you can propose. We've done it before. It's in our memory bank, ready to withdraw and use when needed."

Fred looked doubtful.

"Come into the kitchen and see what I'm doing. It will give you courage. Come on, now." Gorgio steered Fred away from the ethereal table.

"Just because she's switched me to lunch doesn't mean she has Fred for breakfast."

"No, Hank, it means he intends to have her for breakfast. He's been giving her the same looks you used to give her. I tell you he's going to propose. If she says 'yes,' Thompson won't get her— or me. The W ship is all Fred. It will only sink if his new obsession turns away. I'm riding a winner. I'd be a fool to drop out, even for Dad. I'm appreciated, titled, and well paid. And I'm not the boss's son."

"Eve won't marry Fred. At lunch –"

"Lunch may be too late. I may be an artist, but I'm a pragmatic one. My decision will depend on which way the wind blows. And that, Hank, is going to be decided at breakfast today. Yellow pages, Restaurants. Posh."

Hank feverishly turned pages. "But no one will be there at this hour."

"But if someone is..."

"What a luxury to find a parking spot, but not surprising," thought Eve. She glanced at her watch. It was 7:55 A.M. She exited her Lexus and sighed. She knew this was no business meeting, knew that The Four Continents never opened before lunch, knew exactly what Frederick Willard Williams had in mind. Well, she might as well put the stamp of finality on this aspect of their relationship. Gorgio was at the door to greet her, bowed her in, and escorted her to the table set with linens, sparkling glassware, fairy dust, and Fred Williams.

"Good morning, my dear!" Fred beamed as he shot to his feet. "We have a rare treat in store. Gorgio himself is doing the cooking." His bushy eyebrows compressed as he turned to Gorgio. "It is a treat, isn't it?"

"Let's hope so!" replied Gorgio as he bowed again and headed for the kitchen.

Eve gave a half smile of relief. Fred would allow her to eat. He was saving THE question for dessert when she would have more stamina to respond.

As Gorgio entered the kitchen, he stepped back, shocked.

"You left the door open," said Margaret Nelson. "I've always looked forward to breakfast at The Four Continents. I'm sure I'll enjoy it." And she serenely exited the power center of the five-star icon.

Margaret Nelson moved gracefully and slowly around the unset tables and the empty aisles of the restaurant, giving the occupants of the only illuminated table time to gather their wits, exercise basic courtesy, and invite her to join them.

"What are you doing here?" hurled Fred Williams at the smiling matron.

"The same as you, my charming traveling companion. Having breakfast."

His quick glance at Eve produced palms turned outward and a shake of the head.

"Now listen here, Margaret. This is a business breakfast and none of your business." He spoke as graciously as those words would allow.

"Well, don't mind me. I'm used to business breakfasts. Nice suit, Fred." Gorgio pulled a chair out for her, and she sat, wiggling her black skirt comfortably under her before announcing "hot oatmeal with blueberries, strawberries and skim milk, and orange juice and coffee." She gave a smile of finality to Gorgio, whose dismissal was abruptly halted by Fred's strident command.

"Just a minute, Gorgio. I've rented the restaurant, and this woman wasn't invited. I'll thank you to unseat her."

"But Mr. Williams—"

"I said unseat her. I'm paying for my time here, every minute of it. She gets no breakfast and no seat."

Mrs. Nelson looked in shock at her daughter. "And this is someone you would consider marrying, a man who abuses your mother, who would deny her food and a kind word, and who would probably tyrannize his children—if he's still able to have any?"

Eve opened her mouth to speak, but Fred was quicker.

"I'm not traveling with you anymore, you old battle-ax. You're exasperating, opinionated, stubborn, and hellbent on mischief, even on the set. We're having a business meeting here, and you're not welcome. Is that clear?"

"Mother, please!" begged Eve. "We have to get this over with."

Mrs. Nelson's face glowed as Fred Williams' face fell. Mrs. Nelson rose as Hank Martin and Bill Wetcliff approached the table. Bill smiled broadly.

"Room for two more? Now, don't be angry, Fred. We saw your car parked outside and realized that you had achieved the impossible."

"Thank God not yet," murmured Margaret Nelson audibly.

"And since when is The Four Continents on your way to work?"

"Since today, Fred. Nothing like a little change. Are you leaving Mrs. Nelson?"

"I'd rather not. I haven't eaten a thing. But Fred has been eating me alive, so maybe I should. After all, it is his funer - uh, business breakfast."

"And just what are you doing with the competition, Bill?" snapped Williams.

"Uh, well—"

"He's trying to persuade me to return," said Hank.

"You steal the records of our new "senior" branches, and we should ask you to return?"

"He's innocent, Fred, framed, and –"

"Enough! Are you all going to leave so that Eve and I can have this conference?"

"No," said the men in unison.

"We're here, already," protested Margaret Nelson.

"It's a pity to waste the maitre d's time or food," added Bill Wetcliff.

"Why can't you and Eve meet for dinner?" suggested Hank Martin.

Fred turned on Hank. "So you can use your poison fangs on Eve at lunch, and you Bill can have a second chance to win a trophy, and you, Margaret, can try some new outrageous stunt to control your daughter's life?"

Fred Williams firmly gripped Eve's hand and rose to his feet. "Gorgio!"

The hovering maitre d' was instantly at his side.

"Split the bill three ways. They're staying, they're paying. Are you coming, darling?" Fred's stomach shook, but his voice was strong.

Three mouths dropped open, but a fourth responded, "Yes." Fred Williams and Eve Nelson had made a hurried exit from the restaurant, entered Fred's car, and had the chauffer put the motor in gear before the revised breakfast club had digested what had just happened.

"Good lord!" they exclaimed in unison.

"The name is Gorgio," responded the maitre d', nonplussed. "I have Mrs. Nelson's order. What would you gentlemen like?"

Chapter Twenty-Two

"Thank you, Eve."

She looked at Fred questioningly as the car pulled away from the curb.

"For not embarrassing me in front of those characters. But I got the message, not surprising, really." He patted her knee in a fatherly fashion. "You know, getting older doesn't make you any smarter in the love department. Even five wives can't get the message through a skull as thick as mine. But what you persuade yourself you are at fifty is a harder sell at ninety, and I sold myself on it. You know I think the world of you, but you deserve better than what I can give you."

Eve looked into those soulful eyes. "Would you be saying this if you were fifty years younger?"

"No. I'd never have thought of marrying you fifty years ago. Wouldn't have realized what a complement you'd be to this brassy old—then young—coot."

Eve smiled. "Then your timing wasn't wrong."

"What are you saying?"

"If I were fifty years older, the thought of you, of someone like you, would be in outer space. I wouldn't have the patience for you. I wouldn't want the excitement, the world-be-damned attitude, the independent streak ten miles wide. If I were your age, I'd pass you by swifter than one of those lightning bolts you love to hurl."

"But more than what we've got. —"

"Is still out."

They both stared straight ahead at the lineup of yellow taxicabs in the heavy traffic.

"Well," said Fred finally, "may I interest you in Bora Bora, so you can see what your old friend has been up to these past twenty years?"

Eve laughed appreciatively.

"I'm taking that as a 'yes.' And since we have a business to run, why don't we sightsee where we have major branches? After ten U.S. cities' worth of work, we'll be ready for an exotic island. On the plane, we can make lists of what to examine and have Miss Kay forward relevant information to us as we arrive." Fred Williams briskly pulled out his cell phone and dialed.

"Miss Kay, two tickets, first class, flight to Atlanta this evening around 6 o'clock, two hotel suites; executive board meeting this afternoon at 3 o'clock. Topic: pertinent information and ideas about our office management throughout the U.S.A."

"Damn!" he thought, remembering the stack of office information under his mattress, computerized information, fortunately. With a wry smile, he burst into song.

"We're on our way. Pack up your pack. And if we stay, we won't come back. How can we go? We haven't got a dime (he held up his credit card), but we're going, and we're going to have a happy time. Cuanto le gusta, le gusta, le gusta, le gusta, le gusta, le gusta, le gusta..."

"The office may not 'le gusta' it," Eve observed.

"Probably not," cackled Fred. "If we had an office in Brazil and if Carmen Miranda were still around, I'd have her explain the need for fun while one works. Brazil. Hmm. You know—"

"Later, Fred." She passed her car keys to Joseph, who would retrieve her car.

"If there is a later."

"I have a feeling there will be a long stretch of later."

Joseph pulled up in front of Eve's building. "Miss Nelson has to pack, sir, as do you. I assume Los Angeles will be your last U.S. stop. It's closest to Bora Bora. May I suggest ordering your tickets to those destinations now? It's approaching the 'in' season, and flights may be booked if you wait too long. Of course, there is the Queen Mary. Oh, and I haven't heard a word you've said, sir."

"Joseph, you belong in the office!"

"I doubt it, sir. The building is already crowded on every floor. There's certainly no room for a car."

The air was crisp; the day was clear but not in the minds of Thompson's executives.

"Are you crazy, Hank? Where did they go?" George Snell was livid.

"If Eve and Junior don't join us, we won't stop bleeding. We're already swimming in red ink."

"Forget them, Bill. Issue a conference call to all Thompson executives."

"Yes, we need ideas to stall for time."

"No, George. The time is now," asserted Hank, "We don't need bandages. We need ideas to grow Thompson. We'll heal as we go."

"Listen to him!" snorted Snell.

"I think we'd better," said Wetcliff. "Conference call, Miss Kay. To all executives."

"About what?"

"About running this firm. Mr. Williams and Miss Nelson have disappeared."

"Not yet," announced Miss Kay, "but otherwise, you're psychic. Mr. Williams just called for the third time in an hour. He and Miss Nelson will be gone for a few months, with conference calls daily from our branch offices. Farewell meeting with our top brass at 5 P.M. tonight. After that, 'music, mystery; and paradise comes suddenly near.'"

"Have you gone crazy, Miss Kay?"

"Quoting Mr. Williams. From the song 'Stranger in Paradise.'"

"What does it all mean?"

"You're not as psychic as I thought."

"Fred's gone mad!"

"Madder."

Bill Wetcliff Sr. stormed out of Miss Kay's office, followed meekly by George Snell and Hank Martin.

"This job gets more interesting each Williams minute," Miss Kay observed to no one in particular. "I may never take another vacation again." The phone rang.

"Williams, Wetcliff, and Snell."

"Fred here."

"And there and everywhere," Miss Kay almost said aloud instead of "Yes, sir."

"Can't you get rid of bad habits, you foolish woman? It's Williams, Williams, and Williams now. Could I have made it any easier for you?"

"No, sir."

"Move tonight's meeting up one hour. Heads of all departments are required to attend. And you. You're my all-points man now, Kaysee. Need you. Count on you. Huge salary increase ahead. Got it?"

"Got it. Big shots here at 4 o'clock." She hung up. Fred Williams never signed off. Every minute was and would continue to be a Williams minute, whether he was physically present or not. She hoped he lived forever.

Margaret Nelson was trying to help her daughter pack.

"A dozen cities is a lot to cover, Eve, in how many weeks?"

"We're not walking to them, Mother, and the time we spend depends on what we find. We'll have teleconference calls daily at whatever time Fred decides that particular day."

"So, every Williams executive drops whatever he or she is doing — meetings, eatings, greetings, bathroom visits — to be fed whatever information you and Fred discover and get immediate feedback on what it might mean, should mean, can be made to mean for the company."

"Correct."

"Honey, doesn't he think of anyone else?"

"He's company-driven and impatient."

"He's made W.W.&W. a one-man enterprise. What happens to it when he's gone?"

"He's expecting me to carry on."

"The Chief Designate!" Mrs. Nelson was in awe. "Won't Bill Jr. be surprised! But you'll miss Fred's bossing, won't you."

"I'll have yours."

"For personal guidance, yes, of course."

"Not necessarily."

"Is that an invitation?"

"Would you like it to be?"

"I'm in men's clothes, not stocks."

"They're not irreconcilable."

"Oh, darling, I'm too old. Well, I'm not Fred. I can live without more aggravation."

"But not without me."

"No, dear, never without you. Your brother and sister are—well, they're not —"

"Enough of a challenge?"

"Light years away from challenge." Such easy marks.

The packing ritual flowed seamlessly. Margaret Nelson was unusually silent for an unusually long time. She finally spoke to the clothes.

"Are you going to marry him?"

Eve continued packing, and Mrs. Nelson looked up.

"Was that a 'maybe'?"

Eve tucked the last item into a corner of the plaid wardrobe case. It was a bathing suit.

"Maybe it's a 'maybe.' Would you mind very much?"

A slight smile flickered across Margaret Nelson's face.

"Your father was a 'maybe'—to the end of his life."

Eve hugged her mother and opened the window.

"Ready, Joseph!" she called down.

"May I ride with you, dear?"

"It's a meeting."

"Yes, I know, but I'd like to make my peace with Fred. Just in case. Mustn't be denied visits to the grandchildren."

"Mother, aren't you going too far?"

"Look who's talking about going too far! Well, geographically, at least."

Joseph entered humming and put the luggage on the rack. "Will you go to headquarters directly, or should I pick up Mr. Williams first?"

"Headquarters," they said in unison.

Mrs. Nelson laughed heartily. "The boss finds my charm endurable only in small bites, Joseph."

Bill Wetcliff was in the lobby when they arrived.

"I need to talk to you, Eve."

"But the meeting—"

"We've got half an hour, and Fred's not here yet. Please!" He led the familiar way to his office.

Margaret Nelson, unprotesting, watched them go, then sat on the orange sofa, crossed her legs, and reached for the phone.

"W Café, please. Yes, bourbon on the rocks for the lady in the lobby. Very few rocks."

Bill closed the office door behind them and faced Eve.

"Do you know what you are doing?"

"From a business or personal standpoint?"

"Both."

"I'm going on a business trip with my unorthodox, unpredictable boss."

"You can't move up in two directions, Eve. If you marry Fred, you'll have to quit. He's never had a working wife. And if you stay, you won't succeed him. No woman in this company or on this earth will. Fred will see to that, regardless of what he may have told you. You'll lose either way. Maybe not financially. But you're not one of our money-driven zombies."

"Are you thinking of yourself or of me?"

"I'm thinking of both of us. We've got a lot to offer this company. Right now, it's the two of us that have made the difference, the turnaround at W.W&W.—Ego, Inc."

"Don't deny that Fred had a hand, a very significant hand in this."

"A hand we've had to gently ease off the controls to avoid disaster."

"But it was Fred's vision we were working with."

"Vision doesn't increase the bottom line. Time-tested organization, skills, market insight, and common sense do. I thought you understood this, Eve. What's happened to you?"

"And what happened to the creative Bill Wetcliff people loved to hate?"

"He's grown up."

Eve looked into his resolute face, than looked away.

"You were a beautiful baby, Bill," she said softly.

"Eve, I've been a fool to allow this to develop. I've been meaning to tell you this for a long time, but I thought you'd laugh at me." He twisted the button on his shirt collar to the point of its near departure from his shirt.

"I love you. It's been killing me seeing you with Hank and Fred, not knowing if they'd smooth-talked their way into your heart. It's time for me to settle down, and you're the only one I'd want to do that with. Please, Eve! I'll do my best to be worthy of you. It won't be easy, but I'll try, I swear it. Marry me." He saw the faraway look in her eyes. "Have I the least chance in hell You'll have me?" His voice was strong, but he was close to tears.

Eve was touched. She knew the tears were real but was it love or fear that brought them to his eyes? She looked at him silently as he scanned her face, searching eagerly for the longed-for response.

"Do you know how long I've been waiting to hear you say this?"

"Darling—!"

"But I didn't hear it."

"I was a fool. I was afraid you'd say 'no.' I thought that if I postponed asking, I would have a chance."

"Why did you think I would refuse you?"

He blushed. "My reputation was a big minus, and I hadn't achieved anything on my own. Now I have something to offer you. I wanted you to be proud of me, Eve. You couldn't have been before. I'm not Fred in any way, but is that so bad?"

"I didn't want you to be someone else. I wanted you, for better or worse, the way you were."

"Darling! Thank God it's not too late! The meeting! You've got to tell Fred now that you're not going with him."

"But I am."

"But you said –"

"I didn't say I wouldn't go with Fred on this business junket, which will catch our branch offices unawares and reveal what really needs to be done to maximize services and profits there."

Bill grabbed her and kissed her passionately. "Darling, darling," he murmured as he led her down the hall.

Eve needed that time to straighten her head, her heart, and her emotions, which Bill's kiss had knocked in more directions than she knew existed. She hadn't said that she'd marry him. Bill had assumed a lot, and Fred had assumed a lot, both with trepidation. And Hank, what about Hank, whom she had caused to flee to a competitor, where he seemed to be doing quite nicely, no thanks, she was sure, to stolen information about Williams' branch offices. She knew that Fred and the devil were often chummy when a goal had become a fixation. For a thirty-one-year-old woman on a fast career track whom men had easily bypassed before, she was suddenly very much in demand. She had to know why, and she had to know exactly what it was that she wanted. Bill slipped his arm out of hers as he entered the Boardroom. Eve's entrance was delayed by Mrs. Nelson, who grabbed her arm and whispered, "Let Fred sleep on the plane. Insider's tip from his housekeeper. He's been sleeping on Florida, the old fool!"

Chapter Twenty-Three

E ve could see the fuzzy outlines of the half-moon through the gauze draperies in her hotel room.

Fred giggled. "Look at this, Eve. You look quite spiffy and executive in this one, but why can't these newspaper photographers capture me in more elegant poses? I look like the devil's sidekick with my mouth so wide open."

"You were speaking. You can't speak with your mouth closed." She noted his expression. "Well, maybe you can."

"But I like that they're tracking us across the country. It's good publicity. And I could even put up with these ridiculous poses if they'd change the prose."

The photos and headlines papered the table: FATHER KNOWS BEST, BEAUTY AND THE BEAST, TIME WILL TELL, STRANGE BEDFELLOWS.

Eve smiled. "It catches the readers' attention and gets us interviews. Free publicity is a blessing."

"Not when it puts people in the mood to laugh instead of invest. We're an investment management firm, not a comedy routine."

"It's the means to an end."

"Is it?"

Fred Williams slid most of the newspaper clippings into the plastic pouch in his briefcase but fingered one. He looked tired. Eight cities and eight offices had endured, welcomed, blossomed, or withered under their presence. It had been exhilarating, and they had learned a lot.

Fred smiled admiringly at Eve as she grabbed a piece of hotel stationery and began to write.

He looked at her hair, the way she threw back her head when she was thinking, the way she uncrossed her legs, bit the end of the pencil, and said, "Hmm." She passed the paper across to him.

As he read, his head bobbed up and down in a continuous nod until —

"What! Snell and Senior can go take a flying leap for all I care! They've cut and run, and they're not coming back! Let them drown with Thompson!"

"Thompson's the kind of sedate firm we've been for twenty years. There are still people who like conservative investing."

"Old people should think young," insisted Fred.

"Should? What about those who just don't, and who like it that way? And what about the young people who think old, and maybe always will? Perhaps we should entice new but backward-thinking accounts by offering the services of a shrink, whose purpose would be to re-educate and remold our prospective clientele into the kind of customers we would like. Are you proposing that we change them so we can serve them?"

Fred Williams was quiet for a long time. "Sort of, yeah."

He and Eve burst into laughter.

Fred glanced at the news clipping he was still gripping and pushed it toward Eve.

She read, "SOCIALITES INVITED TO BALL TO FUND THE FIRST SEASON OF FLEDGLING OPERA COMPANY."

"So?"

"We're going."

"We haven't been invited."

"So?"

"Why this sudden interest in opera and socialites?"

"You like them, well, opera at least, and it would be good for you to get away from work."

Eve shook her head at the exhausted man before her even as she said, "All right. Thank you, Fred. Pass me the article, and take a nap."

"Just what I had in mind. I'll come by in my tux in two hours."

"Yes, boss."

Eve turned toward the article. Fred had omitted to read the sub-head: JIM AND SUSAN BADDELY SPONSOR THE GALA EVENT OF THE YEAR.

"Baddely, Baddely," murmured Eve. She switched on her laptop.

Eve spotted her almost immediately, her bright red hair piled high, her ears aglow with thick, long diamonds, glitter that announced her presence across the crowded ballroom.

For the tenth time Eve's mind re-read the website story she could not forget:

"John and Samantha Brotherlee of Palm Beach announce the marriage of their daughter Susan, 21, to Frederick Willard Williams. Mr. Brotherlee, an investment banker and partner with his father in Brotherlee and Brotherlee, introduced his daughter to Mr. Williams, 46, a sales executive at the firm, at her coming-out party three years ago. The bride, a graduate of Smith College, has just begun a career in fashion as a buyer for Saks Fifth Avenue, where her mother was formerly a coordinator for individual clients. Mr. Williams' father recently retired as a senior accountant at the Newark, New Jersey, branch of the Veterans Administration. Mr. Williams' mother, the former Gladys Johnson of Ft. Lee, New Jersey, is a lifelong housewife. The young couple will reside in New York City."

Eve's mind did a fast forward:

"Mr. and Mrs. Frederick Williams have announced their divorce. Susan Williams, age 30, is holding a gala "Thank God it's over" celebration for four hundred friends and family at the Ritz Carlton in Naples, Florida. A vice-president at Fashion Fragrances, Inc., her tumultuous marriage to Mr. Williams had become a cottage industry for society gamblers, who began betting on its longevity almost at its inception. Fred Williams, notorious for his short temper and business acumen, is the controlling partner in Williams, Wetcliff, and Snell, an investment management company he started two years ago, which has been seen as his response to his father-in-law's refusal to make him a partner at Brotherlee. Insiders state that Brotherlee is furious at the new company's theft of his clients and its 'aggressive practices and cockeyed management goals.' William Wetcliff and George Snell, former Brotherlee executives, joined Williams in founding the company. The Williamses have lived separately for the past year, during which time Mrs. Williams has often been seen at charity and social events with James Baddely, who recently joined her father's firm. Mr. Williams has evaded invitations to 'these vapid, uppity affairs, where tripe is uttered, and assignations are affected. I'll be the talk-of-the-town, all right, but it will be because of the success of W.W.&S. An honest man does his business in the Boardroom, not the ballroom.' Judging from the nosedive in profits at his new branch in Palm Beach, that may not be the case. When asked about this, Mr. Williams said that he is in business for 'the little investor, who needs me.' Mr. Williams stated that his exclusion from his former wife's gala does not mean that he won't crash the event. 'I've got more to celebrate than that fashion princess has.' We are told that security at the event will be very tight and "Williams-proof."

Fred Williams did not attend, and Eve found no further mention of the former couple on any website. Apparently, their paths diverged, accidentally or on purpose, until now. Fred had knowingly brought her to the kind of event he still despised, and Eve understood why. He hadn't called her "darling" since The Four Continents debacle; he was calling her "darling" now. He was sure of her, and sure she wouldn't let him down. And she wouldn't.

"Do you mind?" asked Fred deferentially as he led Eve onto the dance floor.

How could she mind dancing with "Lightfoot Williams," as he once had been called, and as her earlier evening with him had verified? They sambaed their way across sixty feet of people, not a feat for the faint of heart. Fred pulled up in front of the garrulous redhead and, his hand in Eve's, gushed,

"A magnificent event, Susan. The opera is lucky to have your patronage."

"Amazingly kind of you to say so," she responded.

"It's been a long time since, uh, our last big event."

"Not long enough."

"May I introduce our vice-president, Eve Nelson?" he said, ignoring her reply.

"Do I have a choice?"

"And these charming people?" Fred pointed to her confreres. Susan Baddely sighed in exasperation, but her attempted introduction was aborted by her two friends. "Fred Williams!" exclaimed one,

"You mean I'm still famous in Palm Beach?"

"You've been in the news so much lately that your history has been revived."

"Better his history than him," stated Susan Baddely.

Her friend ignored this. "I'm Jasmine Crackers. You know my husband, Andy."

"Sure do, but it's been a while. Where is old Animal Crackers?" He scanned the room.

"Oh, he couldn't make it. Hates opera, actually. Will you be in town for a while? I'll tell him to call you."

"Do that. I'm at The Palm Hotel. My friend and associate Eve Nelson." He pointed to Eve. "If I can't connect with Andy on this trip..."

Small talk continued while Susan Baddely tapped her stilettos in impatience.

"I don't recall inviting you, Fred," she finally intervened.

"Well, you couldn't, could you? Didn't know I'd be in town, so you're forgiven."

"Forgiven?!" She excused herself with the barest of civility. Fred and Eve watched a red streak shooting toward a heavy-set, white-haired man in the corner. She was voluble, she gesticulated, she gave up and moved toward the abandoned wives whose husbands hers had corralled.

The buzz started slowly, and it was wondrous to see the effect, as glazed eyes began to sparkle, and heads began to turn. Fred glowed. He greeted, as Eve found out later, total strangers, who smiled, asked how he was, and nodded to or were introduced to Eve as he danced her through every beat, whether it was the Samba, the Shrek or The Loony Bin, the latest dance craze. He seemed tireless, but he sensed that Eve was beginning to flag.

"Some wine, darlin'?" and they adjourned to a wall replete with bottles and bartenders. But even as Fred was solicitous, he kept his eyes on Susan Baddely. She was speaking to her husband alone now, and her mood seemed intense. Eve knew that there was no reason for her and Fred to be in Palm Beach. She had been here last month, and she knew that he trusted her report and her judgment. But she realized that a business agenda was not what Fred had in mind for this trip. An unfinished personal agenda, the loose ends of long ago, were to be tidied up and set right, or at least rearranged to her boss' satisfaction. They had been there an hour, and Eve wasn't sure how much more such social electricity she could take when Jim Baddely was upon them. "Mr. Bore and Batter," as he was known, shook Fred's hand like a dog grabs a bone.

"Sorry to hear you're losing Bill Wetcliff Jr. to Thompson. It's not unexpected that he wants to join his father, but it must be difficult losing your advertising genius."

"You're looking at our advertising genius," Fred snapped.

The whisper of a waiter called his adversary away "with regret." Fred contained his anger, allowing himself only a sneer at the backside of the departing Baddely.

"Learned a lot from his wife," he told Eve, who patted his hand before being talked to and walked away by a young woman who begged her for advice since she was starting a career from scratch with only her million-dollar trust fund, and that not until she was twenty-five. Fred headed for the alcove. He whipped out his cell phone.

"Still up, Bill? Oh, I forgot the kind of life you like to lead, all right, used to lead, used to lead. Tell me straight out, are you going to Thompson? I thought not. Go back to bed. You need your beauty sleep, you handsome devil. What? In the middle of the night? I don't like surprises. At least tell me where you're going. I promise, just tell me."

Fred was silent for a full thirty seconds.

"Yes, I'm still here—uh, in Santa Fe. Keep me posted each step of the way, and I mean each. Don't wait 'til you have time. Make time. Of course, I trust you. It's the other people I don't trust. You can still make the midnight flight to Palm Beach. Sure."

Fred Williams was back in the ballroom in a flash. He abruptly reclaimed Eve, and with a "pleasure to see you all, good luck with the opera," and a slight bow to the ladies, whisked Eve to the limo that had been waiting for them all evening.

"Trouble's afoot," he said as they leaned back in their seats. "We have to talk."

Chapter Twenty-Four

They walked the empty beach at 8 a.m., ignoring the softly rippling water and the random clumps of cloud overhead.

"I appreciated your request for secrecy," said Jim Baddely.

"Privacy," corrected Bill Wetcliff.

"Privacy, then, and I appreciated your coming on such short notice and at such a busy time, with your added responsibilities, now that Fred Williams is away."

"I'm reachable here, and Fred's reachable in Santa Fe, should I need him."

"Santa Fe? I see. Unlike W.W. & W. we don't have offices all over the place, not that we'd object to opening some. We've basically been a regional investment management firm, but it's getting a little crowded here, and Williams is to blame for that, expanding a branch right under our hometown's nose. And you're responsible for its success with your senior travel ads. A real coup."

"Thank you, sir," Bill Wetcliff was not about to diminish the compliment by saying that the art was his, but the idea was Fred's.

"Call me Jim. Whether you accept my offer or not, make it, Jim. You're a real catch, you know, and your salary is light years away from reflecting that. You should have been made president already. And the company should have made capital out of your personal art by using it to win over young investors. Saying this may cost me more than I'd like, but you're unique. In financial and other ways, I'd make that very clear. My main ad man is due to retire soon, and I can make it worth his while to make it sooner if you come aboard—as president immediately, as a partner within a year.

It's not common knowledge yet, but we're going public within the next eighteen months. With us, your future is as bright as the sun and as hot as the tropics, another area, by the way, that we can expand into."

"Fred's been good to me. I know him. Outside of what I've read, I don't know you."

"I like that kind of thinking. You'll be detail-oriented as we expand. And as for knowing the boss, Fred and I have lifelong reputations you can compare. We are not about to change. I'm slow, steady, dull. Been in business longer than Fred but haven't been as successful. Successful, mind you, very, but not as successful. More conservative, in hindsight, probably too conservative. That's why we need you and will compensate you accordingly. Fred, we all know, is – how can I put it delicately—not a people-person. He's done well, I give him that, but over the bodies of partners, friends, and employees. Even your father decided to opt-out. I salute him for lasting this long. In addition to all the business benefits, there will be other goodies to enjoy. And let's face it, I have no children, I'm seventy, and I won't last forever."

"Neither will Fred."

"True, but Eve Nelson seems to be on the inside track. Lots to dangle over the old man's head if he wants one final fling."

Bill's face reddened. "Eve's not that kind of woman."

Jim Baddely shrugged. "Her personal life seems to be business-oriented if you believe the stories."

"What are you saying?"

"Only that he didn't ask you to join him on this cross-country tour."

"He needed me to run the company in his absence." Bill was fuming.

"Well, certainly not to take the tour with Eve Nelson. No offense, son, but take off the blinders. What's the chance for upward mobility for a fabulously talented young man when the controlling and very senior CEO is afraid a personal interest will succumb to said talented and handsome young man?"

Bill Wetcliff looked into the now churning water and grey clouds.

"He'll never trust you, Bill. I will. At my stage of life, it's a bigger gamble for me than for you, but I'm very sure you're a winning card."

Bill kicked the sand left and right. "This isn't fair to Eve."

"She's a mature woman, talented, too. She'll find her way. Life throws wrenches into lots of our plans, and we can't control them all. You can't control Eve's future, but you can control your own. There are plenty of wonderful women out here to appreciate you. You should know that from past experience."

"Not the kind of woman I'm looking for."

Jim Baddely stopped walking and faced Bill Wetcliff.

"Lots of people divorce and remarry, so we know that there are others out there who are able to win their hearts. Look at Susan and me. Twenty-five years of understanding and love."

"I didn't know you were married before."

"I wasn't. Susan was."

"A horror story, huh?"

"The worst. An opinionated, irascible, vindictive, tyrannical nightmare."

Bill Wetcliff smiled and uttered a half laugh. "Could have been Fred Williams."

Bill's smile vanished, and his eyes shot wildly open as Jim Baddely responded.

"It was."

Chapter Twenty-Five

They crossed the sand to Jim Baddely's parked car.

"Susan would like to see you." He pulled slowly away from the curb. "She's been badgering me about this ever since she suggested that I interview you."

Bill Wetcliff was astonished. "I don't understand."

"My wife is my partner. Off the books, of course. Opera, ballet, and fashion activities don't encourage confidence in a financial management firm."

"You had a problem fifteen years ago. I understand."

"You certainly do your research. Yes. Susan's trust fund kept us afloat. Now, of course, we're fine. Even finer with you aboard. My wife's very knowledgeable about financial matters and the people in charge of them. She's been on target about people I've hired and haven't hired. Not a single miss. She targeted you. Oh, I did my own checking, of course, but my conclusions were the same." He stopped the Mercedes in front of a red brick mansion full of tiers and cupolas and stained glass windows.

"No need to rush home. You can take an evening flight. No one will know you've been gone. I have another stop to make, but a taxi will be here in one hour. You won't need a formal introduction to Susan. I hope I'll hear from you soon." He shook Bill's hand, watched him exit, and drove off.

Young Bill Wetcliff made his way up the cobblestoned walk. He felt very old. Life was moving fast, faster than he liked, too fast to know if gambles would be safe, if fate was about to punish him for past indiscretions and business mistakes, or if it was about to reward him for his talent and hard work. The door opened before he rang the bell.

"Thanks so much for coming." said a radiant, red-haired woman, much younger-looking than the years Bill knew attached themselves to her. She ushered him into a cavernous living room, a Victorian's artistic haven, full of bric-a-brac and overstuffed chairs. The blue velvet drapes were tied back to the walls. It was like stepping into another world with a woman who seemed the antithesis of it. This was Palm Beach?

"The servants are off on Sunday," explained Susan Baddely, as she motioned him to a yellow brocaded and tasseled sofa. She sat on the other end.

"Sherry, scotch, bourbon?" she asked, reaching toward the bottles and lifting the scotch as he gave his choice.

"You're probably wondering why this meeting." She poured herself a glass of ice water.

"It's natural that you would want to see your investment selection in the flesh to make a final determination."

She had a lilting and very feminine laugh. "We've already made that choice. This is mere denouement. I hope you don't mind."

"On the contrary, I've felt honored down the line since Jim called. I'm overwhelmed that you're so impressed with me. Mind you, I have done some impressive work, but your husband's accolades are a bit, well, over the top. Still, all compliments are very gratefully accepted."

"And all offers from us, too, I hope."

"I need some time."

"I understand; loyalty to your boss, your father, and your female favorite leaves you concerned that a service to us might be a disservice to them."

Bill smiled. "Psychic, too."

Susan Baddely looked at him for a long moment. Her shining blue eyes, her alabaster complexion, her full coral lips, and her unlined face struck him forcefully in the gut. He reddened, swallowed, and looked at his glass, then at the bottles on the table.

"The higher you climb," she said slowly, "the better position you'll be in to help them when they need it." Her voice drew him to her face. "There is more investment money management business than one company can handle. And healthy competition is what has made this country great. No business goes straight up without a crisis. I'm glad I was able to help Jim when help was needed. Your father and Fred Williams have needed help in the distant and recent past and will again. With Baddely and Baddely behind you, you will be in a position to help them in ways beneficial to both companies. Mutual help, mutual rewards. Win-win situations will be possible with you at another firm, with other resources to access."

Bill Wetcliff, even as he took on the glow reflected in Susan Baddely's eyes, turned his eyes away to the blue velvet drapes looking even darker under the antique chandelier.

"Eve Nelson is important to you, isn't she, and you don't see how joining our company can help her."

"She's not ambitious enough to destroy Fred. She loves me, but she thinks Fred needs her. It might work out if I remain at W.W. &S., or we might both be out of jobs. If I leave, she would be torn between Fred and me, and I might not win."

"It's W.W.&W., now, and is that what you want for Eve – a controlling figure to destroy her life? Where is your famous charm, your commanding presence, your romantic invincibility?"

Bill quickly looked her in the face and then down again.

"If you like, Jim can offer her a place at B&B, as well as good reasons for doing so. She's a talented young woman. Win-win. Think of the life you'd be saving, the love you'd be getting, the pride your father will feel knowing that you've made it on your own, without his influence at the former W.W.&S. or Thompson. Join our family, Bill. At this point in your career, can you honestly say you would be made as insanely generous an offer as Jim's made to you?"

Bill's eyes met hers and moved slowly down her face, past the dimpled chin, the voluptuous breasts, the small waist, to the ice water held rock-solid in her hand. "No" hung unexpressed between them as they sat, still at opposite ends of the sofa, a sofa that seemed unbelievably long. Susan Baddely rose slowly, gracefully, one breast at a time.

"You are extremely attractive to us, Bill. I know that we can serve each other to our mutual satisfaction without compromising your other interests."

She held out her hand. What possessed him to kiss it instead of shaking it, he didn't know. His "Goodbye, and thank you" sounded hoarse and gravelly, quite unlike him. Susan Baddely waited seconds that seemed like hours before she slowly lowered her hand to her side. She walked him to the door and pinned his back against its framework as she lightly pressed her bosom into his chest.

"Phone as soon as you decide," she breathed softly.

For a moment, the young man outside the closed door gazed unseeing at the taxicab awaiting him. Fireworks were shooting through his brain, and his heart was beating wildly. Inside the door, Susan Baddely's bosom heaved mightily, and her starburst eyes narrowed to sharp slits. Two men from her past were firmly engraved on the eyelids of her mind, as they often were. Their images would soon be laid to rest. Closure was at hand.

Chapter Twenty-Six

It was a sun-drenched Sunday morning. Fred poured Eve a cup of coffee. "You'd think this was a frickin' paradise," he said, eying the palm trees and the cascading flowers in the near-empty dining room of their hotel. "We're about to be double-crossed. Bill's probably already here. I had told him we wouldn't stop at Palm Beach since you were here last month."

"Where does he think we are?"

"Santa Fe. His evasions oozed guilt. That man is a terrible liar."

"Did he lie?"

"Evasions are lies."

"And lies from 'Santa Fe' are justified?"

"Our lives are at stake."

"You mean W.W.&W's."

"That's exactly what I said. Where are we without this company? Who are we? One cantankerous old mule and one pretty face. Nobody. No identity, no respect, no purpose."

"Without W.W.&W. we die?"

"You bet we do, but if we do live, we don't live well. Bill turned us around with his advertising."

"But it was your idea, and—"

"Ideas are worthless if they're not brought to life. Maybe we can't live forever, but companies can, and we through them."

Eve was silent.

"You're young, Eve. You don't know what it means to give your life to something and lose it all."

She sighed. "Your plan?"

"We become so attractive to Junior that he can't resist. I did that once. I stayed nine long idyllic but excruciating years, and I learned enough to move on. If Bill stays another eight years with us, we'll have time to find a knockout replacement at our leisure to keep our star shining."

"What more can you do to make W irresistible to Bill?"

"I can't do more. You can, but I won't let you. Susan Baddely can, but she won't; she's at the root of the problem. I never told you about Susan and me."

"My computer did."

Fred compressed his lips. "Had to find out sometime, I guess." He was encouraged by Eve's look of curiosity.

"Susan's got a long memory. Of course, it wasn't all her fault. I was pretty hard on her boyfriends, her lovers, her business ideas. She fancied herself a businesswoman. If she hadn't been such a fabulous looker, such a fabulous conversationalist, and such a phenomenal liar, I would have dumped her before she dumped me."

"You knew about her opera gala before we came here, didn't you? You didn't just happen to read about it in the newspaper."

"I hadn't seen Susan for twenty-five years. Oh, yes, in society columns, but not up close. She's still a great looker,"

"Your purpose?"

"Oh, I don't know," he trailed off.

"Yes, you do. She'd see me with you and know that the man she divorced could still get younger women —"

"and prettier."

"—women who could still find the tall, slim business genius fascinating in spite of his money."

"Or his age."

"Fascinating beyond the ability of her dull, uninspired and uninspiring, stocky husband."

"I guess so." Fred looked at a palm tree. "I shouldn't have to, but I'm still the same Fred Williams she once adored. But she's still the same vindictive, spiteful, uppity socialite. It was all I could do to keep from belting her in the jaw. She won't let go until she finishes me off."

"But how can she do that?"

"She can have flat-headed Jim hire Bill away."

"He loves her enough to do anything she says in business?"

"Fears her enough. Baddely and Baddely's survival is based on Susan Brotherlee Baddely's money. They have an understanding. She allows him his young playthings, and he allows her hers, as well as the final say on hiring and firing. At this very moment Bill may be getting a pitch for partner from Jim. But believe me, he'll see Susan, too. I'm not so worried about Jim's offer; I can match that. What I'm worried about is Susan's." His eyebrows suddenly shot up.

"Waiter! Telephone. Quickly! Hello, hello. Long distance, New York City, 212-357-5971." He tapped a foot impatiently. "Bill, Fred. I don't care. You have no business sleeping past 8 o'clock, even on Sunday. You're having something precious stolen right out from under you while you sleep. I'm talking about your son. No, he is not coming to you. Where did you hear that balderdash? Well, he says otherwise. But what he says doesn't mean a tinker's damn if Susan Baddely gets her claws into him. You heard me right. Junior's in Palm Beach, having a friendly little meeting with Jim Baddely. You know it won't stop there. *There* is bad enough for both of us. She'll use Junior to kick me in the business and kick you in the business and the balls. He's booked an evening flight back to New York, but you know a lot can happen in one day. Okay. Make it one o'clock, dining room at The Palm Hotel." Fred hung up.

"Another one of Senior's indiscretions came home to roost." He chuckled, the gravity of it all be damned.

William Wetcliff Sr. paced the room in his pajamas. Then he sat on the edge of the bed, careful not to disturb his flaxen-haired companion. He opened the drawer of his night table and pulled out a small, bulging address book with fraying pages. He quickly thumbed through it. He dialed. His voice was hushed, but very clear.

"Susan. Yes, it is. How much do you want my son?"

Chapter Twenty-Seven

Fred shook his former partner's hand. "I'm glad you realize how serious this is. But why didn't you want Eve in on this? She's tough; she can handle it."

Bill shook his head, "She's part of the problem. She's in love with Bill."

Fred was indignant. "Why should she be?"

"Have you looked in the mirror lately?"

"Eve looks beyond appearances."

"Yes, and she's seen an immature Adonis grow into a more mature young man. The key word here is more. The transformation is not complete. He still has an eye for the passing skirt, and that's our only hope."

"*Our* hope?"

"You have no one in his advertising league, and at Thompson, we have no one in any league. The mega talents want megabucks, and they're worth it, too, if they play out. But it's a gamble, and we can't know for sure. The best of them in the wrong mix can be deadly to the bottom line. We know Bill, know what he can do, but you're going to lose him now to Baddely, and I'm going to lose any chance of winning him over to Thompson. You're hoping that Susan's revenge will shoot me into action to save my son and, more than incidentally, W.W.&W. My son doesn't need saving. He's in a lifelong learning experience. I made a huge mistake in dropping Susan. Huge. She has a right to her revenge. Do I surprise you? Jim's lucky. Susan understands men, accepts, and probably welcomes Jim's affairs so she can have her own. I could have had a very special partner in her, and who knows —," he squared his shoulders and adjusted his tie, a wry smile on his still handsome face—, "we might have had less reason to bed down elsewhere. I'm not concerned about Bill's liaisons. He'll survive them. Haven't we all?"

"I married mine. Don't lump me with you Casanovas."

"Exactly. you married yours. I'm not sure Bill is ready for that, but he thinks he is. If he marries Eve, you lose the rest of your life, even if he stays with W. If he doesn't stay, Thompson benefits, but not enough. We need more."

"What makes you so sure he's got a chance in hell of marrying Eve?"

"Before our meeting last month, he proposed."

"Ha! And Eve turned him down."

"She didn't commit, but she said that she loved him but would go with you on this company tour."

"You're crazy! What did you do, tape them?"

"No, but inadvertently Bill did. Elaine saw the tape and thought it needed transcribing. She called me, and I listened to it."

"She should have told me!"

"There was no sense in upsetting you just yet. You still had a fractional chance with her. She's said she loves Bill, not that she would marry him."

"You're telling me this now?"

"Thompson is sinking fast. When George and I bought the controlling shares, we thought we could turn it around quickly, but it required the speed of light. We've got a great network of clients. More and more have returned since we took over, and we've kept those that fled Fred Williams. But we need the youthful presence and ideas of my wayward son—and we need you. Junior's input can add a lot to our bottom line, partner. I'd say 20% for starters."

"And what's in it for me besides the money?"

They suddenly both laughed heartily.

"A chance, however small, to win Eve."

"And just how do you plan to keep Adonis from pursuing her?"

"I don't plan to persuade him. I can't. But Susan Baddely can."

Fred gave a low whistle.

"Business and pleasure, an irresistible combination, as you now know," Wetcliff said drily.

"But Jim's proposition—"

"Is nothing without Susan's approval. She's willing to postpone the expansion of Jim's business for another day, but she's not willing to postpone Junior. The men in our family could always –"

"All right, all right, all right! Get on with it."

"Eve won't put up with a philanderer, and if I know my son, he knows it too. I'm gambling that he's not as mature as he thinks and, like his dad, not ready for monogamy. There's a whole bunch of little boys running the business world."

"Speak for yourself!" snapped Fred.

"I am. If Eve wants to marry him after a few weeks on tour with you, he'll marry her. He won't back out of his commitment. And my gut tells me he'll try to be faithful. It may kill him, but he'll try. Being unfaithful to Eve would be like slapping the Madonna in the face, and Eve has a very special appeal, not one of ravishing beauty –"

"What do you mean!"

"–but of a mesmerizing combination of good looks, brains, smoldering emotions, and soul."

"Umm." Fred Williams nodded.

"A married Junior appeals to Susan. It provides the ultimate armor against gossip, if you're clever. But a married, faithful Junior does not appeal to her; only a stable marriage that allows him freedom does. So I made her an offer on our behalf."

"*Our*—"

Wetcliff again ignored his former partner's outburst. "She can have Bill if she discourages him from marrying Eve and from joining the Baddely business.

"Can she?"

"What Susan Baddely does, she can undo."

"And she agreed?"

"After a long pause, completely."

"That hot for Junior, huh? But stunning though she is, she's still twenty years his –"

"You've heard Susan breathe,"

"Oh, yes, Jesus, yes." A soft smile lit Fred Williams' face.

The two men rose from the table and headed for the lobby.

"But who's to give Bill that stable marital base?"

Wetcliff pointed to a young woman checking in at reception, "She was near tears when she called me about that tape."

"Fine for us to say, but we can't force Bill to marry Elaine Dawson. And what makes you think that she will? She's no Eve, but she's no fool, either. She won't be used, even for as admirable a reason as the survival of W.W.&W.—all right, W.W.S.&T."

"If she feels like a femme fatale, she'll feel entitled to Bill, and he'll find her attractions admirable—whenever he's home."

"And who can turn this sweet but, relatively speaking, sow's ear into a silk purse?"

"The genius of bed and bath."

"And patron of impossible positions."

The two men whipped out handkerchiefs and wiped their faces.

Chapter Twenty-Eight

The sun rose slowly Monday morning, tired, no doubt, from viewing the exhausting events of the previous day — Elaine balancing books on her head, swiveling her hips just so, raising her arms like a flower bud opening its petals. The temperature rose as, indoors and out, Susan Baddely's instructions to her eager pupil continued. The pupil had a much-needed leisurely plane ride home that evening, and the sun, exhausted too, had set. The relaxing hours aloft that Elaine enjoyed would not have been possible had Bill Jr. not been persuaded to take the flight two hours earlier. So, Monday should have opened well, and it almost did. Bill greeted Elaine warmly as they entered W, as fate would have it, together. At the same time in Palm Beach, Fred Williams and Eve Nelson faced a sudden wind, smiling as they eyed the plane that would take them to Santa Fe, one stop away from Los Angeles, their gateway to blissful Bora Bora. They were almost in paradise. But Fred checked his cell phone before his feet touched the tarmac, and Monday's "almost" vanished.

"What? Why? Damn! Start documenting immediately. Of course, you ninny. Deadline will be—" He turned to Eve. "When the hell's the next flight to New York?"

Frederick Willard Williams stormed into the conference room, his executives already seated and alert, pots of espresso on the table, no milk, no sugar. The real thing.

"I always thought the SEC was inefficient. They're always wasting their time fishing where there are no fish!" His glasses perched low on his nose as he re-read the letter he'd heard read to him on the phone and the documents the staff had assembled.

"It's not enough that William Wetcliff abandoned ship here, now he has to involve us in his sale of W's shares. That man has been nothing but grief to me."

"He wasn't before he left," began Hadley from accounting, but he was cut short by Fred's lethal share.

"And your purchases of company shares are being questioned as well—whether you, Bill, and George made a deal. There weren't many shares available on the open market besides theirs," added public relations chief Bordon.

"I can read, you idiot. No wheeling, dealing here. You don't make deals with a man who forced you to retire."

The door flew open. "For a heavenly twenty years," said Wetcliff Sr., "but it's over. It seems that our partnership is the work of destiny. We can't seem to stay away from each other." Both men fleetingly and simultaneously flashed back to the previous day.

"Humph," grunted Williams grudgingly. "Sit here, Bill."

He pointed to Hadley's chair. "Everyone else out. Let's see how fast we can wrap this up. Can't have the SEC interfering with our lunch."

"You've started eating lunch?" asked Bordon. "Shall I order—"

"It was a metaphor, a metaphor, m-e-t-, God help us! I hope your mind is sharper with the press." He looked at the espresso. "Doesn't this Italian stuff work anymore? You should all be in your offices now, minding your own business, *our* own business. Now scat!"

The door suddenly opened. "Snell! It's about time. Sit next to Godzilla here, and let's get cracking on this waste of time."

Eve thanked Miss Kay for the pile of correspondence on her desk, each envelope carefully slit open, except for those marked "personal," a term she'd found to be generally meaningless, designed to assure the writer of getting her personal attention.

"I took care of those that could be handled by others."

"Thank you. Miss Kay, are you engaged for lunch?"

"No."

"Will you be my guest today?"

"With pleasure. May I ask why?"

"You see things the rest of us can't or won't see. You're a wonderful, unbiased judge of character and behavior. This will just be between you and me."

"Of course."

Eve touched the top of her fountain pen to her chin. She could have been "Eve" to Miss Kay eight years ago at Eve's request, but Miss Kay had chosen to keep her distance, her objectivity, her "place," as she called it, to the woman who trusted her suggestions and advice.

At 12:58, Miss Kay, in her bright red jacket, closed her office door as Elaine passed by. "Still in conference?" she asked the younger woman.

"Yes, but they've moved from coffee to water, so they should be breaking soon. I was wondering, would you have lunch with me tomorrow—privately, some place nice?"

"Well, I—"

"It's very important. It's—personal. You've been so kind to me, and you're so objective, well, I'd really appreciate it."

"Of course, Elaine. Tomorrow. Oh dear," she murmured as Elaine walked away.

Bill Jr. met her in W's lobby. During the elevator ride down, Elaine had undergone a transformation. Gone was the hesitant, uncertain, pretty young lady with the awkward walk. In her place was the best of everything, announced to Bill by swinging hips, a head thrown back, and an expression of both mystery and meaning, opposites reconciled, with hints of surprises to come. ("But Susan, it's impossible!" Elaine had wailed. Susan Baddely had looked at her as you would look at someone beyond naiveté. "Am I impossible?") The composite vision approaching Bill Wetcliff wiped the worry from his mind, but he couldn't understand why. This, after all, was merely Elaine—wasn't it?

"Let's break, boys."

"Tired, Fred?"

"Maybe."

"I didn't think that word was in your vocabulary?"

"Well, now you know that it is, George. How's your wife?"

"Anne is fine, visiting her mother in Phoenix."

"Good woman, Anne. Always thought you were lucky she said yes."

"Not much choice, actually. She was already twenty-nine and no Marilyn Monroe, and my only competition was a diplomat's son who looked like a horse's head and couldn't speak English."

"So, you did her and her ten million dollars a favor and took her off the market."

George Snell laughed. "We got on well as soon as we met, got on even better after we married. Two wonderful sons, four wonderful grandchildren. No complaints on my end. Hers either, I'm sure, if you asked her."

"No men on the side for her, eh?"

"Are you crazy? Oh, don't give me that look. I'd know if there were any. We may not be in heat, but we prize family loyalty above all else."

"Hers, you mean," clarified Bill.

"Lay off it, Bill. You, of all people."

"Hey, I'm divorced."

"And just how sexually loyal were you when you were married?"

"Very. I just had a lot of loyalty in me to spread around. Like you, oh pal and partner, except that Carol wasn't as understanding as Anne. Most women don't seem able to grasp the enormous stresses on a successful businessman and the outlets they require."

Fred Williams looked from George to Bill. "You two are really something. Pardon me if I don't say what."

"Look who's outraged! At least Bill and I have only been married once. Five salads, Fred, five, so hold the sauce."

"I made honest women out of them all and treated them like queens."

"Hard to do that for very long, isn't it, Fred?"

"Maybe. But we sure as hell enjoyed each other. Then we learned and moved on." He looked at the ceiling, a faint smile on his lips. "Alice was a pip. Good sport, but at the hairdresser's a lot and needed too much of my attention. I had a business to run. She went from idle poor to idle rich without understanding tiddledewinks. Runs a talent agency now in Fort Worth. Got a Christmas card from her last year, out of the blue. She understands now. Number four was Joyce. Best waitress in Las Vegas. Liked to flirt too much. Harmless, but still... She wasn't much of an actress, but she tried. Alice is working with her now. She's doing character roles. Gerry was my biggest mistake. I wanted a gorgeous young woman, could afford one, and got one. Unfaithful as hell. Number two seemed to be my dream woman. Remember her, Bill? Beautiful, intelligent, socially active for good causes, adoring. Then—boom! We married, and the angel turned tyrant. Coping with Satan would have been a relief."

Bill Wetcliff laughed heartily. "Carol hid you in our 2x4 cellar closet when she came rampaging in with this huge rolling pin demanding 'Where is he, where is he!'"

Fred had to laugh too. "I don't even remember what I'd done wrong, but it didn't matter. She always seemed to find some excuse for a rolling pin, a chair, a vase. I got a lot of exercise avoiding her aim."

"It was your vocabulary she objected to, wasn't it?"

"Yeah, I guess so. He-man language was beyond her. Don't look so smug. That's why I was always number one in this company, and you boys were numbers two and three."

Bill looked at George. "We won't go into the financial reasons that four-lips, here, was number one. It's all long past anyway, except for wife number one. Her influence lives on."

"Except for Susan," repeated Fred. "I never married a wealthy woman after her. I preferred to marry a kept woman than be a kept man. I still don't want a woman above me financially or socially."

"Or by your side, either, eh, Fred. Still not big on equality."

"One person has to be in charge in every situation. Even in W.W.&S. and now, heaven help us, W.W.S.&T. One mouth has to be bigger than the others, one person's ideas—"

"And investment ownership—"

"—has to be greater than the others."

"*Has* to be or *is*?"

"Boils down to the same thing, George. Too bad Susan couldn't take second place. No, she had to have the money and the affairs. Quite a she-man. Still at it, too."

"And number six, Fred?"

"None of your business, Bill."

"Your wives affect the business."

"This one won't. Early retirement, extremely early, until I'm gone, a true housewife and companion, sharing my interests, exciting me to try some new ones, faithful, loving, supportive, a grand exit for me."

"Eve Nelson is a businesswoman, Fred. You can't ask her to wait five years, maybe ten, you healthy old reprobate, to resume her career. In business if you lose touch for awhile, you're out, unless you buy controlling shares in a company you were once in, like some vocal, aggressive old coot we know. And Eve's not aggressive."

"A few years with me will change that."

"Maybe she'll change you."

"Not a chance. I'm not marrying someone to change me. I've got the money and the seniority. I call the shots."

"Of course, you could have children. That might keep her at home," suggested Snell.

"Children!" barked Fred. "Hell, I don't want competition for Eve's attention. I don't have much longer to go."

"No yen for heirs, Fred?"

"I'll be remembered. My will attends to that."

"Pretty sure Eve will say yes?"

"Not sure of anything, Bill, except that you two had better forget everything we've just been talking about."

"Forgotten," they assured him in chorus.

"And SEC remembered. Be back in an hour." And Fred Williams rose from his magisterial place at the head of the conference table and headed for his office and a nap on the sofa.

Chapter Twenty-Nine

E ve gazed with unfeigned interest at the man in front of her. The clean-cut, wholesome look sat comfortably on a well-chiseled face, with a Grecian nose and hazel eyes under thick eyebrows.

"Notice how I've integrated the fruit orchard and the flower garden," said Hank Martin.

Eve looked again at the winding cobblestone paths through the casual labyrinth of fruit and flowers, the benches strategically placed for views of this charming foreground, the creek in the mid-ground, and the mountains in the background.

"Remember the house in front of it?" He took the sketch of the idyllic cottage from his portfolio. For five days, Eve had seen Hank Martin's paradise unfold. His sketches had revealed him to her as his year at W.W.&S. had not.

"Just the dream of a Midwest boy, to be afforded and enjoyed when the big city dream makes it possible. My near-term heaven will be the New York suburbs."

They finished the pot of coffee they had shared every day that week at 3 o'clock. And then they would separate, he to Thompson, she to W, to complete the day's work.

"You never talk about your dreams, Eve."

"Oh, I don't dream anymore. One day at a time is enough for me. It's sort of a dream-as-you-go policy I've developed."

"Practical. It's hard to be seriously disappointed that way." They concentrated on their coffee. "But you did dream longer term, once?"

"Oh, yes, like everyone else."

Hank Martin did not press her for details that were none of his business, and Eve appreciated his restraint. He was a kind, sweet, young man, who didn't rush, grab, insist.

"You never told me why you switched from construction to finance. There's plenty of money to be made in construction to finance your dream."

"Not fast enough. And New York's an exciting place—The Botanical Garden, The New York Restoration Project, bringing God's nature to human nature. I've got a map of all the pockets of water, trees, plants they've created in Skyscraper City. You've got to let me take you around to see them all someday. New Yorkers have forgotten their roots. You know, you couldn't vote in the colony of New York if you didn't own land, and I don't mean a coop or condo. Someday I'll travel farther, to places like Provence and England's lake district, to get a more rounded view of original creation."

"So, New York's just a part of your journey? Passing through?"

"I guess you could say that, but it's a slow passage, and that's fine with me. You'd love country living, Eve."

"What makes you say that?"

"Because there's no trace of artifice about you. Because you're real. Because natural beauty in all its manifestations is hard to find these days. When people's masks come off, there is nothing underneath, except other masks. And the glue is strong. Let's hope that science can develop the formula that dissolves it. I think if we were truly ourselves, the world would be a better place. We've got to be and stay as real as we can. It's a struggle, a challenge, and that's good. But it's not forever."

Eve looked with envy at Hank's glowing face. "Are you looking for company along the way?"

"Very much," he answered softly.

"No, that's not what I meant."

"Wasn't it?"

"Your world isn't the world I know."

Hank placed the drawings in Eve's lap. "Hank's World: May I introduce you to Eve Nelson? Be advised, H.W., your house's construction and layout are subject to change, your gardens can be reconfigured, and your décor is undecided."

Eve smiled. "It certainly sounds appealing, but to live it—"

"Little by little, conforming the lifestyle to yourself. Bill is reconsidering Elaine. You may want to reconsider him. I'm moving up at Thompson. Snell and Senior find my ideas and their implementation refreshing, and they find me reliable. If ever I want to move out, I'd move up elsewhere. You wouldn't be ashamed of me."

"Ashamed? What a ridiculous word!"

Hank shrugged. "I throw it out just in case it crossed your mind."

"I see what you think of me!"

"No. I don't know what you think of me. I can't see into that fabulously constructed mind and under that serenely beautiful and irresistible exterior."

Eve swallowed hard as Hank leaned across the table. She was about to protest his compliments and his movement when her cell phone rang.

"Eve, are you all right?" It was the wiry voice of Fred Williams.

"Of course."

"I heard you were out with Hank Martin."

"We've been having coffee daily all week."

"Why wasn't I told!"

"You're only told of business affairs, Fred."

There was a shuffling, objects falling, and a bewildered "I-I-I" from the office end.

"I'll be back in twenty minutes. Hank has some work to finish at T, and I've a few things to do at W before I head home. Is the SEC work completed?"

"Yes, yes."

"Good. I'll see you soon."

"Yes." But Fred Williams did not hang up.

Reluctantly, Eve did so. Hank's eyes were glowing as he put his hands on hers.

<h1 style="text-align:center">Chapter Thirty</h1>

An elusive fragrance wafted into the office, accompanied by waves of strawberry hair, a charming little nose and magnetic blue eyes. Eve Nelson walked around the desk to shake the hand of the woman whose beauty could only be called startling. "How may I help you, Mrs. Baddely?"

Susan Baddely smiled a smile that seemed to indicate the irony of the request.

"You are certainly more cordial to me than I was to you in Palm Beach. Thank you. I've come about a matter that is important to both of us, though I've squeezed you in between shopping and the hairdresser. One must always make one's trips do double or triple duty. I know you understand efficiency, and life is relatively short."

"You want Fred back," said Eve matter-of-factly.

A melodic laugh pealed through the office. "Good heavens, no, though after the acrimony of our divorce had dissipated, the thought did come to me—frequently. Fred Williams was probably the best thing that ever happened to me, but I've since moved on, to more malleable and appreciative men."

"Then why did you want to speak to me?"

"I don't want you to marry Bill Wetcliff. You may marry Fred, if you wish. I'd rather you didn't, but my anger towards that miserable, charming ogre only erupts, temporarily, each time he remarries. Your marriage would make five more times in thirty years, so you see, I don't get angry often. And I suppose after surviving ninety years, in spite of his explosive personality and temper tantrums, he is entitled to an attractive, supportive, and stable last hurrah.

"But my last hurrah is many years off, and the Bill Wetcliffs of this world supply what I admit is a voracious need for excitement in all aspects of life, the sexual one being prime. I'm past skydiving and amusement park rides. I require something very personally touching, and often. You smile. You think there are only twenty-four hours in a day, and how can such a small part of it fuel the rest of it. But it's by no means a small part of *my* day. It's an integral part of everything I do *every* day. Intimations, implications, overtures and actions are the mindplay, foreplay and screenplay that make up the fabric of every hour, waking or dreaming. This need permeates my life. Yes, *need*, Eve Nelson. Women who incorporate just a little of my beliefs into each day will feel the transforming power of true intimacy."

"Fascinating."

"The worldly word of an outsider. But most women are outsiders. They miss a lot."

"When you wrap your life around a penis, Mrs. Baddely, you miss the point of God's creation."

"No, I don't. I miss man's. God's creation of male and female formed a unit through which life's joys could unfold. I'm well aware of the traditional beliefs. How could I flout them, otherwise? I know that man was put in control of the earth and in control of women. Well," she laughed, "there's been a little change there that he's still not aware of. I think that's a change even you are pleased with. And do call me Susan. I'm not a total rebel. I lead a well-rounded life. I cook a little, dust a little, work for charity a little, and entertain a little. Quite well-rounded, sometimes too much so. That's when I abstain from pastries—a little." She concluded with another charming laugh. "But in everything I do are sparks of intimacy, and relationships that make life meaningful. Alone with a virile man, all the intimacies of the day converge and explode. I'm not looking for Mr. Permanent. I've got one. I'm content to let him go his way as he lets me go mine. Too bad he lacks the imagination and the capacity to truly enjoy himself. But he doesn't know that, and it's just as well. More women than men have this capacity. How lucky we are!"

"Very interesting. So, you're allowing me to marry Fred, but not Bill."

"Not 'interesting,' my dear. Vital. And yes, though I wouldn't put it quite as dogmatically as that. You're the settle-and-get-married type, but you have potential to be more, to wrest pleasure from other seemingly little things in life. And after Fred, you will even have the wherewithal to do it."

"As you have."

"Yes, though I came into my marriage to Jim with quite a bundle."

"I don't want to live your life."

"And I don't want you to, at least not yet. Handsome hunks are more likely to gravitate to you than to me, otherwise. That's a compliment, my dear."

"Is it?"

"Oh, yes. As is exposing my soul to you. I felt I owed it to Fred's final choice. His final and, I must admit, his wisest. So, having done so, will you at least reveal your intentions toward Bill Wetcliff? His intentions, you know, mean nothing without yours."

"So, you don't want Bill to marry so that he can be free to accommodate you."

"Oh, I do want him to marry, for that very reason. Only men with the veneer of respectability have the freedom I require."

"Elaine!"

"She'll enjoy a very good life and excellent compensation in a divorce, should it come to that. And who knows, maybe their divorce, Fred's demise, and my moving on to fresh territory may coincide. Then Bill would be available to you. Life's coincidences constantly amaze me. You wouldn't appreciate a philandering husband now, anyway. Even later, you would have to keep an eye on Bill."

"Do you really think Elaine can appeal to him?"

"With a lot of help—which she's been getting."

"And you're willing to sacrifice her to Bill's other inclinations, but are willing to spare me."

"I'm not being cruel to Elaine. She'll have a fabulous life. She won't have everything, but who does? I'm sparing you in tribute to Fred."

"And just a little part of Bill will satisfy you?"

"Good heavens, yes! Women fool themselves into thinking that one person can be everything to them. But the truth is, if they're honest and can pull it off, they would do as I do. A little of this, a little of that—small pieces are delicious, small packages more delightful than large ones. Life is made up of lots of little things and little pleasures. I simply get them from different people instead of one. With me it's Christmas all the time. I give and I receive. I've fed a lot of men with more than money and more than sex—with confidence and hope and joy. Bill will be a better husband to Elaine because of me. I can be very practical, you see. Like you, my dear, just not as often. I've heard that Bill proposed marriage to you and that you accepted. Will you drop him for the sake of Fred and yourself, if not for me?"

Eve's eyes locked onto Susan Baddely's. She would make no comment about the presumed acceptance. "You are right about my appreciation for the practical. I am eminently, overwhelmingly practical in most ways. But I will marry only, exclusively for love."

"Which means—"

Eve examined the most fabulously put together and confident female she had ever met. Finally, she said, "That's a haunting fragrance you're wearing. What is it?"

"Capricci, by Nina Ricci. Easy to wear, hard to find. The favor of an answer would be appreciated—when you discover what it is. I don't think life will allow you the luxury of much time."

Chapter Thirty-One

"**W**hat in blazes is this?" Fred Williams jumped aside to avoid being run over by a table-sized cake being wheeled in by two men in baker's hats.

"It's for the celebration," stated Miss Kay.

"We're cementing a partnership at 7 o'clock, and swallowing the Queen Mary in red roses and pink icing is not the way I want it done. Who ordered this?"

"I did, and it's not for the Williams-Thompson marriage. Oh, do be careful, Mr. Williams. Those ambrosial canapés are easily damaged. Ah, here comes the wine."

"All right, out with it."

Miss Kay walked toward a sleek wallboard of buttons connecting the ballroom to loudspeakers on all floors of the Williams-Thompson buildings. She flipped switches.

"Attention all members of the Williams and Thompson money management families. In addition to the 7 P.M. celebration of the merger of our companies, you are invited to an earlier happy event at 5 P.M. in Williams Ballroom A to celebrate the upcoming marriage of vice-president Eve Nelson."

Miss Kay showed no emotion as she turned toward Fred Williams, whose face turned white. In his office, young Bill Wetcliff's face turned a vivid pink. Through the ballroom's speakers, Hank Martin's anguished voice seemed unnaturally loud.

"Miss Kay, Miss Kay, I know you're there!"

And at their desks two women sat shocked—frozen.

As Miss Kay reentered her office, she saw the unwavering green light that indicated her boss wanted to see her immediately.

When she entered Eve Nelson's office, steno pad in hand, she saw that Eve's finger was still on the button, her face a picture of the Ten Furies combined.

"Miss Kay, what have you done!"

Miss Kay ignored the tone and replied serenely, "What you asked me to do. I distinctly recall you saying at lunch earlier this week, 'Find a way to help me decide,' and I've done that. Oh, don't try to reach your mother. She's been on the phone since I called her at 6 A.M. Zillions of her friends will descend on Ballroom A at 5 o'clock to wish you joy."

"But I'm not engaged to anyone, and I may never be!" she cried.

"Never is not an option. None of the men who want you could survive it. A 'yes' or 'no,' they will be able to manage. The merger of W and T has gotten off to a rocky start. The principles don't seem to know their asses from their elbows, if you'll pardon the expression, and it's your fault. You have seven hours to prepare for the celebration. You look lovely, so that's not an issue. Your preparation consists solely in deciding whose proposal you are accepting. Your other work can wait. The choice of a lifetime takes priority. I'll order your lunch. No calls, of course." And without awaiting a response, she marched smartly from the room.

Eve Nelson had never put her personal affairs before business, but concentrating on anything but 5 o'clock would be insane, as well as impossible. She had always counted on Miss Kay as a stabilizing office force that brought others to heel with her professionalism and good sense. Others, not her boss. And what good sense was there in forcing her to do the impossible, to make her the butt of office jokes forever. And what a field day the media would have with this! It would make a mockery of what the company stood for, make it look unreliable and unstable. She would have to quit, leave the lucrative position she had worked so hard to reach, and take a job in a small company, hidden away in the backwoods somewhere, as she ran from the shameful, laughable position that Miss Kay had gotten her into. But why should she suffer because Miss Kay had gone berserk?

Let Miss Kay take the blame. She'd earned it! Eve thought of all the business decisions she had made, some fair, some superb and, on the whole, most astonishingly prescient and wise. She had been so busy working that she had never recapped her accomplishments. Others had, ergo her promotions, but her vanity never had required it. Vanity! What did she know of that? What *should* she know of that? Susan Baddely knew a lot about it, though it was more a matter of justifiable pride. But her pride and attendant vanity had not made her fuel for laughter. Gossip, yes, but not laughter. And having met her, it was impossible not to admire one of the most dangerous women in the world, in whom personal and professional concerns could overlap and cause havoc beyond her person. Susan Baddely always got her men, one at a time, to enjoy before moving on to other attractions, other adventures, always with some mutuality of benefit on multiple levels. She was a good businesswoman, even if, at bottom, she was in business for herself. And there lay the unbreachable distance between them, for Eve knew that she was mainly in business for W&T, that her life was unbalanced, and that at 5 o'clock, there would be an attempt to even the scales. But to act in haste on such an important decision... Yet in the back of her mind, Eve heard a blend of Margaret Nelson and Miss Kay: "You've been preparing for this for thirty-one years. If not now, when?" The clock struck noon. Two hours of mental activity in romantic territory had left her exhausted. There was a large, brown, paper lunch bag on the entry table. When Miss Kay had placed it there, she did not know. She took the bag, slowly opened the door, and peeked into her secretary's office. Miss Kay was not there, gone, no doubt to lunch. Eve put the brown bag in her leather tote, hurried to the elevator, and hailed a taxi. She needed Central Park.

Brown paper bags were everywhere, on laps, benches, occasionally on the grass, reminders of a meal gone by. Eve removed her lunch from the tote. Why a tote? Leather, no less. What was wrong being seen with a naked, plain brown bag?

Was Saks so important on a bench in Central Park? Did the ever-practical Eve Nelson want practicality encased in "class"? Did she want her marriage that way, too? Then Bill would certainly be her choice. Fred was hardly "class," and a Hank without money would never be considered classy, either. But Eve knew that she was not a woman of appearances, and that a concern for them could only and always be a temporary aberration. The appearance of the bag paled beside the importance of its contents. And Miss Kay had provided Eve's usual lunch of choice: tuna and egg salad. Very elegant. But she knew very well that she didn't want a man who would provide as simply for her as she would for herself. Oh, she would shake her head, perhaps, complain gently, but she wanted to be someone's queen, an independent queen, to be sure, but a queen all the same to someone who could see in her what she could not see in herself, who not only believed in her, but who loved her for who she was—Margaret Nelson's quiet, confident, practical, but assertive daughter, attractive to herself in the right clothes, but to him, always. A blind, adoring mate she could both respect and love. She knew that she wanted the impossible, but the possible wasn't worth the troubles, the responsibilities that marriage imposed—putting the "other" before oneself (and praying that he would do likewise), putting up with in-laws and extended family. Better to remain alone and free. She reflected that she might change her mind in thirty years, but time enough to worry about that. Or there would have been if Miss Kay had not short-circuited destiny. Eve sighed. She would start the selection process with "character," and then move on to the rewards the relationship offered.

Fred was certainly a character. His character was being a "character," designed to wake you completely, including your blushing mechanism. Bill was, at heart, good-natured and thoughtful, but playful in ways more appropriate to youth. Only Hank had the kind of character that made you feel good about yourself. Like Bill, he was handsome, but it was the kind of handsome that was more genteel and quietly reassuring. Of course, Bill's good looks got your senses churning. They teemed with the promise of excitement. They were dangerous and appealing. You go through life but once, she thought. Fred was exciting, too. But if he got your heart pumping because you were the object of his scorn, that pump could be your last. It was handsome, reliable Hank who was best for the long haul, especially if your heart was set on country living. Eve rifled her handbag for an aspirin. A headache had sprung full blown and could not be ignored. What had she told Susan Baddely—that she would marry only for love. The lake in Central Park gently bubbled her the question, the softly blowing leaves and blades of grass echoed it. "Whom do you love?" Not whom do you think you should love. "Let me rephrase that," said an ancient tree trunk that insisted on her attention. "Whom would you prefer not to live without? Whose life touches yours beautifully and the most?" Eve looked at the brown paper bags, the rippling water, the waving grass and the sky full of slow moving clouds. Heads were bent over books, fingers were blindly digging into paper for the midday meal, figures in shorts were running, despite the cool weather. The answer to the question was obvious, as natural as a stroll through Central Park.

Miss Kay was excited. It was almost 5 o'clock. The hour of insanity was approaching. An ultimatum would be met—or not. She prayed that Eve was not boarding a plane to the North Pole. The guests had begun to arrive. "Just in time," said Miss Kay, with a hint of reprimand, as Eve took her place at the door to greet the well-wishers. Margaret Nelson arrived promptly at 5 o'clock.

"Hello, dear. Everything looks wonderful. Umm, smell those hors d'oeuvres! That's a lovely dress, Eve. Not too frilly, not too severe."

"It's a pre-Miss-Kay-announcement dress. What I wore to work this morning."

"Well, it's just right."

Eve stood there calmly—gracious, smiling, laughing, shaking hands, expressing gratitude for kind words, for their coming. Miss Kay flew around the ballroom like a cyclone making sure platters were refilled and wine and whiskey bottles never empty. Mrs. Nelson stared in wonder at the dynamo.

"She's me under another name!"

"No, Mother. She only gives opinions when asked, and then with reluctance."

"A strange creature, then," observed Margaret Nelson, who kissed her daughter lightly on the cheek and, with difficulty, refrained from asking the question in everyone's mind, and moved on to nibble food and make small talk with total strangers, very much a prerogative of the mother of the bride-to-be. A jazz quartet in the middle of the ballroom kept spirits high and feet tapping, a few pairs dancing. Pastel balloons blowing across the ceiling on long ribbons were shouting "Congratulations," "Have a ball." "Lucky guy," and "Finally!" Eve shook her head at the last. "Mother!" she mumbled, as she saw that eminent lady greeting her social and business friends who had just begun to arrive. Eve could have continued that way forever, wanted to, but when Miss Kay's voice boomed through the speakers. "The time has come," she knew it had. As Miss Kay stepped aside. Eve walked briskly to the microphone.

"Thank you again for coming. This occasion is as much a surprise to me as it is to you. I'll still be Eve Nelson here at W.W.S.&T, and I look forward to working with our expanded team. But privately, I will be part of another team. You probably have never met the handsome, charming, exciting man I am about to marry, and you never may again, but for a few minutes—seconds?—you shall." She reached her hand out to him. "Mr. Frederick Willard Williams."

Fred Williams, in shock, nearly keeled over, and hands reached out to steady him. "I thought marriage to someone this young might kill him, but not this soon," can a voice from the crowd.

Fred Williams was still beaming at the merger celebration. His words had more to do with his personal merger than with his professional one.

"I will not have my wife working"—he glanced at Eve, "at this company—" he glanced again "directly. She'll be moving over to Thompson"—another glance—and then more strongly, "which needs a lot of help. And don't think that marriage is going to soften me. Too old to change. Don't want to change.

And I expect when we return from our honeymoon in Bora Bora, you will all have some exciting ideas when we discuss new beginnings."

"Redundant," said George Snell softly, but audibly.

"I like redundant!" boomed Fred Williams.

"I guess you do. Six wives."

"What was that?"

"I said I guess you do. Seems wise."

Fred's head gave a short, vigorous shake.

It was 8 o'clock, and bleary-eyed employees, who had already missed innumerable trains, applauded Williams's words enthusiastically, even as they rapidly headed for the exits. Eve saw Elaine and Bill exit together, she looking adoringly into his face as he spoke to her.

"Poor Elaine," said Eve. As Bill turned for a word to a colleague, she saw Elaine shoot an admiring glance at a departing, sullen Hank Martin.

"Well, maybe not!"

Morning marked the beginning of a new day and a new relationship, as Eve Nelson and Frederick Willard Williams became husband and wife. The City Hall ceremony was short, the friends and family attending few, just as the couple had wanted. The only business associate present was Miss Kay, who gripped Fred Williams' hand tightly as he said, "Well, two days in L.A. and we're off to Bora Bora."

"And back," added Miss Kay.

Fred kissed Miss Kay gently on the cheek. "Yes, Miss Kay, thank you. And back."

Margaret Nelson brushed aside tears and kissed her daughter. "God bless you, darling. And you too, Fred."

"Thank you, Mother," he responded solemnly.

Margaret Nelson swiped at him with her bag, and he laughed. "Come on, darlin'. We have a ship to catch."

"Oh, do be careful!"

"Too late. She's already married me." Fred Williams hugged his laughing wife, and with his arm around her waist, steered her out the door and down the hall, as he waved backwards to the wedding party.

Margaret Nelson's face was scrunched in consternation, and Miss Kay patted her hand. "It won't be boring," she said. "You wouldn't enjoy boring."

THE END